A City
Full of Rain

A City
Full of Rain

Collected Stories

[handwritten inscription: To Miriam, We wrote for the common images of friendship, mutual support & admiration for the gift of language. Thanks for the years of all of the above.]

❦

GARY EBERLE

To order additional copies of this book, contact:
Xlibris Corporation
1-888-7-XLIBRIS
www.Xlibris.com
Orders@Xlibris.com

Contents

IN ANOTHER COUNTRY 9

TANABATA 11

ORIGAMI OR THE SADNESS OF
PAPER BIRDS 29

STES. MARIES-DE-LA-MER 36

"IN THE STILL-VEX'D BERMOOTHES" 57

READING *CARMINA BURANA* AT
THE BEACH 67

FIVE ROOMS IN A CITY FULL OF RAIN 75

A CITY FULL OF RAIN 77

HASTE TO THE WEDDING 85

DIANA CLOAKS HERSELF IN MOONLIGHT 92

THE MERMAID'S SONG 102

CHIAROSCURO 110

MISTAKEN IDENTITIES 123

THE ART OF THE FUGUE 125

THE THEORY OF CHAOS 137

FIRST PERSON, SINGULAR 149

HOLY TOLEDO 151

MILK 165

ORGAN WORKS *A Story in Four Movements* 178

ALTERNATE LIVES 197
TRAJECTORY 199
HOUSE OF DREAMS 204

Most of these stories have appeared in print in the following journals: *Nexus, West Branch, Willow Spring, The MacGuffin, Crosscurrents: A Quarterly, The Grand Rapids College Review, On-the-Town Magazine.* "Stes. Maries de-la-Mer" appeared in *The PrePress Awards 1992-93.* "Holy Toledo," which first appeared in *The MacGuffin,* was nominated for a Pushcart Prize.

IN ANOTHER COUNTRY

TANABATA

I heard Fiona McKay before I actually saw her. I had taken the bullet train from Tokyo to Kyoto, then an inter-city north to Kanazawa, switching there to a small and, by Japanese standards, not very clean two-car local train to Hakui on the Chirihama coast of the Noto Peninsula. The Noto juts out into the Sea of Japan from the northern coast of Honshu like an unfinished thought, and I thought it might be one of the few regions of Japan which had been left relatively unspoiled by the postwar industrialization.

As I switched from train to train, the number of foreigners progressively decreased until, after Kanazawa, I was the only *gaijin* left on the train. During my two years in Japan, I had gotten out of Tokyo as much as possible, mainly to get away from people like me. Being a foreigner is a strange experience on an island as homogenous as Japan. Since, in my work, I dealt mainly with Japanese I sometimes found my looks somewhat repulsive when I caught a glimpse of myself in a mirror or store window. I looked pale, almost green, and far too large, with hay-colored hair sprouting out of my face and head. My blue eyes reminded me of the eyes of a dead fish. I wished I looked otherwise.

After two years of being among the Japanese, I had grown impatient at the stupidity of the American tourists, people like me, I was constantly bumping into on the streets of Tokyo. I found myself looking at the *gaijin* like a Japanese. We were large, ungainly, loud, barbarous, demanding too much space to swing our legs and arms in, like hairy apes set loose in Tokyo with cameras. Fortunately, since most of the *gaijin* stayed in Tokyo or Kyoto, escape was possible.

But at Hakui, a small town that serves as little more than a railway transfer point, I was surprised to hear an English speaking voice rising above the general hum of traffic outside the train station.

"Buh-loody hell! No, no, no!" the voice exploded in frustration, and I turned to see a towering red-headed Australian woman gesturing at a large backpack and two wooden boxes that lay beside a local bus. She held a Berlitz phrase book open in one hand and between bursts of English profanity she was trying to get the bus driver to allow her to take the pack and the odd boxes onto the crowded bus that was going out to the nine-mile stretch of rocky coast on the western side of the peninsula known as the Noto Kongo.

Without knowing it, she was trapped in an embarrassing dilemma. As a foreigner, she should have been accorded the utmost courtesy and allowed to do as she pleased. The driver, who probably had never encountered a Westerner before, much less a six foot redhead, had politely offered to load her heavy things into the baggage compartment outside the bus, but she had apparently misinterpreted his gesture as an attempt to prevent her from taking her gear with her.

By the time I saw them, a sizeable crowd had gathered to observe the bus driver do battle with this strapping Amazon whose flying red hair probably made the peasants among them think she was part dragon.

My first impulse was to turn away, thinking she was just another stupid tourist, but the bus driver just then caught my eye and looked at me with such an expression of faceless embarrassment that I went over to see what I could do.

The arrival of a second *gaijin*, as tall and wild haired as the first, sent a ripple of murmurs through the crowd gathered on the sidewalk. The murmurs were silenced, however, when I bowed deeply to the driver, deeper than necessary, actually, and addressed him in Japanese. I took care to use a polite form of the verb, not too polite, of course, but enough to indicate that I didn't wish to cause him any further discomfort.

"Well, thank Christ," the red-haired woman said, "Would you tell this bloke I need my bloody gear and want to take it on board?"

I turned to her after bowing to the driver again and said, slowly, as if she didn't understand English, "He knows that. He is only offering to load it into the baggage compartment beneath the bus for you."

The driver fired off something in Japanese and I caught most of it, though his accent was a little rough.

"He says he would be most pleased if you would allow him to take the burden of your heavy pack personally and that if you would take a seat on his humble bus and make yourself comfortable and all that he would be most honored."

"Oh," she said, blinking as if just waking up, "Oh, Christ, is that all? Well then, tell him to load it on and let's get on then."

Then she threw back her head and let out a loud laugh. Some of the older peasants on the sidewalk backed away, perhaps fearing that flames would come from this dragon's mouth. I translated her comment, loosely, and added a thanks to the driver who smiled and laughed and bowed himself at the misunderstanding. The crowd tittered and dispersed as the large pack and the two boxes were absorbed into Japanese efficiency beneath the bus. No one lost face.

"Fiona McKay," she said, extending her hand. Her last name rhymed with sky and her handshake was firm. It was strange to be staring into the eyes of a woman half an inch taller than I. After seeing mostly the ink dark eyes of Japanese for two years, I had forgotten just how bright and varied the pigments in our eyes are. In Japan, drivers' licenses don't even have a space for eye or hair color since everyone's is the same. Fiona's eyes were a surprisingly deep green with flecks of gold in the irises. "Harry Dean," I said, "On vacation?"

"Don't I wish," she replied, "I'm hiking up the Noto for research. Finishing up my dissertation."

"On?"

"Entomology at U-Syd."

"Sounds interesting," I said, to be polite.

"Too right," she replied. She had a wide open smile the way many Aussies do, and her teeth were large and white. "Specially here. They've got some Japanese *coleoptera* here as big as your bloody hand, regular samurai. Wish I spoke the local lingo better, though. Thanks for your help." She jerked her thumb back at the bus. "Ridin' out?"

"No, I said, "Not today anyway. I'm staying at a *ryokan* here tonight, then tomorrow I'm going north a bit to Myojoji temple. It's supposed to have an exquisite founders' hall and pagoda."

"Ah," she said, with about the same tone of feigned interest as I had used when commenting on her bugs. "Well, ta, then."

And with that, she turned and mounted the bus. I couldn't help but wonder how she'd do out there. I wasn't concerned about her physically. She was a strong woman, about twenty-eight years old, with a lean and wiry build over firm bones. She was dressed all right, too, for the rugged Noto, in hiking boots, khaki walking shorts and cotton shirt.

But the Noto wasn't the outback. There was really no place you could go in Japan anymore to be totally away from people and Fiona McKay struck me as the sort of person who would have difficulty with the layers of politeness even the most rural Japanese expect. After two years, I hadn't mastered it myself, and I always felt awkward, even with my colleagues.

But, as I never expected to see her again, I didn't give it much more thought. I was wrapping up my two-year stint teaching English at the Meiji Institute in Tokyo, and this visit to the Noto was my last chance to find what I imagined was the "real" Japan. It was nearly impossible to encounter it in any form anymore. It had all been Westernized until the cultural contamination was like the pollution in the ocean. It was worst closest to Tokyo, but there was nowhere you could go without meeting it. I loathed what we had done to Japan, even if most of the Japanese didn't.

The hall of the ancestors at Myojoji was a perfect example of what had happened. Its ceiling had a magnificent heron on it carved from a single piece of cypress. The ceiling was painted a deep cerulean and the gray heron, symbol of long life, seemed to fly across it. But there in the corner of the room hung a smoke detector, its bright red eye detracting from the otherwise perfect blue of the false sky.

The new ugly Japan kept intruding itself that way everywhere. Just the week before, a tea ceremony at a friend's house was interrupted three times by the telephone. At Nikko, Buddhist monks carried SLR's around their necks, and I'd found lunches in exquisite bento boxes garnished with plastic bamboo leaves.

My desperate attempt to find the Japan of my imagination in Hakui failed, and after two days there I pushed my search halfway out the Noto peninsula and across Nanao Bay to the island of Noto, hoping to find some untouched remnant there. Just eighty years ago, the island was inhabited only by primitive tribes of pearl divers. To my disappointment, the small bays of the island were now covered with the ugly grids of commercial pearl growers, and at the small *minshuku*, or guest house, where I stayed, the owner ran the TV day and night.

Disappointed, I decided to drive the coast highway back to Hakui even though it was out of the way. I wasn't thinking of Fiona McKay at all at that point, but was just trying to find something of the lost Japan of Utamaro and Basho. I still hoped to discover some unblemished corner on the back roads.

Then, just north of Tatsurahama, I ran into Fiona again. Actually, I didn't see her at first, only a bizarre apparition that I thought might have been the last hallucination of a desperate traveller. A gaggle of schoolchildren in Girl Scout uniforms was following someone carrying a large ungainly bamboo rack. They were laughing and waving their hands. Attached to the rack, which was about four feet square, were perhaps one hundred small tubes made of bamboo. The bearer carried the whole contraption on her back using a headstrap to take the extra weight. It looked like something from Hiroshige's Tokaido series. The whole gang was approaching a small roadside shrine to Jizo-bosatsu, patron of children and travellers, when I passed them. I had gone about fifty yards when I noticed that it was Fiona in the middle of the children.

I stopped and backed up to them. Fiona had a great big smile on her face and, through gestures and a few words of Japanese, she and the children were carrying on an animated conversation. They crowded around her and asked for her autograph as if she were a celebrity. All my fears about her fitting in were apparently wasted.

"'Lo," she said, recognizing me, "You again, eh? Me and me chums were just hiking to the bus stop. How about a lift to Hakui?"

I got out of the car and saw that the weird contraption around which the children were gathered was actually a rack for carrying her specimens. She had run out of collecting bottles, and then had run into the Girl Scouts who used their scout knives to fashion boxes for her out of bamboo. The little bamboo tubes were full of insects that she and the children, whom she'd met and befriended when she'd stumbled on their campground, had collected. Their teacher, Mrs. Yamaguchi, had spoken a little English and among them they had gathered far more insects than Fiona had ever anticipated getting on such a short field trip.

"*Arigato, domo arigato,*" Fiona said, bowing deeply to the children who did not want to let her go. They lit some incense in Jizo's small shrine and rang the bells to get the god's attention as, somehow, we managed to jam the specimen rack, her boxes and her backpack into the hatchback of the little Toyota I was driving. As we left, the children and Mrs. Yamamoto all shouted "Bye-bye, bye-bye," and waved. I cringed at the children's "bye-bye's," a creeping Americanism my Japanese intellectual friends regularly railed about.

Fiona smelled all sour of sweat and wood smoke after a week of camping on the coast, and before we'd driven more than ten kilometers she'd fallen asleep, her head rolled back in a great snore which continued until we hit the outskirts of Hakui where I had to slam on the brakes. The streets were jammed with people and the area around the station was filled with small stalls and booths selling everything from fresh fruit to rubber sandals.

"What's this?" she asked, stretching out as she woke up. Her long arms filled the small car and went out the windows on either side. The car was filled with the spicy odor of her underarms.

"A midsummer festival," I said. "*Tanabata-matsuri.* It must be seventh night. It looks like all the farmers have come in for the fireworks. I hope we can find rooms. There's no train out till morning."

We tried every one of the few hotels around the stations, but they were all booked solid. Tries at more outlying ones failed, too. Finally I dropped the Toyota at the station rental place because the festival traffic made driving absurd and a friendly cab driver took us to a small *ryokan*, or traditional inn, he knew of on the southern edge of town. It was on a backstreet, only a block away from some gaudy festival stalls. The door was unmarked and dark. The proprietress turned out to be an old woman, bent double, like many Japanese women, from years of hard labor. She walked with her hand in the small of her back, and had to take great pains to bend up to see my face. Her teeth were all golden with metal bridgework and when she spoke the smell of Suntory whiskey filled the cluttered vestibule.

She nervously whispered something to the taxi driver, the only word of which I caught was *gaijin*. The driver replied that I understood Japanese and had lived in Japan for two years. This seemed to placate her somewhat. Perhaps she had dealt with Westerners before who did not know proper shoe etiquette or who refused to eat raw fish. Then they had another whispered conversation at the end of which the old lady gave a hissing laugh.

When I went back to the taxi, Fiona was attempting to shoo off an aggressive salesman who was trying to sell her a couple of sticky rice balls wrapped in seaweed. She looked very tired in spite of her nap, and I got rid of the salesman by giving him the two hundred yen he wanted for the snack. I put the rice balls in my jacket pocket and said, "The good news is they seem to have room for us."

"What's the bad news?" Fiona asked.

"It's kind of a dive. The proprietress says there's only one room left, so we'll have to share. Also, the driver seems to think we're married."

"Christ," Fiona said wearily rubbing the back of her hands across her eyes.

"There's really no other room in town," I explained.

Fiona looked at me from the back seat of the cab. Her long legs were folded up uncomfortably and her face was drawn and tired from the week's camping on the Noto. Her large hands fluttered in front of her face for a moment in a helpless gesture that seemed oddly feminine in a woman her size. Finally, she sighed. "Well, I suppose I can stand it if you can," she said.

At the registration desk, the awkwardness of the situation got even worse. I saw the hunched old proprietress cast a quick look at Fiona's ring finger, and smile. A sudden lowering of her head told me that she had just erected one of the those invisible psychological walls the Japanese build when they don't wish to be embarrassed. I had seen it happen on a subway in Tokyo once when a drunken man lurched on to our car and made as if he were going to relieve himself in a corner. The air in the car seemed to turn ten degrees colder and I heard the walls snap into place with the finality of metal doors sliding to. They had rendered the man invisible. Good God, I swore to myself, she thinks Fiona's a prostitute. I felt acutely uncomfortable, but Fiona seemed not to mind or notice.

She had kicked off her hiking boots in the entry way and lined them up with my shoes. The boots looked gigantic next to the loafers I wore constantly in Japan to make the endless shoe rituals easier. I noticed the maid's startled expression when she saw those boots standing there on their own, looming over the tiny tennis shoes and slip-ons of the staff and other guests. I myself was somewhat surprised to notice that, in our stocking feet, Fiona was still a half-inch taller than I. After two years of looking at Japanese, I found her body all out of proportion. The paleness of her skin and the redness of her hair startled me every time I looked at her.

The maid, in a cheap yellow kimono with a flower on the *obi*, wordlessly led us across a small bridge over an indoor carp pond and up a few steps to a narrow hallway. Her *tabi*, stockings with toes in them, swept noisily over the tatami. Her steps were large and heavy, and I thought she could use some training in tea ceremony to teach her to walk better. She stopped in front of a shoji door and slid it open. The door glided smoothly on its runners making a sibilant sound that magnified the silence of the old inn.

The room we entered was a small one even by Japanese standards, with a pair of water-stained shoji at the far end. It was sparsely furnished with only a small imitation laquerware table of the sort you could pick up at any department store. The *takanoma*, or niche, had an old silk flower in a vase and painted scroll with a reproduction of old calligraphy on it. On the table was a tall plastic thermos with hot water and two handleless cups. Though the room was rather expensive, the furnishings were cheap imitations of traditional Japanese crafts, a distinct disappointment, but as it was the only place left in town it would have to do.

"Tea?" I asked Fiona as the maid bustled about the room touching a thing here and there to make sure I noticed it.

"I'd kill for some," she said, thumping her backpack with its odd rack of insect cages against the wall. "Then a bath. After a week in the bush I'm about due, eh?"

"*Furo, kudasai,*" I said to the maid as I put a bag of green tea into each of the cups. The maid disappeared into the bathroom, and a moment later, we heard the sound of water splashing into the deep cube of the tub. The maid came back out gesturing and chattering excitedly.

"*Wakarimasu,*" I said, smiling and bowing. "*Wakarimasu.*" I understand.

"What's that then?" Fiona asked. She had sat herself on one of the cushions by the low table and stretched her legs out straight beneath it. Her feet in their ragg hiking socks flopped on the tatami and looked disembodied, like the lower half of a magician's illusion, and her legs seemed to reach halfway across the small room.

"She's telling us how to take a bath," I explained. "You're to wash first and then get in the tub. There's a stool you can sit on, and a bucket."

"Been through that before," Fiona said. "Thank her and tell her we'll manage."

After tea, Fiona took one of the *yukata* or summer kimonos that had been provided us and headed for the bathroom. I heard her dip the plastic bucket into the hot water of the tub. That was followed by a short shriek. "Ooowww!," she whined, "Poached like an egg! Why do they keep it so bloody hot?" I heard her run some cold water into the tub and then climb in.

As she soaked, the maid returned and efficiently laid out the futons. There was one blue one and one red one, both of them ornately decorated with dragons more in the Chinese style than the Japanese. She put them side by side, and I decided Fiona and I could move them whatever chaste distance apart we wanted when we went to sleep, though the room was so small it would hardly make any difference.

The maid bowed and left silently, and when she'd gone I was surprised at the quietness of the *ryokan*. Even at the best of the old ones these days, the calm studied atmosphere was usually destroyed by the muffled noise of television sets behind the shoji, but this one was oddly silent for such a third class place. Either all the other guests were out on the street enjoying the festival or the rooms had been rented to a convention of deaf mutes.

I listened hard, then (almost reassuringly) heard the distant crackle of laughter from a TV game show. The truly profound quiet of traditional Japan was a thing of the past. I had only experienced it twice in my two years there; once at the stone garden of Ryoanji in Kyoto when I accidentally found myself alone on the porch for a few moments between tour buses, and once at an old inn similar to this one high up in the mountains overlooking a busy harbor when I awoke in the middle of the night from a dream and found myself immersed in an inky quiet I found almost terrifying.

Other than the TV, easily ignored, there seemed to be no sound at all in the old inn except an occasional drip from the bathroom as Fiona changed positions in the tub. The sound of her in the water reminded me, for some reason, of the splash of the tail of one of the ornamental carp I'd seen earlier that year in a pond near Nara. There was also an occasional rustle or chirp from within the bamboo cages she'd improvised to hold her specimens.

I squatted down beside the pack to examine the boxes more closely. It was quite ingenious what she and the scouts had done. Each box was formed of one cell of bamboo about four inches long and two inches in diameter. With pocket knives they had cut out sections of the sides of the tubes to serve as doors, then held the hatches secure with twine. Air holes were bored into the cells with awls and the whole thing had been arranged on the rack and tied onto her backpack. I'm sure the scout master had been proud to show off her children's dexterity with bamboo. The orientals never stopped telling you about the wonders of bamboo. It's a grass, not a tree, they tell you, and it grows up to forty feet high, each cell of it as hollow as the Tao. You can eat it, build with it, make musical instruments with it. You find it everywhere. They use it for making drinking cups at temples, handles on trays, paintbrushes, furniture and everything else. Every Japanese construction worker has at least one story about bamboo scaffolding standing up during an earthquake while the Western-style steel pipe scaffolding came tumbling down around them. Now Fiona and the girl scouts had made insect specimen boxes out of it.

I heard something behind me and turned, startled to see Fiona watching me from the door of the bathroom.

"Don't set 'em free," she said walking towards me across the tatami, "It took me and the girls all week to catch 'em."

The blue and white *yukata* she was wearing was much too short for her, though it fit her well enough around. As she strode across the floor in her bare feet, a flash of white thigh showed through the opening of the *yukata*. She tossed her crumpled khaki shorts and T-shirt into a heap beside the backpack, and looked down at the futons laid side by side in the center of the room.

"Cozy, eh?" she smiled, "Just like Mr. and Mrs. Yamamoto."

"We can move them, if you like," I said, surprised to find myself suddenly nervous. The tightly knotted *yukata* emphasized the flair of her hips and the swell of her breasts in a way that her hiking outfit had not, and now that there were no Japanese present, I was not even struck by her size so much, though the too-small bathrobe should have emphasized it more. In fact, if anything, she looked smaller and more feminine in it. The open V formed by the crossing sides of the garment revealed a large expanse of pale skin above her breasts, the whiteness of which reminded me of Northern snowdrifts, and I realized that though she was a tall woman she was not out of proportion at all. I had merely forgotten what a white woman's body looks like.

"I've left the water in if you'd like a bath yourself," she said, rubbing her hair vigorously with the thick white towel. "Local custom, isn't it?"

Even now, I could smell the steam of the bathroom coming into the main room. It carried the sweet sour scent of Fiona's body. The idea of sitting in the same bath water Fiona had just come out of unnerved me somehow, though I had almost grown used to the custom in the time I'd spent with Japanese women and friends.

"I think . . . maybe later," I found myself stammering, "Did you cover it so it stays hot?"

She nodded. I had no idea what she was thinking or if the half smile that seemed to play over her lips constantly was mocking me or not. I was saved from finding out by the maid who entered with a meal. Two cups of miso soup, a square of tofu in soy sauce, a few pieces of sushi, rice and saki. The maid left it on the low table and bowed out. Fiona dug in with relish, handling her chopsticks deftly. *Jozu*, the Japanese would have said, she was very skillful, and her long pale fingers manipulated the sticks delicately.

By the time we'd finished, talking of this and that, it was nearly nine o'clock and I heard a few stirrings in the bamboo insect boxes behind me. Fiona's eyes brightened.

"They know it's dusk even though we're in here with lights on. Circadian rhythms. Amazing, isn't it?"

She unfurled herself from the table and padded across the tatami to her pack. She untied a few of the bamboo tubes and brought them back. Until this time we had managed to keep the table between us, but when she returned she sat down right next to me and set the little cages on the table. She brushed her hair back with her hand (it smelled like wet wool) and then, using a chopstick from dinner, she popped open one of the tubes. She turned it over and a three-inch long beetle fell scrabbling onto the table. Its back was the color of an emerald, and its curving mandibles were as long as the rest of its body. Fiona pinned it in place gently with her chopstick and held it on the small pile of rotting leaves and moss she'd packed in with it to serve as food.

I had jumped aside when the thing started scuttling towards my end of the table and Fiona laughed. "This one's an old Tokugawa warrior all right," she said as the beetle kicked furiously trying to escape her chopstick. "Don't worry though, those choppers are purely ornamental. They're rigid, don't close at all."

I looked more closely. I had seen prints of such insects and of crabs done up so the plates of chitin covering their bodies looked like samurai armor. Now for the first time I saw how little the artists had to exaggerate. Using her fingers, she carefully lifted the bug up by its hard shell and slipped it back into its cage, put the cover on and tied it closed.

"I can hardly wait to get back to the lab and study them," she said. She rattled off a dozen names of species she had found: *matsu mushi, kutsuma mushi, kusa hibari, kin hibari*. The Japanese girls taught her the local names. She undid another cage and emptied onto the table a green swordtailed grasshopper.

"*Munin*," Fiona said. The grasshopper looked around itself and took one or two tentative steps with its frail legs. Then it arched its legs like tiny flying buttresses and the room was filled with a strange, disembodied sound. It was a mournful melody, just three notes, long and slow, that came out of the *munin* and seemed to permeate the room like the odor of incense.

It was exquisite music, full of *mono-no-aware*, that "sadness of things" that the Japanese used to treasure so much in their art. It was something deep out of old Japan, like the moan of the wind through the branches of a thousand year old cypress tree or the whining song of a Noh actor.

"Every night at this time, right as a clock," she whispered. She seemed rapt by the sound, sitting there on her heels, like a Japanese woman, her hands on her thighs, the light summer kimono slightly open. She reminded me of a figure from an *ukiyo-e* print by Utamaro, *Girl with Grasshopper.*

"What's it singing about?" I asked.

"What's it singing about?" she repeated softly, not taking her eyes off the insect. "What do we all sing about? Loneliness, life, all that." She shook her hair back. "Sorry," she said, changing her tone.

"What for?"

"Not too scientific, that bit, was it?" She smiled, but her lips twisted up in a funny way. "I've just felt lonely lately," she continued. "I broke up with someone back at U-Syd just before I came here. The *munin's* probably just getting ready to molt or mate or something, nothing romantic about it."

Suddenly the room was jolted by a series of explosions. The Tanabata fireworks had begun. The paper of the outside *shoji* windows turned blue, red and white. Fiona slid the *munin* back into its box and joined me at the window. Over the ridge poles and tiled roofs of the houses across the street we could see the fireworks lighting up the sky. Fiona had turned her face up and I could see her pulse beneath the pale skin where the arc of her neck met the jaw. Her red hair was drying now and the light of the fireworks threw deep shadows into the whorls of its layers.

"What is *Tanabata* anyway?" she asked, "They have so many festivals here I don't know how they keep track."

"Seventh night of the seventh moon," I said, "An old legend. The star of the cowherd Tanabata meets the constellation of the Spinning Maiden over the River of heaven. They were separated by her father or something. The two lovers can meet only on this night. It's a very romantic holiday, for the Japanese, anyway."

Fiona sighed. "I was looking at the sky all week out on the Noto, flat on my back. One night I suddenly started to cry, just like that. I felt lost among the Northern constellations. They make no sense to me. God, how I missed the Southern Cross."

For some reason, her comment startled me. There was a note of sadness in her voice, and I could see her eyes straining up beyond the fireworks to the sky, trying to pick out the stars made invisible by the streetlights of Hakui. I had never thought much about the fact that Fiona, whom I had considered so like me, had grown up under a different sky on the bottom of the world. Her winter was my summer; her day my night. In the flickering light of the fireworks I suddenly found this woman, whom I thought I knew through and through because she was white like me, was very foreign to me.

In the narrow street beneath us, a gang of schoolgirls turned a corner and ran down the rain-damp pavement in blue sailor uniforms. They were carrying slips of paper and they gathered in a clutch around a small tree that stuck up incongruously from a hole in the sidewalk across the narrow back street our room faced. We watched as they tied the papers, prayers to the Spinning Maiden to bring them good husbands and lovers, onto the branches of the tree with pieces of colored yarn. The girls giggled and made bawdy jokes as they tied their prayers to the small tree. They were just ready to run off when an old woman in a frayed green kimono rounded the corner into the narrow street below us. She was carrying a *samisen* and she was accompanied by a younger man, an intellectual type, who carried a small tape recorder in his hand. The schoolgirls bowed before the old woman, apparently an old performer, and begged her for a Tanabata song. The *samisen* player exchanged a few words with the man, who, I guessed, was an ethnologist or folklorist from some university. (There was a push to save whatever bits and pieces they could of the past folk arts before they were all swallowed up by Japanese versions of American television.) The young man turned on his tape recorder as the old woman joked with the girls a bit about their boyfriends then struck her *samisen* with a large black plectrum and began to sing. Her old cracked voice and the sharp banjo-like twang of the instrument filled the empty street below.

Fiona edged closer to me. "What's she singing?" she whispered. The old woman looked up at us standing above her and seemed to smile, a bit embarrassed at having an alien audience. I bowed slightly and Fiona smiled and the old woman projected her voice up to us. It was a special moment for her. From the looks of the old kimono she wore, she was not well off, probably a singer who in the pre-war days had been popular in the entertainment districts but who had since fallen on hard times.

I translated as best I could as she sang plaintively:

> "*Would that I might become a star,*
> *The star of Tanabata!*
> *The crimson leaves of the maple tree*
> *Might bridge the River of Heaven*
> *and carry my love to me.*
> *The colored strings of the Tanabata festival*
> *Might bind my longing and desire*
> *To his handsome heart!*"

When the old woman finished, the girls bowed respectfully and Fiona and I applauded. When the girls saw us they squealed "bye-bye" and skittered off in a flurry of giggles to the next tree. We thanked the old singer, and she and her companion disappeared into a nearly deserted *yaki-tori* bar across the way, and the street was empty again, as if the scene below had been made of clouds. The fireworks had ended and I noticed that Fiona had looped her arm through mine as we stood at the window.

The sad song of the *munin* once again filled the silence and she turned her face to mine and said, "How about a kiss, Harry Dean? Japan's too damned beautiful to face alone."

As we made love on the dragon-embroidered futons, I was surprised at Fiona's strength. She was so different from the Japanese women (prostitutes whom my friends had arranged for me) I had made love to in the past two years. They were small-breasted and slim hipped, their arms no bigger around than wands of young bamboo. They were suffused with the taste that was not there. Their touch was so fine it had brought me as close as I ever thought I would get to being fully satisfied. But now I realized it had been like dining in Tokyo gourmet restaurants where the delicate taste was so tightly wrapped in a jacket of ceremony and ritual and artistic presentation you never really tasted anything. The women were highly polished surfaces, formed, like laquerware, by putting thin layer over thin layer until they were hard and cold and brittle. But Fiona's lovemaking was as straightforward as herself, blunt, athletic, and intoxicating, with nothing understated about it. Making love to her was like wrestling with something big and powerful. In the tight embrace of her arms and legs, I felt surrounded by something sure and oddly familiar I had been away from for a long time. The paper-thin walls of the old *ryokan* seemed to shake as we two big *gaijin* rolled on the blue and red dragons of the futons.

Afterwards, we lay on the tatami tangled in our yukata like two characters from an old erotic print. The *munin*'s song was finished and we heard only an occasional sound of movement from within the cages, soft sibilant sounds of hard shell against bamboo in the darkness. Blue light from the streetlight, not the moon, filtered through the shoji doors and the night was growing cooler. In the distance, the television still mumbled.

Without a word, Fiona turned toward me and fell asleep, her red hair tumbling over the silk cover of the futon. Her lips were parted slightly, revealing the white of her teeth. The blue light through the paper doors and windows threw the shadows of her breasts across her white skin and cast into darkness the rough triangle between her legs.

In the deep and strange calm that embraced us, I remembered the *munin*. In spite of the fireworks and the television and the cheapness of the room, it had filled the night with a sound as old as Japan itself, echoing from the time when the divine couple, Izanami and Izanagi, dipped their spear into the ocean at the beginning of time and drew up mud to form the islands. Beside me, a beetle scratched inside its cage with a sound like a fingernail against bamboo. I felt I had arrived in Japan even as I was preparing to leave it.

Three days later I was on a plane headed back to the United States. Fiona and I had parted with just a handshake at the train station in Hakui. It seemed oddly impersonal after the night before.

"Genji used to leave his lovers with a poem when they parted," I said as she boarded the train for Kanazawa. (I was heading up to Niigata to get the bullet back to Tokyo.)

Fiona shrugged and waved from the steps. "Well, give my love to old Genj if you see 'im," she said. "Meanwhile, bye-bye."

As I packed my books back at the Meiji Institute, I found a postcard from Tokyo Disneyland a friend had given me. On it, a Japanese school girl, in kimono, embraced Mickey Mouse as though there had never been anything else in the history of the entire world. I sent the card to Fiona at the University of Sydney, and on the back I copied some lines from *Genji monogatari* that I had looked up when I had gotten back to Tokyo:

> *The dew upon the locust wing*
> *Is lost among the leaves–*
> *So are my tears lost.*

On the plane, I wondered how she would react, back in the lab with her tubes of insects, when she received the card with Mickey Mouse on one side and Lady Murasaki's nine hundred year old verse on the other. I thought it strange that both those things were Japan, and then I thought it even more strange that I was sitting in a big aluminum tube hurtling through the sky listening to Bach and thinking of all this. From the ground, I realized, the plane I rode in was just a small white dot, making its way from star to star across the dark Pacific sky like the lost lover Tanabata.

ORIGAMI OR THE SADNESS OF PAPER BIRDS

Kathleen watched Reiko's fingers and tried to copy their movements, but her hands felt too large. Reiko's hands were small and delicate, almost like a child's, though she had just turned thirty, and the nails looked like ten crescent moons playing over the surface of the rice paper, folding and unfolding, creasing and bending until, with a slight tug at the ends, the bent paper was transformed into a flying crane. Kathleen's fingers were reddish and freckled, the nails too long to work the fine tissue. They looked like carrot stubs by comparison. The skin was beginning to hang loose on them.

Reiko set her bird aside on the lacquered table where it seemed to float as if on a small pond beside the other birds they had made that morning for the wedding of a friend of Reiko's, a young girl named Tomoko whose parents had forced her into an arranged marriage. Relatives and friends were making strings of paper cranes to hang in the shrine of *Ojizo-bosatsu*, the Buddhist god of good fortune. Reiko's own marriage had been the result of an *o-miai*, too. When she had returned from the United States after three years of college, she discovered that in her absence her parents had arranged a marriage for her to the son of friends of theirs. Though in Tokyo such a practice would be considered old fashioned, in the small town of Nishi-Maizuru matchmakers and arranged marriages were still common.

Reiko wrote long desperate letters to Kathleen, her former teacher, begging her for advice, but what advice could she give? Kathleen herself had married for love, but when Reiko's first letter had arrived it was just after Brad had decided something was missing in his life and had moved out, leaving her with a six year old and half a career. Marriage in general, whether for love or by arrangement, seemed like a bad idea at the time and she had encouraged Reiko to emigrate and pursue her interests. The young girl was a talented photographer and wanted to work for a magazine. Instead, she gave in to pressure from her family and had married Yasuhiro, an officer in a bank in the city of Nishi-Maizuru. The town was in a Japanese backwater, a four hour train ride from Kanazawa and a world away from the sophisticated Tokyo-Osaka corridor where a talented woman like Reiko might have had a chance to live and work on her own.

"Tea?" Reiko asked.

Kathleen nodded. "*Hai, ocha,*" she said.

Reiko smiled. "Very good," she said. "You are speaking Japanese very well."

Kathleen felt herself blush. The Japanese were incessantly flattering her for the slightest thing. That she used chopsticks amazed them, and, in one house she had visited, a mother scolded her son for not using his chopsticks as skillfully as the *gaijin.* They would applaud when she parroted the phrases she had learned. But in fact she knew she had the vocabulary of a two year old and was no more skillful eating Japanese style than anyone could be who had grown up eating with a knife and fork.

Reiko turned on her cushion and took a tin of green tea from a cabinet. Kneeling on the tatami, she opened the canister, pinched a bit of the tea between her thumb and forefinger, then put the tea in a small earthenware pot. After she had poured the water, she fanned herself with the side of her hand.

"Hot, no?" she asked.

"Yes, very," Kathleen said. "Why can't the Japanese do without tea even on days like this?"

Reiko looked embarrassed. "You don't want tea," she said.

"No, no," Kathleen answered. "It's not that. Please, *dozo*, it won't make it any hotter than it already is."

The morning's meal had consisted of a few dried fish encrusted with salt, some pickled vegetables, rice, hot tea and miso soup. The air already hung thickly about them. Yasu, in his white shirt and tie, quickly slurped his tea and soup and headed for work. Like most Japanese men, he seemed to drink very much at night, but somehow in the morning he was always ready for work, charging out the door with the energetic Japanese quick-step that would carry him through the day.

Reiko was left behind, a housewife, an *okusan*, something Kathleen thought would never happen to her.

She recalled the first time she had seen Reiko walking into her English class with the shy mincing steps of a Japanese schoolgirl, cradling the whole semester's worth of books. She had actually paused in front of the lectern and bowed stiffly. The quick awkward bow had taken Kathleen totally by surprise. No American student would do anything remotely resembling it. She was lucky if they even grunted. Even Reiko seemed to sense it was out of place, but she had just arrived in America and couldn't help herself. When she stood up from the bow, she gave a slight embarrassed smile, tucked her body sideways and hurried to her seat, sliding into it quickly because she was aware others were looking at her. She had stood out. The one thing the Japanese seemed to want more than anything else was not to stand out. They told one another, "The nail that stands up gets hammered down," and so wherever they went, they tried relentlessly to look and act like everyone else, but, being Japanese, they always failed. Only at home, on the island, could they blend in and be invisible.

Outside Reiko's house it was raining as it had ever since Kathleen had arrived in Japan two weeks before. She had added a new word to her small Japanese vocabulary, *tsuyu*, the rainy season. A fine mist hung in the air constantly. If not for the intense heat it would have been picturesque. The mist muted the colors all around, and in the distance outside the window she could see patches of cloud hovering around the top of a cone shaped mountain. It reminded her of a scroll painting she had seen in the National Museum in Tokyo. But the heat made it unbearable. And everywhere she had to drink tea, hot steaming tea.

"You don't do photography anymore?" Kathleen asked as Reiko handed her a cup of tea. She set it on the table to let it cool before drinking it. Her head and hair felt damp in the heat.

"Only of family, things like these," she said. She pointed to photos of her two children, now in school, hanging on the wall.

"Don't you miss it?"

"No," said Reiko as if it was something she had long ago taken for granted. She picked up another square of paper, folded it in half corner to corner then paused. "Yes, I mean. I do miss it. That is, sometimes. I don't know. Do you understand?" Then she muttered a few more words in Japanese, the only ones of which Kathleen caught were "*so desu ne?*" which the Japanese use to end every sentence the way some Americans use "you know?"

"I don't think I do understand," Kathleen said.

"There is no word, exactly," Reiko said.

Kathleen imagined there existed one word in Japanese that could encapsulate all the contradictory things Reiko wanted to say. English seemed so awkward sometimes, a big clunking language with no way of expressing finer shades of meaning the way Japanese could. Silence fell between them for a moment, and a momentary sadness hung in the air like the hot mist. Kathleen tasted her hot tea and looked out the window. Behind the house, a farmer was tending a small vegetable patch of cabbage, potatoes and soy beans. The metallic thump of his hoe made a dull rhythm that reminded her of the clack of the bamboo *shishi odoshi* against the stone in the stream of the monastery at Ryoanji in Kyoto. The sharp crack that came as the hollow bamboo rhythmically filled with water and swung down upon the river stone was originally used to frighten deer away, but in time it came to be appreciated for its abstract beauty, the sudden flash of sound that served to remind the listener of the eternal silence surrounding everything.

The farmer had arrived early this morning on his bicycle. A Japanese farmer might have many fields this size, and he would ride from one to another throughout the day. No land was wasted in Japan. Every open patch along the railroad tracks, behind houses and even between factories was used for food. The rice fields everywhere reminded her, for some reason, of the way cornfields dot everyplace in the midwest.

"I sometimes think I should not have gone to America," Reiko said. "When I came back I felt strange, like a foreigner. It is very hard for Japanese to come back to Japan." She made a sharp crease in the paper with her thumbnail. The sound it made was like a letter opener slitting open an envelope. Kathleen went back to her own bird. Her large fingers worked the paper clumsily, and her cranes were coming out lopsided. They leaned on the table as if wounded. Fortunately, she was slow and only a few lame birds swam among the flotilla of a perfectly formed ones that Reiko had made. When they put them on the string for the wedding, she would hang hers on the inside so people couldn't see.

"Are you happy, Reiko?" Kathleen asked. It was a question she wanted to ask since she had arrived at the house three days before.

Reiko looked surprised she would ask such a question, then she looked puzzled, much as she had back in her student days when Kathleen would try to explain to her some confused meaning in English. Reiko's voice went soft and her eyes turned away to the floor. "I think I was happy here until you came, Kathleen-san."

Kathleen sensed her coming had brought back too many memories of Reiko's student days. She feared her presence might have shamed Reiko by pointing out the difference between what she had wanted to be ten years before and what she had become. Though they had corresponded regularly over the years, this was their first meeting in all that time.

"I'm sorry," Kathleen said.

"Oh, no" said Reiko. "I didn't mean . . . I mean, I am very happy to see you again, but I have not spoken English for a long time. I am understanding that I am not unhappy in Japanese. I am not happy only in English." Again she chewed her lower lip and then spoke in hurried Japanese, obviously frustrated she could not explain herself. "I am not happy in English because in Japanese we have no way of saying the kind of unhappy I am. There are no words for the feelings I learned in America, does this make sense?"

"Can't you speak to Yasu?"

"It is not Yasu," she said, "I am disappointed, that's all."

"In what?"

"*Hoyoma!*" Reiko exclaimed. "I cannot say."

Kathleen looked past her out the window again. The farmer was wearing a straw hat to shed the light rain that was falling. The rhythm of his hoe continued, patiently, endlessly. The simple scene, framed by the open shoji window, reminded her of the *ukiyo-e* prints she had seen in the National Museum. They were genre pieces, drawings of everyday life, and the word *ukiyo-e* meant, in English, "pictures of the floating world," as though those pictures of everyday life were representations of a world that was really just an illusion. This world of appearances was believed to be afloat on a timeless sea that, in the end, was utterly indifferent to the fates and unhappinesses of human beings. The two of them in the room, sitting on the tatami, making paper birds, could be a scene from *ukiyo-e*. The word *ukiyo*, she had learned, also meant "sad."

Looking out the window at the farmer and at the mist-enshrouded mountains behind him, the world did in fact seem to be floating and insubstantial, and even her existence in the middle of it seemed to be unsure. Two weeks before she had been home in her apartment, planning for this trip, a way of celebrating her forty-fifth birthday, a sign of independence or something. She had lunch with her sixteen year old daughter who was going to live with Brad for the summer. Then she had flown to Seattle and from there to Tokyo. She had started out in high spirits. It was her first trip alone in nearly twenty years. Then, on the plane, somewhere high above the Pacific, she had suddenly felt. . .what did she feel? Disappointed? Was Reiko's word the correct one after all? Was that the only word to describe the feeling of getting older, of having watched the expectations of your younger self fall away one by one?

Reiko left the room and came back a moment later with her dual text edition of Shakespeare, the one they had used together ten years before. Reiko had marked a place in *The Tempest* and she showed it to Kathleen. It was the line where Caliban, infuriated with Prospero, explodes:

> *You taught me language; and my profit on it*
> *Is I know how to curse. The red plague rid you*
> *For learning me your language!*

"I'm sorry Reiko, I'm so sorry," Kathleen said.

Together the two women cried in the hot moist room as the farmer outside continued to hoe. Tears fell on the rice paper. They folded more and still more paper cranes in silence, bending them into the intricate folds and creases that make up the floating world, folding them desperately to make a string of paper birds, a frail wish for someone else's good fortune.

STES. MARIES-DE-LA-MER

Marc had a thing about looking like a tourist so he had tucked himself into a doorway across from the railway station in Arles and was thumbing through his Frommer's with his back turned to the street. Virginia sat on her bright purple *Ciao* bag that, after two weeks of travel, looked something like a rumpled eggplant. She watched the parade of brightly colored Mopeds, Renaults and Citroens as they rumbled noisily through the broad main street. She had given up trying to get Marc to ask questions or refer to a map in train stations.

"I don't want to look like a tourist," he snapped the last time she had brought it up.

"Look at us!" she'd replied, "Suitcases, cameras, maps, guidebooks—what the hell do you think we look like? What the hell do you think we *are?*"

"You know what I mean," he said. His voice took on that waspish tone it got whenever she had him cornered. She knew better than to push it further. If she did, he would close the guide book, throw it in the day bag and pinch the bridge of his nose in that long-suffering way he had and, in complete control, he would say something like, "Well, we could just go home, you know," or "We don't *have* to travel, do we?" and then he'd be impossible for the rest of the day. He'd get solicitous.

"Is your *citron presse* lemony enough, dear?" he would ask. He did it just to aggravate her.

She often thought of just staying home alone.

"Married people shouldn't travel together," her friend Rosalee had said. Rosalee went to Puerta Vallarta every February without Ron. He went to Vail. It saved their marriage, Rosalee said. Virginia would have listened but she found it difficult to take advice from someone who painted her toenails red. Besides, Marc would never stand for it. "You stay home?" he asked in disbelief when she'd brought it up one time, "What would people think?"

And so she'd learned to follow him in his mad dashes from the railroad stations. He'd walk blindly for one or two blocks in any direction to get away from other tourists and only then would he stop and figure out where they needed to go. It didn't matter they often had to backtrack through the station again because they had lit out in the wrong direction in the first place. Marc would not, under any circumstances, pull out a map in a station. Perhaps he wanted people to think he was a native just returning from a trip, that he lived in Strasbourg or Edinburgh or wherever, and so he would just walk confidently right out of the station with her behind him as if he knew exactly where he was headed, though he really didn't have the slightest idea.

They had just come down the Rhone. The previous year they had done an oenophile's tour of Bordeaux. This year they were doing Burgundy and the Cotes du Rhone. They had eaten their way through Lyons and Dijon then had slowly worked their way down the river valley, stopping at Chateauneuf du Pape for two days though there was nothing to do there really.

The train ran between the steep vineyard-covered slopes of the Rhone valley. As they came towards Arles, they watched the broad brown river spend itself, growing wide and warm like the Mississippi in its more flaccid bends. The swift flow cut a deep trough through the hillsides south of Lyons then gradually slowed and broadened as the land grew flat. Downstream from Arles the river oozed slowly into the broad delta of the Camargue and, in that great flood plain, gradually emptied itself into the Mediterranean.

Virginia had covered her eyes with her hand, making a visor to shield her from the glare as she watched the street. Marc refused to let her wear sunglasses when they traveled abroad. ("For Christ' sakes," he said, "You may as well wear a sign around your neck.")

"You're looking for a place to stay?" a man asked.

Marc turned quickly from the doorway, his finger jammed into the Frommer's. "No," he said, tucking the book behind his back. "What makes you think that?"

Virginia rolled her eyes. "We're tourists," she said.

"Virginia!" snapped Marc.

"I have a place," the man replied. He was tall and tanned, in his forties, American by his accent. His narrowly-striped cotton shirt had no collar and the cuffs were turned one-quarter up his forearms. His light hair was longish and there was something suggesting the 1960's in the flatness of his rounded steelrims. He wore khaki pants and the hair on his forearms had been turned the color of sand by the hot sun of the *midi*. Virginia stood so she would not have to be looking up into the sun at him. If she had looked more closely, she might have noticed something tired about him, as if he were searching for inspiration. It was not clear, however, whether he was really looking or whether he had given up and had simply maintained the world-weary look as a way of attracting women.

"I'm Jeremy," he said, reaching out and shaking her hand.

He was keeping house for a couple of French friends, Arlesiennes, he said, who were up in Strasbourg for a couple of weeks to visit a sick aunt or something and they gave him permission to rent out the room and keep the money.

It was only a short walk away, and Marc quickly slipped his Frommer's into the day pack as they fell in beside Jeremy.

Jeremy walked slowly, with flowing steps, his sandaled feet leisurely sweeping above the concrete. Along the way he pointed out directions in a peculiar offhand way. "To the Roman ruins," he said, vaguely flicking his hand towards a narrow street that angled off to the right. Then he added, "They use the arena for bullfights. Provençal usually. They don't kill the bull. Sometimes Spanish-style, with killing."

Pause. "If you're into that." He talked in a laid back way, self-consciously and excruciatingly cool, like someone who had seen too much, like a person who's overeaten and can't even think about food anymore.

They walked through a couple of narrow streets, little more than alleys really, that finally gave way to the broad boulevard where the house was located. As they approached an open-fronted bar, she noticed several swarthy men in brightly-colored shirts staring at her. The men leaned back on their elbows on the mahogany bar and their eyes frankly and forthrightly went over her body bottom to top and back again, stopping at each way station—ankles, calves, bottom, breasts—long enough to appraise, compare, and imagine before moving on again. She tried staring back but couldn't maintain eye contact. Her eyes kept drifting to the large patches of black wiry hair that spilled out the open V's of their shirts, and she felt afraid and vaguely threatened.

"Is this a particularly rough neighborhood?" she asked Jeremy as they got closer to the bar.

"No, why?"

"Those men, the way they stare."

He shrugged. "The men are different here," he said, "Pretty unevolved, you know. It's their Mediterranean thing. They don't mean anything by it."

"It makes me feel like a piece of meat."

"Virginia," said Marc, "It's called *machismo*. It's older than the hills around here. You can't expect to liberate them. You don't even speak the local dialect for Christ's sake. When in Rome, you know."

In an angry flash, she decided to show him how a woman should react to machismo, and she stopped in her tracks, set down her *Ciao* bag, put her arms akimbo and stared hard at one of the men, face to face about fifteen feet away. Without blinking his eyes or turning them away for a moment, the man curled up his lip in a half smile, his head nodding almost imperceptibly in appreciation of her boldness. He then lowered his gaze, stared for a moment at the triangle formed by the crotch of her jeans and then back up at her. He stuck out his tongue and licked. She felt her face go red and she tucked her head down and charged after the others, forgetting her bag which she had to go back for as the men in the cafe laughed.

"For God's sake, Virginia," Marc snapped.

"You might have done something, Marc," she said.

"What? Go *mano a mano* with one of those Spaniards? Are you out of your mind?"

"They aren't Spaniards," Jeremy said. "Probably Algerian."

"Whatever. They probably carry knives. I don't."

The trio walked the rest of the way in silence. Perhaps Rosalee was right about separate vacations saving marriages, Virginia thought as she watched Marc stroll along the street beside Jeremy as if he lived there. The house they eventually arrived at almost made her forget the men in the bar. It was a white-washed two storey place in the middle of a line of similar houses that stood in a semi-detached line along the boulevard. A couple of palm trees stood at the curb where a line of cars had angled up. In spite of the business of the street, the house had a sort of charm to it. Its white walls reflected the bright sunlight as Jeremy opened a large double door made of a light varnished wood and led them into a dark and separate-feeling foyer.

The interior of the house was cool, the shutters being closed against the heat of the early afternoon sun. Virginia could feel the coldness of the foyer's red tiles through the rope soles of her espadrilles. At the end of the hallway was a small courtyard behind the house with a green box of geraniums hung on the high white stucco wall. The geraniums glowed like neon in the sunlight and sent a pink reflection into the house.

She had forgotten how introverted French houses were. Behind the plain facades, hidden by the ever-present *grils* and shutters, the interiors were rich and colorful. Unlike American houses with their big picture windows inviting neighbors to look in, French houses turned in on themselves, saving their most interesting parts for private viewing only.

Jeremy showed them their room at the top of the stairs and left them. He and Marc had agreed on a ridiculously low price on the way over. Marc sat on the edge of the bed. The antique frame was made of a dark wood and the mattress was covered with a light bedspread made of Indian cotton woven in a loose pattern of red and orange.

"Do you think it's all right?" she asked.

"What do you mean?" asked Marc, falling back on the bed full length and staring at the ceiling. "Look at that plasterwork, lost art," he muttered.

"I mean we don't know who this man is," she said. "This could be anything. Drugs. Weird sex. Who knows? People don't just come up to you on the street and offer you cheap rooms, do they?" She was unusually nervous, still remembering the men in the bar.

"Oh, stop talking like a tourist," he said. "Where's your sense of adventure?"

"Well at least there's a lock on the bedroom door," she said, "We can sleep anyway."

Once they had washed up, they had lunch at a small cafe near the Place du Forum and then spent the early afternoon shopping for supper at an outdoor market and the local Monoprix. Then, while Marc went off to see the baths of Constantine, she sat in the small courtyard reading Simenon's *Le Fou de Bergerac* and tanning her legs. Jeremy was out for the afternoon. He had not said where he was going. He was vague, as usual, and only said he had some "things" to do. There was a small washing machine on the patio and she threw a few things in, deciphering as best she could the instructions which had been partly scraped off the metal. The small washer growled and wobbled as it ran, and during the wash cycle, a small rivulet of suds spilled out the top but then stopped.

Halfway through the first rinse, Jeremy returned. He startled her. She had not heard him come in the front door and she got the uneasy feeling he may have been there all along, in some room they hadn't discovered yet.

"Hi," he said. His smile was half on, and the flat round lenses of his steelrims made his eyes seem bigger than they were and gave him an air of innocence that nothing else about him suggested. Now, closer, she could see his light sandy hair was partially shot through with flecks of silver.

"So, how did you get this place?" she asked, putting her book self-consciously on her knees and sitting up straight in her chair.

"I meet people," he said. "It's what I do, all over the place. You know how you do."

"Uh-hum," she said. She caught a glimpse of herself in the French window. She was sitting in the sunlight and the window reflection clearly showed her white blouse and the cotton skirt she had pulled up to expose her legs. She was wearing her round tortoise shell reading sunglasses and was surprised how cool she looked, dressed in white against the white stucco wall of the courtyard with the glasses on. She thought she looked European, like someone she had never been. She mentioned how the courtyard didn't seem so hot.

"The stone holds the cool of the night," he said, "Then tonight, it will hold the heat so it'll be warm enough out here. It works quite well that way, the house I mean. Don't need air conditioning or heat."

"Oh," she said, and there was an awkward silence during which the wash machine suddenly kicked two spurts of gray water out of the hose. It gurgled down the drain.

"Temperamental thing," Jeremy said, walking up to it and softly nudging it a quarter inch to the left. The machine grew a little quieter. She cleared her throat. He didn't seem to need to talk. He was one of those men who are comfortable with long silences, or who at least seem that way. She tentatively went to pick her novel up again, but hesitated, her hands fluttering for a moment above the cover, then she folded them in the lap of her skirt. She wanted to brush the skirt down below her knees again but felt too self-conscious, vaguely uncomfortable and even vaguely threatened by Jeremy. She wanted to know more about him, if only to ease her fears.

"So, where you from anyway?" she asked.

"All over," Jeremy said flopping his hand back and forth a couple of times. He looked at her without blinking in the bright Mediterranean sun, as if his eyes had grown used to it. She found his stare unnerving.

"Well, yes," she said, "but you must be from some place. Everybody's from someplace. I'm from Lansing, originally. We're from East Grand Rapids now. Michigan."

He nodded to indicate he had heard of it. Then he shrugged, and, as if pulling a name out of a hat, said, "I spent some time in Vancouver, I guess."

"That's someplace," she said, "but I thought you were American."

"I am," he said, running his finger beneath his nose like an embarrassed schoolboy, "or was, sort of anyway."

"Are you from the Northwest, then?"

"O.K.," Jeremy said, smiling agreeably as if that was as good an idea as any.

She laughed nervously. "No really. Where are you from?"

"Memphis," he said, "I'm from Memphis."

"You're not southern," she said, "Come on." She looked at him again. His features were fine, the bones on his face clearly outlined and his forehead high. His lips were thin and when he opened his mouth, he had teeth as straight as a fence, amazingly good teeth. "I'll bet New England, I'd guess Connecticut."

"All right," he said, "You got me."

"Really?"

He laughed and she blushed, fearing he was starting to make fun of her. She noticed she had slumped down into the chair, so she stiffened in her chair, her voice cooler now. "I was only trying to make conversation," she said, sounding more hurt than she wanted.

"I'm sorry," he said, "It's just that after so long it doesn't matter. Where I'm from isn't me anymore, you know?"

"So what about you?" he asked, "Do you, like, work or anything?"

What should she say? She had spent nearly thirteen years in the same city, married to the same man, Marc, who would soon take over the family's small furniture business from his father. What she had seen of the world had been with Marc, but she did not want to tell Jeremy this.

"I volunteer. I direct the World Humanities Council back home. We bring in speakers, lectures, films, that sort of thing once a month." She felt small and unimportant suddenly, imagining that Jeremy, who had been all over the world, couldn't possibly find her life at home at all intriguing. "It's very interesting, really, my work I mean."

"I'll bet," he said, smiling.

She saw herself again in the mirror-like window. She noticed that a small window had opened on her blouse front through which the top of her bra and the curve of a breast could be seen. If she was alone, she would have thought it made her look seductive and interesting, but now she straightened up her back to close the blouse and used the opportunity to pull her skirt back down over her legs.

The small washer finished its spin cycle and stopped. A buzzer went off, making Virginia flinch a bit. For some reason she felt like a boxer at the end of a round, though she had not known they had been sparring. Jeremy stood there, his hand on his hip, smiling at her in a way she felt mocked her. She disliked his insolent maleness, his chic Euro-cool.

"Well, I have some things to do," Jeremy said, jerking his thumb towards the inside of the house. But he didn't move. It was as if he were waiting for her to ask him to stay and talk. Things hung there for a second, suspended, and she wanted to ask him something else—the meaning of a French word she had just run across in her book, anything to break the silence—but she really wanted him to go so she remained silent. She was afraid he was going to come towards her, even touch her, in the tense silence. Just then, however, Marc came back. She had not heard him come in either and realized that the courtyard was built in such a way that it muffled sound. Marc came over to her chair and his lips hovered like a helicopter about three inches above her head. He made a smacking sound that passed for a kiss.

"What have you two been up to?" he asked.

"Nothing. Nothing at all," she said, again straightening her skirt that no longer needed straightening. "Just laundry."

They planned to eat a late supper, Provençal style, starting about nine-thirty, just the two of them, she and Marc. Jeremy had said he had made plans to be out for the evening. She found herself singing in the kitchen as she made *poulet basquaise* with the peppers, chili and chicken they had bought from the market. This was the kind of vacation she longed for, she told herself, the two of them alone in an old house in France.

Then, about a half and hour before dinner time, Marc came in.
"Guess what?" he said, pecking her on the cheek, "I met Jeremy in town and talked him into joining us. What a fascinating guy."

She felt the song go right out of her. During dinner, she found herself watching Jeremy closely. She noticed small things about him. He ate European style, not like an American. He smoked Gitaines. She watched him nod appreciatively as Marc spent the whole meal going over their wine itinerary bottle by bottle from the time their plane left Detroit Metro ("You can't get good wine on an airplane, of course, but you'd think Air France, for God's sake, would stock a decent house white, wouldn't you?") to their sojourn at Chateauneuf du Pape. ("A couple of amusing little houses, but no depth, not like the Bordeaux.")

After they had finished the *poulet basquaise*, Jeremy said, "I have some wine you should try." Marc, who had been drifting off during dinner, suddenly perked up a little as Jeremy got up from the table and opened a small cabinet in the corner of the kitchen. Inside were two dozen or so large green bottles standing in ranks like a slope-shouldered regiment. None of the bottles had labels. Jeremy lifted two of them with one hand and they clinked together. They had drunk two bottles of white with dinner and Marc had begun to slur.

"You'll like this Marc," he said, twisting in the corkscrew. The meat of the cork squeaked as the screw bit into it. "I get it straight from the *caves*. I met the proprietor. It's his special reserve. No preservatives. He lets me bring my own bottles and the cellar master fills them right from the casks."

The cork came out with a resonant pop that filled the kitchen. Marc picked it from the table and sniffed. His eyebrows lifted. They let the wine breathe while they cleaned up then Jeremy set three glasses on the table and filled them up. All during dinner, he had let little bits about himself drop whenever Marc gave him a chance. Vague things that hinted at a mysterious past. It was almost calculated, she thought. "*Cha*," he said at one point apropos of nothing in particular, "If you know only that one word you can travel from Turkey to Japan to Mongolia and always get tea and a meal. *Cha, chai, o-cha.*" He also let fall names of other cities and countries in such a casual way that she assembled from the pieces a picture of him rather aimlessly and romantically wandering the world since about the time she had graduated from high school fifteen years before. He seemed to her to be rootless, floating, open to anything, as if he hadn't aged at all in those years on the road while she and Marc, who were seven or eight years younger than he, were beginning to flatten out already, weighed down by the gravity of sitting in one place too long. Even in their trips abroad, they never seemed to get anywhere. They got home and it seemed sometimes as if they had never left. Nothing had changed except they added one new photo album to the shelf in the study.

Jeremy slid the glasses in front of them.

"It's not a dessert wine, of course," he said, "but . . ."

Marc lifted his glass and swirled it a bit to see how well the deep scarlet wine clung to the sides.

"Good nose, eh?" Jeremy asked, sniffing the aroma above the rim.

"Uh-hum," Marc nodded, imitating him. "Great nose."

"Go ahead," Jeremy said.

Marc drank, smacking his lips and clucking his tongue against his palate. His face melted. "Jesus," he said. His eyes were closed.

She tasted. It seemed no better or worse than many of the other wines they'd been drinking for the past two weeks.

"It gets better as the bottle goes down," Jeremy said.

"Honey, isn't this incredible?" Marc asked. "Why haven't we had this before? Jesus, if I could ship this back home, I could make a fortune."

"Doesn't travel well," Jeremy said.

"Of course," Marc sighed. He tasted again and ran his tongue over the roof of his mouth as if licking velvet.

Virginia could hear him practicing already for the story he would tell at the Grapevine the next time they went there when they got home. "You can't get it anywhere else in the friggin' world," he would say, knowing none of the others would ever get a chance to contradict him. "Best red I've ever tasted." Half of the reason he traveled the way he did was so he could have these little half-adventures with which to lord it over his stockbroker friends at the yuppie bars. It was a safe bet none of them would ever travel second class or stay at the house of someone who picked them up at the railroad station, and so he was free to invent. In every retelling the trains got a little more like the Orient Express, the one-star hotels got more quaint and, she knew, this wine Jeremy had poured into balloon glasses would get richer, deeper, and more profound each year as it aged in the cellerage of Marc's imagination.

"More?" Jeremy asked, sliding the bottle across the table. Marc poured eagerly, but filled the glass only half way to let the aroma fill the void. She couldn't stand it anymore.

"I'm going to take a bath," Virginia said.

When she returned, one bottle was empty and Marc was clearly drunk. Jeremy had popped an Edith Piaf tape into his casette deck and Marc was loudly humming along to *La Vie en Rose.* "Isn't this great, honey?" he asked, his voice thick. "Isn't this . . ." he searched for a word, ". . .European?" Jeremy, too, was drunk, though more controlled than Marc. She could only tell because his normally pale face was a little flushed and the corner of his mouth was turned up in a smile.

"Tomorrow," he said, "You must go to Stes. Maries de la Mer. It's a neat town, painted by Van Gogh." He pronounced the artist's name "fan Hoch," the final sound degenerating into a guttural clatter. "The town's in the Camargue, right on the sea." He waved his hand as he had when pointing to the Roman ruins. "The Camargue: flamingoes, wild horses, the whole shot."

"Right," slurred Marc, "We'll do that, eh, honey?" By this time, he was swilling down the wine like a cheap house red. She knew his sinuses would kill him in the morning because of the histamines in the red, but it would do no good to remind him. "Here's to Stes. Maries de la Mer," he said as he pounded back another glass. "Where is it again?"

"You just go to the Mediterranean and hang a left," Jeremy said. While she was taking her bath, they had become like two boys in that peculiar male-bonding way that alcohol does to men. She felt closed out as they looked at each other and laughed.

"'To the Mediterranean and hang a left,'" Marc repeated, "I love that. Here's to the friggin' Mediterranean!"

"I'll get the map," she said, going out for the day bag. When she got back, Marc had laid his head down on the table. His eyes were bleary and his neck was floppy and she knew he would be asleep soon. As she straightened the accordion folds of the map on the table top, his eyes closed and his breathing changed. She located the blue line of the Rhone and followed it down through Arles and into the Camargue, seeing Stes. Maries de la Mer on the coast between the Petit Rhone on the east and the Grand Rhone on the west.

The Piaf tape played out and in the silence, Jeremy had moved behind her and leaned over, his long finger running along the coast until it lighted on the spot.

"There," he said. His arm was over her shoulder. "You take a bus down from the Place du Forum, I forget the number, but it's marked Camargue."

Marc's deep bronchitic snore started. It was the histamines in the red wines. He always said red wine made his lungs feel like fluffy flannel but he didn't let that stop him from drinking.

"A bus to the . . .?"

"Camargue," he said. His hand had slid around behind her and under her arm. He lifted her from the chair. Now he ran his hand up under her hair and lifted it, his face a few inches from hers. She could see the lines more clearly now. Though he looked like a boy from a few feet away, up close he was clearly aging.

"Don't," she said.

"Don't what?"

"Don't this." Her eyes flicked over to Marc, asleep on the table.

"Oh, married, eh?" Jeremy asked, not moving his hand. His fingers played with the ends of her hair.

"You knew I was married."

"I didn't think you were *that* married," he said.

She wanted Marc to do something, to wake up and lift his head and see her like this. Why? What did she expect him to do? Did she think he would leap up, as she imagined one of the swarthy men in the bar might do, and shout something about the honor of his woman? Did she really expect Marc, her Marc, to jump up and break one of the empty wine bottles and twist it into Jeremy's face? She knew he never would. He would merely look up, blink once or twice, twitch his lips and then say something like "Virginia, for cripes' sake." And that would be the end of it.

She brushed Jeremy's arm away and felt his fingers slide through her hair.

"I don't do this kind of thing," she said, steeling herself for a struggle. Like all men, she thought, he would prod, he'd push, he'd cajole, he'd try again, but she would be ready. She would be firm and consistent. What made men act like this around women anyway, sniffing up their crotches like dogs, looking for the—to them—dark and mysterious place. She wouldn't put up with it. She was ready.

"Okay," he shrugged, "That's cool. I can respect that." And he picked up the bottles and put them away. "Gotta return the empties," he said, scratching his head sleepily. "Listen, would you mind turning out the light?" And he was gone.

The following morning, Marc sat beside her on the bus, his hand spanning his forehead from temple to temple, squeezing tight as if to prevent it from exploding. Marc at first refused to go to Stes. Maries. He said he felt as if someone were driving a wedge between his eyebrows, but she forced him out of bed.

"We're going," she'd said, yanking the covers off him early. "You seemed to think it was a great idea last night when you and Jeremy were drunk. The bus leaves the Place du Forum at 10. We're going to be on it, Marc. Now up."

The bus was not marked Camargue. It was marked Stes. Maries de-la-Mer. Jeremy was gone by the time they got up that morning. There was only a note, scrawled in French, "*Je vous souhaite un jour tres agreable.*" "Have a nice day," with a French accent, she thought. She found the note when she came down for coffee and she threw it in the trash. She was glad he was not there.

She was still angry with him, and with herself, for the night before. She told herself nothing had happened, but that only made her angrier.

They caught the bus and the city of Arles gave way to a winding white road. Marc tried to sleep, but his head kept banging against the window of the bus. Beyond him, in the brilliant sunlight, the land flattened out and the horizon grew big and round. In the wet flood plains, rice grew, and here and there she began to see the stocky white horses of the Camargue looking as though they'd been dipped in chalk dust. A flamingo stood knee deep in a ditch beside the road as if someone had planted it there. The land was primitive and she began to get a giddy sense that the bus was taking them to the edge of a flat earth or that they would just keep driving out to the bright white rim of the horizon and disappear there as into a vanishing point on a painting.

When the bus stopped at the main square on the edge of the Mediterranean, Marc pulled her to a table at an outdoor cafe.

"I've *got* to get my fluids up," he said, ordering two Cokes with ice, something he would never do unless the situation were grave.

The square was hot and dry, yellow with dust though the great aqua sea was only a few feet away over a breakwall.

"He tried to kiss me last night," Virginia said when the Cokes came.

"Jeremy?"

"After you passed out."

"I didn't pass out," Marc said, "I fell asleep." He sipped his Coke and chewed a couple of ice cubes with his eyes closed against the bright sunlight. She waited.

"Well?"

"Well what?" he asked.

"He tried to kiss me, Marc!"

"Of course he tried to kiss you."

"You don't believe me?"

He shrugged as he put the cold glass against his forehead. "You just don't do that sort of thing, Virginia, not you."

She stood up angrily from the table. "I'm going to the church. Right now." She marched across the hot square towards the church of Stes. Maries de la Mer. Marc got up and fumbled in his pocket for change to leave on the table.

"Wait, honey!" he called.

But she did not want to wait. She wanted to get as far away from him as she could. The old 12th century church with its thick masonry walls promised relief. It had been fortified against the Moslems, perhaps it could protect her from Marc. What did he think anyway, that she wasn't attractive to men anymore, that she never wondered what it was like to sleep with another man? Couldn't he be at least a little jealous?

Her eyes focused on a dark cool doorway in the side of the white wall of the church. She vaguely heard the clatter of hooves against the cobblestones of the square but didn't really notice them until she received a rough shove.

"*Tiens!*" A policeman prodded her out of the way with a push from his baton. "*Gardez, madam!*" he said, pointing towards a gypsy processional that was rounding the corner and coming right at her. Two dozen laughing men sitting astride white horses cantered across the square and had almost run over her. They were dark-skinned and passed a leather wineskin among them, shooting long lines of red into their open mouths. One man sang. They passed so near she could smell the sour sweat of the horses and the leather of the reins and saddles. Only the policeman's arm kept her from falling into their path.

One of the gypsy men looked down at her and grinned, revealing a gold tooth in the bottom of his mouth. Another nudged him–the horses were that close together–and they laughed, tossing back their heads in their funny little hats that were like a cross between fedoras and Stetsons.

She wheeled around on her heel furiously, running from the smell of the men and their horses and their coarse rough laughter. The entrance of the crypt looked dark and cool and she headed for it. But it was not cool. As she set her foot on the first step down, she was hit with a wall of heat that pushed against her like a hand. The narrow stairwell was like a chimney and the smell of beeswax and the smoke of guttering candles filled her nostrils. She started to turn back but then heard Marc call her. He was trapped on the other side of the small parade of horses which now was cantering and galloping in circles to the accompaniment of gypsy songs.

"Honey!" he called, straining his neck upwards to see over the horses' backs, "Wait, honey!"

She hated him calling her honey, and she plunged down the stairs.

It was quiet there, like a tomb, with the gagging smell of underground mold. The crypt was lit with the yellow flickering of candles, thousands of them, stuck on spikes, guttering away in the darkness. Their heat is what she had felt as she came down the stairs. They formed a large semi-circle around a strange icon standing in the corner.

The statue was the size of a small woman, dressed in a long flowing gown filigreed with gold and red and black. Her face was black, like clarinet wood. Virginia felt drawn to it and as she wandered over and stared at it, the heat and close air of the crypt seemed less stifling.

The figure wore an ornate golden crown with jewels enclosing the temples. Virginia gazed at the statue's golden eyes until they seemed to gaze back. The expression on the statue's face unnerved her and she turned to the plaque on the smoke-blackened wall beside the statue.

This was St. Sara, patroness of gypsies, the plaque explained. She had come to the Camargue sometime during the first century when the two Maries who had found Christ's empty tomb had been set adrift in a leaky skiff during a persecution. The two virgins and their servant had floated for weeks until, famished, exhausted, they washed ashore here where the Rhone filtered into the sea. The church above was dedicated to the two Maries. Sara's shrine was here in the crypt. Once a year the gypsies came and took her out of this vault and bathed her in the sea and then brought her back to the dim candlelight and perpetual heat of the underchurch.

Virginia stared again at the troubling statue and then looked at her own image in the glass of a case that displayed other of Sara's gowns. Her reflection was ghostly. She was dressed in cool white cotton. Her skin was as pale as shaved ice, her hair the light blond color of pearwood. She felt fragile and brittle in front of the statue of Sara, like twice-fired porcelain, vitreous, so pale light would go right through her.

It would have been so easy to kiss him, she thought now as she turned her eyes back to the golden unblinking eyes of Sara. It would have been so easy to fall, to relax into the pull of his arms, but she had not. She had held there, suspended, crisp, controlled.

"I don't do this," she had said, "I don't do this kind of thing." Marc was right about her.

But it had not been a *kind* of thing at all. It had been one thing only, one time only, irredeemably past now, a thing that would not return again.

She stared again at Sara. Yes, she admitted, she had wanted to feel another pair of lips and arms around her than Marc's. She had wanted to give in to the fullness and heaviness she felt inside her, but she had grown brittle. "I don't do this kind of thing," she had said and regretted it almost immediately.

Sara's cheeks had a patina that glowed softly in the flickering yellow light. The dark wood seemed to pulse as if blood flowed beneath it. She understood. Sara understood. Virginia suddenly found herself crawling over the small grill separating her from the statue. She was crying and wanted to fall into the dark arms of Sara as the ancient Maries must have done when they needed comfort all those hundreds of years ago.

Why can't we be more like men?, Virginia wondered as she reached out tentatively to put her palm against the filigreed fabric of the dress. Things fall off them. Nothing seems to stick to them, not where they're from, not any of the places they've been, not any of the people they've met. It all fell away and they shined like new copper pots.

But things cling to us. All sorts of things hang on us, so we can't give in to them, ever. We don't dare because if we do we will carry it with us forever like the smell of bacon on our clothes.

Quite suddenly, Virginia felt herself being pulled back by several pairs of rough hands. An explosion of language with the foul smell of garlic and wine erupted around her, rough voices in a language she did not understand. Several gypsy men had come into the crypt and had seen her touching the statue. Now they pushed at her and shook blunt fingers at her.

"No, no, no, you don't understand," she said. She tried to back away, but several men blocked her way. More angry shouting in a rough babble that frightened her.

"Marc!" she shouted, but he was not there.

One of the men grabbed her by the sleeve of her white dress, and as she tried to twist away her shoe caught in a crack of the flagstones. She felt a sharp heat in her ankle and then she stumbled, striking her head on the edge of a wooden *priedieu* as she fell. For a moment, she felt the cool of the worn flagstones on her cheek, and then everything seemed to float away.

She looked up. The gypsy men murmured together for a moment then they doffed their funny black hats and bowed. They looked repentant, frightened, then two of them lifted her up from the floor and sat her on a chair. For a moment she felt relieved, but then she realized they had put her on the palanquin they used to carry Sara to the sea. The gypsy men lifted her up on high and carried the palanquin out of the dark crypt into the harsh white light above ground. She shielded her eyes. She could not find her sunglasses. The men's breath smelled of garlic and wine and rose up around her like the hot waxy breath of the candles. They were carrying her to the sea. She tried to scream but was not able. She saw Marc standing there and tried to reach out to him, but he merely said, "Smile, honey, smile" as he took her picture over and over. Then the men were knee deep, then waist deep in the sea. Marc continued to snap her picture. "This will look great at home!" They were lowering her, chair and all, into the Mediterranean. She felt the water rising but she could not move. She watched as the salt crusted on her white dress and made a line that ran ahead of the water the way the dark line of moisture runs ahead of a burning match flame. Finally, the water came up to her mouth then filled her nostrils, suffocating her. Her blond hair waved in the current like fine sea grass, and she felt her eyes go pearl white in the undersea and still she could not move. She felt the dark swirls of salt entering her lungs, making her liquid inside and out.

She looked up and there was Sara standing on the surface of the water. Her image was rippling, her gold crown gleaming and her face as black as smoke-burnished wood. She was smiling. Smiling!

"Marc!" Virginia called out. She smelled him before she saw him. His after shave. She was swimming, coming back. She opened her eyes and he was there, leaning over her in the crypt. She was still on the floor, but someone had thrown a jacket over her. A *gendarme* stood there, too, his radio crackling on his belt, keeping back the circle of gypsy men. Marc had come into the crypt behind her, just as she fell. Now he held her hand as a nurse from the nearby aid station bathed her temples with alcohol swabs. She had not hit her head that hard, but the smell and the heat and the confusion had caused her to black out.

"I'll sue, by God," Marc was saying as she came around, "I'll find somebody to sue, I will." But no one seemed to speak any English.

"Get me out of here, please," she gasped. The nurse sensed her meaning and nodded. It was all right if she could manage. Marc helped her up. There was a slight twinge in her ankle, but she tried to walk without a limp so no one would try to keep her from getting out of the crypt. She wanted to run away from them all.

The light in the square above stabbed her eyes like knife points. She fumbled in her bag and found her sunglasses as they crossed the plaza to the small cafe. Marc held on to her arm and led her to a chair. She was still wobbly. He ordered her an orange squash. It was cold and pure, cleansing the smoke from her palate. Her hands were still shaking, but her head did not hurt beyond a dull throb where she'd struck the kneeler. A few feet away, the light glittered on the Mediterranean as though nothing had happened. Along the quay there was an art show, pastel seascapes leaning on easels, hanging from lines, fluttering in the breeze like confetti. The orange was fresh and sunny on her tongue.

"Better?" Marc asked. His hand came across the table and lay on top of hers. It was pale and cold and reassuring.

"Better," she nodded. She watched rather abstractedly as a fat French man in a small black bikini bottom plunged his hands into a crack between two rocks on the breakwall. She sipped her orange drink and felt the muscles in her shoulders begin to relax. She thought it was all over. Dark-haired children, their bodies tanned, lines of pale sand clinging to their legs, stood around the man as he groped in the warm water. After a moment he straightened up, raising his hands–doubled together, dripping seaweed, sand and water–in a triumphal gesture above his head.

"*Moules!*" he shouted. Mussels! He pronounced it in the southern French way so it came out sounding like "mooleh!" and the children began to dance around him on their toes, chanting "Mooleh, mooleh, mooleh!" as they tried to climb the fat man's legs and grab the cold mussels from his hands. Virginia smiled. Then one of the dancing boys grabbed the edge of the man's bathing suit to help him climb, but the suit slipped down and the man's penis fell out and hung there in the bright sun of the quay. He was helpless, his hands in the air above him dripping with mussels. There was a moment of silence along the crowded quay but then, all around him, people began to laugh and finally the fat man himself shrugged and burst into laughter, laughing at himself, at the red-faced and giggling boys, at the way of things. The gypsy men applauded, but Virginia turned her eyes away.

"IN THE STILL-VEX'D BERMOOTHES"

Randall sat beside the kidney shaped pool and watched the horizon bob up and down over the swimmers' heads. He sipped the rum concoction the waitress had recommended for him and made a face. Too much grenadine or something, like laced fruit punch. (Besides he could never take a drink seriously that was served in a plastic coconut.)

Because he had not yet delivered his lecture, none of the passengers stopped to say hello or to ask him questions about art or the meaning of life. It was an occupational hazard that he had eluded for the moment. He idly watched the Caribbean as it flashed around him and he tried to name its exact color. Blue, aquamarine, azure, sapphire, cerulean, no, that color they paint suburban California swimming pools. He had expected it to look more like the Mediterranean and was disappointed it didn't. Ever since he had signed up as the cruise's guest lecturer on art, he'd freshened himself on memories of the Mediterranean, thinking it would be that way again. But the Caribbean islands, when they first appeared on the horizon, were just dark clumps of vegetation rising up from the blue. He missed the sparse craggy whiteness of Corfu where he'd spent a summer when he was young.

The light here was different from the Mediterranean, more humid, if light could be humid. The nearly naked bodies around him on the lounge chairs and the pool edges seemed like pieces of frying meat, oiled and glistening in the light, some turning to pink on this, the third day out. It seemed strange to be spending Christmas vacation this way, in heat and sun instead of snow. The tropical humidity was overpowering, and his flowered cotton shirt clung to him, but he would not take it off. He lately found himself embarrassed to be naked or even half naked in front of others. That, too, had started with Rachel, like much else.

In middle age, he finally grew to feel some sympathy for all those models from his early years, forced to lie unclothed in uncomfortable poses in drafty studios. He used to tell them to feel relaxed because they were participating in the "great tradition of the nude," but he found that tradition to be of little comfort when he first stood before Rachel without his clothes on and read in her disappointed look just how old he really was, with tufts of gray hair sprouting from odd parts of his body, with his pectorals sagging in their middle aged way.

It was Rachel for whom Jacob labored for fourteen years, was it not? He was young when he started.

Randall had first seen her body in terms of triangles. She was, in the beginning anyway, just another geometric painter's problem to be worked out. So many curvilinear roughly triangular shapes and forms—the delta of her pubic hair, her triangular torso, her two arms held akimbo, her one leg bent up behind the other as she lay on her back on the couch. When she first came to his studio and posed, he realized how difficult it would be to freeze on canvas what he saw before him. A challenge, a problem. She was in her early twenties, halfway into adulthood, the flesh was still in transition, not yet launched into the decline brought on by the inevitable subtractive process of time.

When students, he and his friends had disdained the human figure, using it for compulsory figure drawing courses then abandoning it. It was a dead letter, a subject used up by generations of geniuses. It was exhausted, old fashioned, unmodern, even bourgeois, and so throughout his career he purposely engineered his paintings to be stark and startling against austere gallery walls, the antithesis of human. Then, abruptly—or so it seemed to the critics—he had returned to the figure when he reached middle age. The art monthlies could not understand why. He hardly knew himself, except that abstract work had suddenly ceased to satisfy, despite the moderate success he had with it.

He decided to walk around the deck, leaving his coconut beside the canvas chair.

He wondered where Rachel was spending her Christmas. He had seen her on campus only once since she had finally left him that fall. He had masochistically gone to the university's production of a Feydeau comedy in which she had played the ingenue. The butt of the three-act joke had been a middle-aged man who lusted after the young girl played by Rachel. The old graybeard ogled and drooled and rubbed his hands with rapacious desire every time she walked onstage, and every time she slapped him with her folded fan, the audience howled. It was more than he could stand, thinking that living with him had prepared her for the part, and he slunk out at intermission, went home, poured a stiff drink and spent a morose hour grieving over the ways life imitates art.

For the part, Rachel wore her hair in Second Empire style, all ringlets around her face. Girdled and bonneted, followed around by an outrageous bustle, she hardly looked like herself at all, but that didn't ease the sting of the satire. When they lived together the previous year, she had worn only blue jeans and a whole wardrobe of T-shirts with slogans. In the mornings, she would stick her fingers into the mass of thick brown hair that cascaded down her back and would draw it back behind her ears, binding it with two twists into a thick rope. Then she'd flip it up with one hand from her nape and pin it in place with a leather and wood barrette in a French twist.

Two middle-aged women waddled down the deck towards him in brightly flowered muu-muus and straw hats they must have picked up on their first stopover. Both of them gave him a quick once-over from behind their narrow sunglasses. He nodded uneasily as he passed them, unsure whether they recognized him or not. The cruise was filled with minor celebrities, a first novelist, a singer who hadn't had a hit record in years, himself. He was certain the two women would be at his lecture and would almost certainly take his course in sketching to pass the time between islands.

Beneath a canvas canopy, shaded from the sun, he stopped and sat in a deck chair to collect himself before the talk. The title—"Whither Modern Art?"—had been the cruise social director's. He cringed.

The horizon was a distant blue line, barely visible, separating sea from sky. On what seemed the very rim of the world, he could make out one small island, a black dot that seemed not to be moving at all, though he knew the ship was sailing as quickly as possible to take them from one island to the next. The sun, the brilliant sea and that immobile dot soon became hypnotic and his eyes closed.

He must have slept, for when he opened them again, a girl and a young ship's officer had materialized in front of him and leaned against the varnished rail looking out to sea. The young officer—he was little more than a boy, really—seemed to be pointing something out to her, something that perhaps lay beyond the horizon and that they would reach the following day. The boy spoke halting English and the girl nodded encouragement and tried to help by supplying him with the words she thought he wanted to say. Randall had seen the girl at dinner, a rather plain type who always sat with her parents, but now he was startled to see how closely, from behind anyway, she resembled Rachel. Perhaps it was merely because she had done her hair up in a French twist of the sort Rachel used to wear. Many of the girls on the boat did that, to tan their necks and to keep cool, but this one had done it precisely as Rachel had, and even had a matching barrette to hold it in place.

He was about to say something but held back. Other passengers sat around him on lounge chairs, and the young couple seemed oblivious of him and probably assumed he was still sleeping. Too much of the dirty old man in saying anything to her, he thought. Besides, speaking might drive them away, and he wanted them to stay. With their backs turned to him, they seemed almost chimeral, a metaphor starkly outlined against the glittering aqua of the sea and the darker blue of the sky. They formed a tableau: the Sailor and the Maiden.

"Oh yes," Rachel had said the day he interviewed her for the modeling job, "I want to be an actress, but not *just* an actress, you understand, a truly great one."

He paid little attention to what she was saying as his hand quickly sketched her with pencil, though later, after she left, he wondered whether anyone could be that young.

The live-in arrangement had not even entered his mind at first. She seemed to show no interest in him, merely accepting her weekly modeling fee with a simple thanks. It was the night of the opening that things changed.

The show opened at the University's gallery and there was a small reception, with other faculty, the local newspaper art critic, friends and a few enemies. And she came, too, to see herself on the walls, a whole room full of portraits of herself. She was flattered by the comments of the audience, and after the reception, a few friends returned to the studio for an afterglow. She stayed on.

It seemed odd to be there with her without a brush or pencil in his hand, without her sitting in a pose he had set. There was only one work light on, a bare bulb, and it threw shadows of scattered canvasses and easels against the walls in German Expressionist shapes.

Rachel now seemed someone else, not the young woman he had painted for so many weeks, and he realized that he had missed something essential in her. She was usually stiff and formal when posing. Now she was herself, and he thought of the canvasses in the gallery and realized with a shock that every one of them was missing something vital.

The next morning, she was still there.

The campus gossip spread fairly quickly. Over coffee, passed with the cream and sugar, went the information that old Thorndyke was shacking up with a girl from the theater. He sensed he had become a sort of walking joke, and it hurt him even more than he thought it would.

It had been different when he was the young one. Nell was thirty-eight when he knew her, and he was only a little older than Rachel at the time, fresh out of art school.

Nell, broad hipped, with salt-strewn black hair and a loud spontaneous laugh, took him in like a puppy when he arrived in the Village. She chain-smoked cigarets as she sculpted and held them like a Spaniard. She said—or had he imagined this—that she had some connection with the Spanish Civil War. She was of that generation anyway and had been in Spain near that time. When he finally left her to go to Paris, she gave him no words of wisdom, only the hastily scrawled address of an old friend of hers who lived near Montparnasse, but when he arrived there no one had ever heard of the man who must have left years before.

Nell's sculpture grew angry near the end of her life. He didn't understand the change in her. She spent hours railing against time and mortality and the gallery owners who took half the asking price for her work. And when he last saw her, as he passed through New York just before he took the teaching job in Chicago, she seemed old and shriveled to him.

She couldn't afford an operation for her cataracts, and her hands worked like two blind spiders over the lump of clay in front of her. It was good she was a sculptor, he thought, not a painter. He didn't feel right offering her money, though his work had begun to sell and he could afford it. She refused to take it anyway. She had always been the giver, not him. The old always gave to the young. He understood that better now.

He wondered if he had given anything to Rachel. He never could tell what she was thinking, what was going on inside. She seemed to give the illusion of motion even when she sat perfectly still. More than once he had accused her of changing position even when she swore she had not. Maybe it was just her youth that seemed to elude him.

Once when she was feeling philosophical, she stretched her arms towards the ceiling. "I'm going to have it all, Randall," she said. She'd just come from a dance rehearsal and her leotard was sweaty with dark circles beneath the armpits. Even though she must have been fatigued, she couldn't lie still. She had the restless energy of youth and she honestly believed she could have it all, whatever she meant by "all."

Randall looked at the young couple in front of him at the ship's rail. The sailor couldn't have been more than twenty-two. He was tanned and youthfully toned, and occasionally the girl would turn halfway around to catch a coy glimpse of him from the corner of her eye. They both were looking over the bow as the ship rolled gently on the blue

Caribbean swells, as if they were looking into the future. Perhaps they *want* to grow older, he thought. He had noticed the older passengers tended to stand on the fantail looking at the wake.

"Do you think I'm, well, too old for you?" he asked one time. "I mean, I'd understand if. . ."

"Of course not, Randy," she said, quickly pecking him on the cheek, but she seemed vaguely disturbed the rest of that evening and before bed she rearranged all the plants. Perhaps she had never thought of it before, and he hated himself for even raising the question.

Two weeks later, she suddenly announced she had auditioned for summer stock and had a chance to work at some summer actors' retreat in Montana for the summer. Did he understand why she had to go, she asked, but then, before he could say anything, she answered herself. She was sure he understood, being an artist himself and all, and it was only then, twenty-five years later, he finally sympathized with Nell and felt ashamed of how he had treated her when he was Rachel's age. He remembered how she had sat there quietly when he announced that he simply had to get to Paris, that his very life depended on it. He thought he was being emotionally honest, but it felt very callous now. She had looked shell-shocked, a little time-worn. The blue smoke from her cigaret curled up past her head and she said, without much emphasis, "Yes, of course, you have to go to Paris, Randall, but you won't find anything there. Of course, you don't believe that, do you?" Then she scrawled the address of her former lover in Montparnasse who had long since gone.

He gave nothing at all to Rachel, only a ride to Union Station, a brief kiss.

Her first postcard said, "Am working with Jerry Hobarth, the British director. Have you heard of him? He's done movies in England and studied at RADA. He's wonderful! (As an artist, I mean. Hey, I miss you, Randy. Really.) Rachel."

Things too horrible to contemplate were writ large between the widely spaced lines of Rachel's sprawling handwriting.

For the first three weeks or so, cards continued to come full of news, but full of blanks, too. Like the obligatory letters kids write home from camp, they did not reveal what he really wanted to know. She told of parts she had gotten, classes she was in and so on, but he wanted to know what was happening outside school. Little by little he inferred. She wrote about how this Hobarth person was coaching her on the side. He was *such* a help to her though she only had small parts. He took *such* a personal interest, and blah, blah, blah. Then she sent along a clipping from a local paper showing herself and others in the company attending a movement class conducted by Hobarth. A circle was drawn around her head with a superfluous and childish ME next to it. An arrow pointed to Hobarth. He was young and trim, with a dancer's body, not over thirty-two, with black hair that swooped down over his forehead dramatically. HIM she had written next to his picture. HIM, what a primitive word, he thought. ME, HIM. Me Jane, him Tarzan. He angrily crumpled the clipping and then impaled it with an Exacto knife against his drawing table so hard that the knife stuck upright in the board.

There was nothing for the rest of the summer. He knew there would not be. He himself had never written to Nell until a full year later—nothing beyond a postcard of the Eiffel Tower that cost him only a few centimes. Finally, feeling nostalgic for New York, he sent her a letter one day from his Greek island. It was full of impersonal newsy stuff that neither needed nor expected an answer. He never thought before how she must have felt receiving it. It was so cold, so full of art theory, so empty of himself.

When he first saw Rachel again, she looked a little older than she had at the beginning of the summer. She carried herself a little differently, with less spring in her step. Hobarth must have dropped her hard. That was inevitable. But she didn't come running back to him. She merely showed up at the door of his apartment one day with an empty suitcase to fetch her things.

He asked why she was going, but, as he expected, she gave him some vague answer about her career and how she had to work without any distractions. Roughly the same answer he had given Nell.

"Besides," she finally added, as if it was merely an afterthought (perhaps it was), "You're older than I am Randy." It was a simple enough declarative sentence but devastating. She left with her bag, holding it closed because it was overstuffed with things she had kept there.

The sailor and the girl finally turned from the rail and walked past him. She really looked nothing like Rachel at all, despite her twist of hair. On her, it was just hair. Rachel's twist had always caused him trouble when he tried to paint or sketch it. It whorled like a vortex. He tried doing separate sketches of it, drawing it on paper alone and he found when he disembodied it that way, disconnected it from her head, it became almost abstract, the way electron microscope studies of common objects make them seem like alien worlds, seen clearly but by that very fact becoming something unknown. It had reminded him of the tangled liana vines outside an old friend's home in New Orleans, or of the climbing ladder of the DNA molecule, or of seaweed, or of rope, or of how youth was mysteriously sucked out of us, never to return again.

He arrived too late to see the Paris of legend. Nell must have known he would. In the late '50's Montparnasse was only a parody of its heyday. All that remained, oddly, was Alice B. Toklas and he got to see her shortly before she died. He had only intended to stand in front of the house where she lay bed-ridden, just to see the outside, as if it were a shrine. It was not the famous 27 Rue de Fleurus, of course. That was long gone. Gertrude had died long before, too, he knew, but he had heard that Alice was still alive. He wanted at least to see the house where she lay, this living link to that giddy period between the wars that he had just missed. He had gotten the address from an old American when he had espresso at the Deux Magots. He wouldn't have had the nerve to go to the door at all except that he saw a drape move slightly on the upper floor. Hardly a flicker, but it seemed to beckon. (He later realized it could not have been her.)

The concierge was brusk, but disappeared upstairs with this bold young American's request. She came back a few moments later and admitted him, muttering in French. As he mounted the narrow stairs to the room where she lay, he realized he had prepared nothing to say to her. He thought briefly of the people she had known, lived among, all dead now, and he grew frightened and tongue-tied. The concierge had pulled a black straight-backed chair up to the bedside and he sat down in it, his hands suddenly grown large on his knees. He knew he must look awkward and stiff, like a young Spanish suitor facing his fiance with a whole roomful of relatives and duennas present, listening. Up close, one did not mind Alice's homeliness.

"I . . . I've come to see Gertrude's grave," he stammered and immediately felt how awful a comment it was. But she said nothing for a moment, only looked at him with those intense hawk's eyes that seemed undiminished by her illness, as though she had made peace with death.

"But she's not buried here," she said simply.

They had tea and she talked of the young boys who used to come—Picasso, Braque, Hemingway.

Shortly after, he took what little money he had and left for the Greek islands.

For a moment, it seemed his early life had been nothing but turning away from people and things, a series of missed connections, harsh unfeeling leave-takings in pursuit of some ill-defined and unclear goal. Being young meant being discontent with everything, but he realized that flying from thing to thing you only ended up with a handful of air—or a pile of canvases that recorded lost opportunities. Yet, he thought, something was left behind, a residue, not like ashes exactly but like the strong odor of an expensive perfume that from time to time spontaneously revives itself in a room. Memory.

He glanced at his watch. It was time for his speech. "Whither Modern Art?" He rose from the deck chair and headed for the lounge. The sun was high and hot, glancing off the brilliant water of the Caribbean in points so sharp his eyes hurt. As he passed the lifeboats, he smelled the resins used to preserve the davit ropes. He closed his eyes and smiled. The odor reminded him of the way the aroma of wild thyme would rise to meet him when he was twenty-five and walked the craggy hills of Corfu with his paint kit beneath his arm.

READING *CARMINA BURANA* AT THE BEACH

The manuscript of the Carmina Burana, written ca. AD 1230, was found at the Benedictbeuren monastery in Bavaria in 1803 by...

Harry dozed. The light breeze coming off the lake blew cool air through the webbing of the hammock and lulled him. He moved just enough to sway the hammock gently. He could feel the dappled sunlight filtering down through the trees on to his face. His finger was tucked between the covers of the book laid on his stomach. In the distance, the screech of a gull broke the soft rhythm of the Lake Michigan waves. A riffle of laughter flew up from the girls down on the beach. He was drifting off, floating on the line that stretches between waking and sleep like a surface film.

Then Pauline called from the porch.

"Harry, it's the Nelsons, they want to know if we want to meet them at the Hatch on Macatawa."

He snorted, pushed his pork pie hat back on his head and sat up. His eyes felt cool and the beach below looked pale, as if the color had been drained out.

"Christ, all they can talk about is golf," he said. Behind him he heard the light tinkle of the girls' laughter again, but he did not turn, not with Pauline looking, not after Stephanie last fall. "All right," he mumbled, "I'll go."

"You don't have to."

"I'll go," he repeated, a little irritably, "Christ, how do we meet these people anyway?" He read.

The Goliardists, mostly defrocked clerics, wandered the roads of Europe from university town to university town, composing their often-obscene and disrespectful poems in macaronic verse, a mixture of debased church Latin and . . .

He flipped through the pages. The girls who had rented the cottage next door must have been planning a bonfire for that night. All afternoon they and some boys they had met had been carting firewood like a row of ants down the long, steep stairway that clung to the bluff. Three years before, when Lake Michigan was at high water, the stairs had washed away, but since then the water level had gone down and now there was plenty of beach down below. The owner had rebuilt the stairs and rented the place out.

He sat up and watched the girls down on the sand, fifty feet below him. Their suits looked metallic and glittered in the sun. They probed the sand with their toes, and as they looked down, they held their long hair back from their faces with their hands.

> *Stetit puella*
> *Rufa tunica;*
> *Si quis eam tetigit,*
> *Tunica crepuit.*
> *Eia!*
> *Stetit puella,*
> *tamquam rosula;*
> *Facie splenduit,*
> *os eius florvit.*
> *Eia!*

> *There stood a girl*
> *In a red tunic*
> *When it was touched,*
> *The tunic rustled.*
> *Ah!*

There stood a girl,
Like a rose,
Her face was radiant,
Her mouth bloomed.
Ah!

"Six o'clock at the Hatch," Pauline called, coming down the wood walkway with a towel. "I'm going for a swim, care to join me?"

He shook his head, smiled rather lamely and held up the book. Not that he was actually reading it, but as he had pawed through the shelf of books in the house, it was the only one that seemed to interest him. There were a few fat Ludlumesque thrillers, but now that the Cold War was over, there didn't seem to be much point. He'd never liked mysteries or westerns. Then he'd come upon this, stuck in the midst of the other stuff. He figured it was one of his daughter's textbooks from college. He flipped through it and decided it was the book he wanted for the hammock. For starters, it was thin and half the pages were in Latin so he could skip them, and they were poems so he could read them in little gulps without worrying about having to plow through the whole thing.

He watched Pauline descend the long wooden staircase to the beach. She still walked with a limp from the accident. The doctor said she should wait at least six more weeks before stressing the leg with dance, but already Harry had caught her in the basement limbering up, trying a step or two, nothing with high impact, nothing where she'd twist the tibia which had shattered in so many places just the previous summer.

She walked as though she had lost more than just a quarter inch of height in that leg. The doctors said she would recover from that. A crack physical therapist at Blodgett Hospital said eventually the muscles in her leg would compensate and the limp would disappear altogether. But Harry wondered if the other break, the one between the two of them, would ever heal. She carried it behind her like a sadness, dragging it with each fall of her foot. He had broken his leg when he was a boy and he still had an ache there when the cold damp days came, a soreness just below the skin, a thing that most of the time he could forget about, but that kept coming back when the conditions were right. He thought it would be that way with them from now on, a mark deep in the bone that would never go away. He wished he had never laid eyes on Stephanie.

> *The roasted cygnet sings:*
> *Olim lacus colveram,*
> *Olim pulcher extiteram,*
> *dum cignus ego fueram.*
> *Miser! Miser!*
> *Modo niger*
> *et ustus fortiter!*
> *Nunc in scutella iaceo*
> *et volitare nequeo,*
> *dentes fredentes video.*

> *Once I dwelt in the lakes,*
> *Once I was*
> *A beautiful swan!*
> *O miserable me!*
> *Now I am*
> *Roasted black!*
> *I am borne in upon a platter*
> *and can no longer fly.*
> *I can see the gnashing teeth.*

He watched as Pauline dropped her towel and knifed into the water. He did not know how she could stand it. Lake Michigan never got warm enough for him, not even in July and August. The water was so cold it made his feet cramp the moment he stepped in. She was wearing a black tank suit. She'd been swimming at the high school pool ever since the cast came off, and her body, always trim, now had the look of a swimmer's body. Her shoulders, somehow, had gotten bigger, stronger, not that she looked like one of those East German Olympic mutants, but she was holding on to herself better than he was.

He rolled off the hammock and went up to the house to get ready for dinner at the Hatch and caught sight of himself in the mirror. They shouldn't put mirrors in beach houses, he thought. He was spreading out at the bottom, taking on the shape of his desk chair, getting a little frog necked. He realized he was beginning to look like what he was: a middle-aged man who spent most of his time behind a desk.

Ego sum abbas Cucaniensis
Et consulium meum est bibulis
Et in secta Decii voluntas mea est,
Et qui mane me quesierit in taberna,
Post vesperam nudus egredietur
Et sic denudatus veste clamabit:
Wafna! Wafna!
Quid fecisti sors turpissima?
Nostre vite gaudia,
Abstulisti omnia!

I am the abbot of Cockaigne
And my advice is be a drunkard
And in the sect of Decius is my will:
Whoever gambles with me in the tavern,
By vespers will be stripped bare,
And naked he will leave shouting:
Wafna! Wafna!
Shameful fate, what have you done?
Wafna! Wafna!
All the joys of our lives, you have taken away,
every one!

The sun was setting by the time they got back from the Hatch. They had both drunk a little too much, it was one way of dealing with the Nelsons, and now they leaned against the rail of the deck, watching the sun go down like a big beachball. It was so cool and red you could look at it and not hurt your eyes. It seemed to set quickly, so swiftly they could actually see it move. Broad bands of orange and yellow lay all along the horizon with darker colors layered above. Down below on the beach, it was darker than above, and the girls pulled long university sweatshirts over their bathing suits. The boys who had helped them haul the firewood down the steps were nowhere to be seen and the girls looked somehow incomplete. One walked along the water gazing at the sunset, another stared down towards the lighthouse at Holland. The third listlessly rearranged the sticks on the bonfire pile for the hundredth time. They seemed to be waiting for something.

> *Swaz hie gat umbe,*
> *Daz sint alles megede*
> *die wellent an man*
> *allen disen sumer gan!*

> *Here are the maidens*
> *all in a circle,*
> *Wishing to be without a man*
> *all the summer long!*

There was no breeze, but it was growing cooler, a relief after the heat of the day. Suddenly the girl at the shoreline shrieked, a short yip quickly squelched by her hands flying to her mouth. The others came over and gathered around something at the water's edge. They all squealed and Harry squinted to see what they were looking at. A dark wet ball of fur or feathers lay in a lump at the girls' feet. Probably a dead gull, he thought.

Three college-age boys came running down the beach towards the girls, kicking the wet sand high above their bare legs. When they reached the girls, they stopped. They talked for a moment over the dead thing, then one of the boys grabbed a stick and took whatever it was and flung it back into the water. The girls squealed again, then laughed and the boys joined them by the piled wood of the bonfire, apparently no longer interested in where they had been running to a moment before. Harry heard the sound of beer cans opening and laughter.

Chume, chume, geselle min,
ih enbite harte din,
ih enbite harte din,
chum, chum, geselle min.

   Suzer rosenvarwer munt,
   chum unde mache mich gesunt
   chum unde mache mich gesunt
   Suzer rosenvarver munt.

   Come, come, my love,
I wait for you,
I wait for you,
come, come, my love.

   Sweet, rosy mouth,
   Come make me whole
   Come make me whole
   Sweet rosy mouth.

"I'm cool," Pauline said, "Could you go back up to the house for a sweater, Harry? I don't want to leave the sunset."

As Harry came back from the cottage with Pauline's sweater, the last rays of the sun made an X-ray of her younger self through the light summer dress she wore. The dress was belted at the middle, and a slight breeze came up the bluff and lifted the corner of the hem just a bit. In the dim light, he could not see the scars from where the surgeon's pins had been. He remembered making love to her when they were young and their bodies had been firm and thin and full of hope, lying on the bed in the afternoon, their fingers tracing each other's names on their flesh. He had even written her poetry, bad poetry, but she didn't seem to mind. Harry put the sweater over Pauline's shoulders and she leaned her head over towards him. He pulled her closer.

From below, there came a sudden cheer as the bonfire blazed up. It was dark down there already, though up on the bluff Harry and Pauline could still see a bit of light lying along the horizon like a strip of fat. One of the girls began to sing a children's campfire song, some doggerel nonsense that the others knew and joined in. In a moment, they were all singing faster and had joined hands in a circle dance around the fire, lifting their legs high to drive their feet better into the sand. Soon they were whirling around the flames, laughing, giddy, out of breath, almost off balance. One of the girls cried, "Stop!" but the boys, with their big clunking steps, kept pulling them faster and faster and the girls did not protest any further, knowing this was part of an ancient game they were all playing.

They are young enough, Harry thought, to *want* to fall, to want to tumble on to the sand in a heap, to risk someone's getting thrown in the fire. They had not yet hurt or been hurt, so they didn't know about the dangers of dancing that way. He wanted to call out, "Be careful," but he knew they would not listen any more than he would have listened at their age, and he felt sad.

He looked out at the horizon where the last light had finally gone off the west. The reckless laughter of the girls filled the night. He looked up and saw Pauline had been watching him watch the girls dance. The night breeze was raising some waves below and the slow rhythm of the surf made a counterpoint to the silly students' song. He smiled, in embarrassment, thinking he knew what Pauline was thinking of him.

The light wind blew a bit of Pauline's hair, just the tips, across her face and into her mouth. She cleared it away with her hand and smiled at him. He held his wife closer. He had never wanted her more.

Were diu welt alle min
Von deme mere unze an den Rin,
des wolt ih mih darben
daz diu chunigen von Engellant
lege in minen armen!

O, if all the world were mine
From the ocean to the Rhine,
I would gladly give it up
To have the Queen of England
Lying in my arms!

FIVE ROOMS IN A CITY FULL OF RAIN

A CITY FULL OF RAIN

Lowell was not sleeping well. Not that he slept well as a rule, but this was more than his usual insomnia. He was lying on the Murphy bed he had folded down from the closet of the old apartment he lived in. He had tossed and turned on it all night. He inhaled its sour smells for the thousandth time. It was the night before his wedding, and he felt something uncomfortable entering through his skin as if he were an amphibian breathing through his pores.

The sounds of the night scratched at him and kept him awake. It was after midnight. Someone in the building across the alleyway flushed a toilet. A cat yowled in heat beneath the window. On Woodward Avenue, muscle cars roared through the dark. And then the moaning started in the next apartment.

In the two years he had lived in the studio flat he had never heard the moaning before. He only began to hear it after he had sold his single bed in preparation for his marriage and slept on the Murphy bed. The bed's thick mattress, upright in the closet between his apartment and the old Jews', had acted as a sound barrier.

Now he tried pulling a pillow over his ears to silence the moans, but in the heat of the night it quickly grew unbearable. It was even worse than the moaning. Besides, with the pillow over his ears, he could hear his own heartbeat and the persistent ringing in the ears that lets us know we're still alive.

He tried to lie on his back, his side, on the other side. Nothing worked at all. Nothing was comfortable. It felt as though gravity were a little stronger than usual that night. Maybe it was the weight of his impending marriage, he thought, and it surprised him to be thinking of marriage to Carol as a weight or doom. He had never thought of it that way before. It was too late for second thoughts. In the morning he would take the leap off the ledge that almost everybody takes sooner or later.

Beneath the window, the cat continued to yowl. Its voice seemed nearly human as it echoed off the canyon walls of the alleyway. The whole city seemed to coil as restlessly as the cat, its concrete shoulders tight, its behind hunched squat, nervous, plagued with insomnia.

"Ooooooooooooooooooooooo!"

From the next apartment, the old Jew's moans continued, melting into the hot night.

Lowell got up from his bed and padded barefoot across the wooden floor of the apartment to the window where he sat on the flat metal shelf that covered the radiator there. It was the dead of the night, and he felt half dead himself. His flesh was prickly with the heat, and he felt a slimy sweat beneath his pajamas. He tried to look out over the city. By putting his head close to the screen and peering at an angle, he could just see a thin wedge of Palmer Park, a dark rough shape of trees, beyond the next building's parking lot. Security lights threw a strange pink glow over everything, as if the whole city were burning with a smokeless fire. He listened for noises above the steady white noise of the traffic from Woodward Avenue.

There was nothing for a moment. Then, far off, a laugh flitting through the night like a bat. Then breaking glass and a slurred word somewhere else. Farthest off, like the muted roar of surf, he could hear the beginnings of the storm that was rumbling towards the city. He could still hear the Jew's moan coming through the wall. Lowell waited for the rain. The first drops of it would hit the concrete and disappear like spit on an iron, but then the cool damp tide would come and cover everything. He wanted it badly, but until it came all he could do was wait.

He wondered, as he sat, whether the widow across the way waited for the rain, too, pacing back and forth across her apartment as she often did at night. She seemed to share his general insomnia and on hot summer nights he had seen her walking back and forth from one room to the other of her large apartment, dressed only in her underwear, trying to keep cool. As Lowell's was the only apartment looking into hers, she was careless about drawing her shades, especially since he often wasn't home. He had been spending the night with Carol more frequently, but these past few nights, as the wedding approached, she wanted to be alone.

The widow was an overweight woman, fiftyish, her flesh yellowed by the light of her lamp, her large yet empty breasts sagging against the cups of her bra. Sometimes it seemed to Lowell as though her flesh had lost the will to resist the pull of the earth any longer. She walked solidly through her apartment in the heat, swaying from side to side flat-footed, like a cow. Carol, when she walked naked, pranced on her toes like a young girl. He could not imagine her ever getting like the woman across the way, yet, he realized, she probably would.

He knew little about the widow or about the old Jew next door. He didn't even know if the widow was a widow. He merely assumed so because she lived alone and occasionally had visits from a woman young enough to be her daughter.

The old Jew had a wife, Lowell knew that, but almost everyone had a wife at one time or another. He would have a wife himself in the morning. So, what else did he know about the man who moaned nightly on the other side of the wall? A silver *mesuza* was nailed to the doorjamb of the Jews' apartment, and when the husband came home from his long solitary walks through the city, he would rub his thumb roughly over it, not so much to take a blessing, it seemed, as to mash it into the wood, to crush it the way you crush a garlic clove to release its odor. He was a large man. His wife was tiny, shrivelled almost. The old man walked stiffly, as if wearing a back brace, and for a long time Lowell thought he was totally mute for he never opened his mouth when he passed him in the hallway or on the street. His eyes were vacant, staring, and the only sign of recognition he gave Lowell was a quick upward jerk of his right arm, as if it was connected to a cable.

As Lowell sat there listening to the old man moan, he realized that he had not invited any of these neighbors to his wedding. It had never even occurred to him. Yet there were many people coming whom he saw less often, uncles, aunts, distant cousins from the hometown he'd left years before. Why not invite the neighbors as well? Was it only because he did not know their names? The city was only superficially anonymous that way, he realized. He did not know things like his neighbors' last names, but he had witnessed some of their most private moments. He had seen the widow when she must have thought she was absolutely alone, and he was also privy to his other neighbor's bad dreams. How many relatives did he know that well?

He listened again. There had been a brief pause in the moaning. The night was strangely calm otherwise, quieter than usual at this hour, with the sudden silence that often precedes a night storm as anyone yet awake tries to find shelter from it. There was no sound but the intermittent thunder above the hiss of traffic a block away. Then a siren, far off and unconnected; then the sound of an empty truck rattling into the bottomless sack of the night.

Then the moans resumed softly, mingled with the sound of approaching thunder. The trees over in Palmer Park, weirdly pink from the halogen vapor security lights, began to rustle in the premonitory way trees often do before a storm.

Would the old Jew enjoy the wedding? he wondered. Did the old man enjoy anything? His face was always expressionless, like a wall, the wailing wall, impassive. He constantly wore his yarmulke beneath a battered fedora that looked like it came from the forties, and the tassles of his prayer shawl hung from beneath the hem of his black coat. His thick gray beard was suspended like a beehive from his jaw, and there was always the look of a drowned man in his pale silver eyes that stared not ahead but inward.

The first night Lowell heard him moaning, he woke in a sweat. He knew immediately they were not moans of pleasure like the ones that regularly came from the college students' apartment above his. The moans from the Jews' side of the wall were long, sustained, dirge-like, occasionally punctuated with speech in a language Lowell couldn't understand. It could have been Hebrew, Yiddish, perhaps Czech or Polish. There was no way to tell through the wall, but the voice was impassioned, angry and pleading all at once. It droned on and on, as if reciting a litany of pain against God.

The next morning, Lowell saw the manager about it.

"Leave the man alone," the manager said.

"He moaned all night," Lowell told him.

"So plug your ears."

"That's not what I meant," Lowell explained. "We should do something, shouldn't we?"

"Leave him alone," the manager repeated.

The rising wind of the coming storm started a can rolling down the alley beneath his window. Rrrrrrrr. Empty tin on the prowl, spinning, turning, then rounding a corner somewhere, driven by a cross current, caught in an eddy or swirl of wind formed by the building. He felt the cool coming through the fine mesh of the window screen. The cat had long since gone, prowling elsewhere in her heat, still yowling somewhere, hoping, perhaps, to unite herself with some tomcat before the rain. Lowell imagined the widow pacing restlessly across the way, moving nunlike from room to room in silent meditation. Perhaps the whole city was awake.

Would Carol put up with his insomnia? he wondered. Would she nag, or, worse, would she feel compelled to sit up with him all night to keep him company? The last thing an insomniac wants is company. Sitting all alone in the silence of a sleeping house is the only reward of the affliction.

The second night that he slept on the Murphy bed, the Jew moaned again, until long after midnight. Did the old man want company, Lowell wondered, or did he, like Lowell himself, enjoy the loneliness of facing the night alone, wrestling with it like Jacob with the angel? Could he do anything for the old man anyway? Lowell and the old man shared no language. Should he go to the wife then? He had seen her only once, on her knees, wearing a pale yellow babushka, washing the doorsill. He barely caught a glimpse of her before she slammed the door, frightened of him, of anyone.

Now the first cold gusts of wind swept through the corners of the city and whistled through the alleyway. The breeze whipped the edges of the curtains like swatting hands. In the next room, the old Jew's moaning continued in apparent indifference to the storm. It droned on, rhythmically, liturgically, in a tongue Lowell could not understand any more than he understood the exact meaning of the cat's meowing. Only, as with the cat, he sensed in it a painful desire to unite with something or someone beyond itself. And yet, it was still more. It was far more than an animal sound. It was a uniquely human moan the old man made, a noise with the sad persistence of memory in it, memory that could not, in the end, be shared.

Lowell finally asked his friend Barry Stein about the Jewish couple.

"Oh, them," he said, shaking his head. Barry worked with Jewish Social Services out of Temple Israel in Palmer Park. "The usual thing," he added, as if it didn't need more explanation.

The usual thing, that phrase had filled several hours of insomnia since. Both the man and his wife had their entire families wiped out in the Holocaust. Only the two of them survived. They had known one another slightly before the war. Then they had met again afterwards when they were brought to America by a relief agency.

"They live off us now," Barry said. "They can't manage any real work of any kind. We pay the rent, try to find counseling and so on."

"Why does he moan like that?" Lowell asked.

"He was barely alive when the camp he was in was liberated," Barry said, "Broken vertebrae in the lower back, probably from a rifle butt as the Germans tried to kill off whatever few remained in the camps. I think he may have already counted himself among the dead. Maybe he's disappointed."

The usual thing. Lowell remembered Barry's phrase as the brunt of the storm finally swept down on the city. Lowell had to close the windows to keep out the wet. The rain struck against the panes like waves beating against a ship's portholes, and the building seemed to toss on the streams of water that swirled through the alley three stories below. It was as if the clouds' swollen bellies had been slit by a bayonet and their entrails showered down, splashing against the window panes, threatening to break in. As in the Book of Job, God was revealing his darker side in the storm.

Lowell's future suddenly seemed as frightening as the storm outside. In a few hours he would be married and gone, different from what he had been yet the same. Marriage always ends badly, he thought, it was the usual thing. The death of one spouse, a bad divorce. One or the other was the inevitable end of it. Marriage could not end well. There was sadness accompanying it, always.

And? Beyond that normal disappointment? Was there was still worse waiting for them? Could the Jew have foreseen the camps when he was Lowell's age? As a twenty-five-year old man could he ever have imagined that he would end his life in a large American city howling into the night from his reservoir of bad dreams? Had he considered the tremendous risk of it all?

Suddenly, there was a tremendous flash of lightning that made him jump. It was long, lingering chain lightning that seemed to form a web over the entire city, sweeping everything up the way a seine picks up everything undersea. For a moment, everything was silent, suspended in the breathless blue light.

Across from him, in the window of her apartment, the widow appeared. Her skin was turned blue by the lightning, and she seemed frozen to the window, her arms folded into herself, staring up in fear at the bright sky. Her eyes caught his, but instead of turning away, she looked oddly relieved. She lifted one hand and seemed to wave, a slight helpless smile in the midst of the storm.

And then the lightning stopped and, as if a giant hand had swept across the world, the city was plunged into darkness. The bright pink security lights went black, the numerals on his digital clock disappeared, and nothing remained of the widow across the way and her desperate gesture except the dull image of it etched on his retina.

Then the thunder was let loose and the windows shook in the darkness. He was alone.

By dawn, the storm had passed. From the apartment next to Lowell's came only muffled weeping and then silence. The widow came to her window again, but she didn't look out. Instead she pulled the shade down. At dawn, Carol called. Her voice sounded different to him now, like a stranger's.

"More people?" she asked, a little shocked at his sudden request. Before that he had taken little interest in who came to the wedding.

"Not now, darling," she insisted, "It's too late, you know that. Absolutely not. The caterer would have a fit." Then she said, "I'm glad you're awake, though. Yes, the power was off here, too. I was afraid you might oversleep, you know how you are. That's why I called. Wasn't it a horrible storm? I've got to go now. Don't forget to brush your tux. Bye."

As the smell of coffee filled the kitchen, Lowell opened the windows to let in some wet morning air. By looking out at a sharp angle from where he sat at the kitchen table, he could just see a small corner of Palmer Park and a piece of the street that ran by it. It was a view he had enjoyed every morning. Though it was after dawn now, the world still had the dull color of the storm. It was the color of a drained pond, as though the buildings of the city had been exposed on a low tide, flotsam left by the storm, waiting to be salvaged while still wet.

As he watched, a young couple on ten-speeds flashed through the narrow view he had of Palmer Park. They were laughing. Their tires went "Ssssssssss" on the still-wet pavement.

HASTE TO THE WEDDING

The light from the digital clock tinted the bedroom pale green. Beneath the open window, crickets rasped their legs together. In the distance Harry heard the rumble of thunder, deep and growling over Lake St. Clair.

He was glad he lived close enough to the lake to smell the storm as it came. In the yard, the leaves rustled in the rising wind. Already Harry could feel an uneasy bristling on his arms as the temperature dipped, as if someone had passed near him. But no one was near him except Pauline who slept beside him.

She lay with her back turned to him, the thin sheet pulled up to her shoulders as though she had sensed the cool while still asleep. The white sheet ran down the length of her body, over the curve of her hips, and down to a point at her feet. Harry cleared his head and stared at her sillhouette in the pale green light of the clock. The strange light made the curves and shadows of the sheet over her body look like a far-off mountain range, like the rounded, treeless mountains of England's Lake District.

He tried to gauge the approaching storm. It was a gift he had since childhood. He could measure the severity of storms by the changed smell of the air, by how the electricity charged the small hairs on the back of his neck and arms and made them stand up straight. He could tell it would be a bad one. The hair follicles on his forearm actually ached, like a thousand needle points. He was ready for a thick rain driven on the shoulder of the strong wind, a rain like the ones that would sweep off Lake Erie when he was a kid and make the corn and wheat fields around Monroe stir like an ocean, ending summer hot spells, dumping cold pure water from the sky as from a deep well. He was ready for a good cleansing storm. It had been building in his skin and hair for weeks, perhaps years.

In the distance, thunder rumbled again. Through the twisted branches of the tree in the yard, he saw the horizon lit up in a blue line. The lightning was beyond the lake yet, somewhere over Canada, coming fast. It rumbled like the empty coal cars that rolled through the farmlands when he was young.

Beside him, Pauline continued to sleep, breathing regularly, her long body in its shroud. She murmured slightly. It was a pathetic sound, as if she were dreaming of spiders. She rolled into a fetal position, and he reached over and touched her on the shoulder, trying to reassure her. Pauline's thin hand slipped up to his, though she still slept, and gripped hard. Her hand was warm, almost hot, and he held it dumbly, afraid to let go and wake her. She smacked her lips sleepily.

Soon, he felt a damp wind wash over his shoulders from the open window. Pauline stirred, let go of his hand and rolled on her back. Her face made a pale oval amidst the spray of black hair on the pillow.

The first raindrops fell and the smell of dust rose into the air. Big drops, like pearls, exploded on the windowsill and tossed flecks on the web of the screen.

Harry went to the window and tried to pull it closed, but the humidity had swelled it open. Pauline sleepily stuck out her hand to rub the sheet where he should have been. Finding him missing, she opened her eyes. They glinted in the green light of the clock.

"What's going on?" she asked.

"Damn thing's stuck," he said, pulling at the window. He strained again. Sweat broke out on his forehead. The window refused to budge. Spray from rain hitting the window wet his pajamas at the waist. Harry looked up at the clouds and hung on the window. They were great dark shapes, giant potatoes that had been grown in the earth and released. He tugged again, holding his breath and straining.

"Don't hurt yourself, Harry," Pauline said, getting up from the bed and coming to the window beside him. She grabbed one side of the sash and they pulled together. She clenched her teeth and pressed her lips shut as she pulled. He stopped to look at her, his hands limp on the windowframe. He was thinking of how she had looked when he first saw her.

"Pull, Harry," she said, "Help me."

He hauled down on his side of the window and suddenly it gave, slamming shut so hard that the counterweights hidden in the sash bounced with a clang. They bumped into one another, but Pauline, the dancer, got her footing back first. He leaned against the wall, slightly out of breath, as she straightened her hair and walked back to bed on tip-toe. The long white nightgown she was wearing clung to her and formed a sickle's curve of white down which her black hair fell.

"That was nice," Harry said.

"What?"

"That. That was the first thing we've done together in a while."

Pauline looked hurt for a moment, then turned and crawled back to her side of the bed. She looked tired, fatigued, as if the bed were a desert she had to get across with no provisions. She fell in a lump on her side and pulled the sheet up to her shoulders again. Her voice was slightly cracked, as if talking around a lump in her throat. "We'd better get to sleep if we're going to this wedding tomorrow morning."

"I'm sorry," Harry said, still by the window.

She said nothing.

"I'll check the rest of the house."

"Mmmmph," said Pauline.

Summer thunder filled the air. Giant hands were ripping the clouds in half, and the house shook when there was a close hit.

In the morning, on their way to his niece Carol's wedding, they would drive past the spot near the lakeshore where he and Pauline had kissed on a hot summer night. It was just after they had met. It wasn't their first kiss, but it was the one that stayed strongest in his memory. It had rained that night, too. They were out walking along the lakeshore in Grosse Pointe. The water of Lake St. Clair was dark and the waves beat against the rock breakwall. The storm burst suddenly, and they ran, soaking wet, up to the porch of St. Paul's church and took shelter there. Pauline's lips were blue and her teeth chattered. Her hair was streaming with the rain and Harry's lips were cold, too, and his skin was covered with goose bumps. Then she held her face up for a kiss there in the church doorway, and he found her lips hard and cold. They were so wet that they slid around in one another's arms, and they laughed and kissed again, shivering, then stopped laughing as their lips stayed together. Only later, remembering, was Harry aware that the rain beat against the church roof like drummers and heartbeats, and that the smell of stale incense and beeswax candles seemed to come through the dry wood of the doorway where they stood.

Harry shut the downstairs windows on his own. They had replaced the old wooden sashes with Anderson windows after he was made editor. He realized the closed-up house had the musty smell of Pauline's body and perfume, but not much of his smell at all. Hard rain beat on the windows as he walked back upstairs.

He looked at her, asleep again, or pretending to be asleep, with the folds of the thin sheet covering her like water. He tried again to remember what she looked like the first time her saw her.

It was at a dance concert he was reviewing for the *Varsity News* at the University of Detroit. She danced an adagio, choreographed by a mutual friend, and her thin legs were outlined clearly against the deep blue of the cyclorama. It looked as though she danced against the sky, moving swiftly through the air. Her calves had fist-like knots of muscle when she went on toe, but it did not make her look less graceful to him. He wrote her a rave review and then called her for a date.

His reminiscences were punctuated by explosions of lightning and rumbling thunder. He lay down beside her and curled up into the spaces left by her body. He inhaled the familiar odor of her body and smelled the herbal shampoo she used. He could tell she wasn't really sleeping for she flinched with each flash of lightning and he could feel the goose bumps rising on her arms as she pulled closer to him.

He remembered most her eyes. They were big, dark, Mediterranean—she was Italian. What else did he remember? Honesty. Her eyes were honest. A bolt of lightning lit the sky and she twitched beneath his arm. Honest. The thunder rumbled. Pauline had been honest when they first met. Well, what of it? He thought. For that matter, so had he. They agreed before they got married that they would tell one another of all their past lovers. They were only twenty-three; there wasn't much to tell then. Youth can afford honesty; there's time to rebuild.

He gave Pauline a tug towards him. She resisted. He tugged again with gently increasing pressure until at last she rolled over on her back. She was crying. Her cheeks glistened when the lightning came.

"What's the matter?" he asked.

"The storm," she said, "You know how thunder frightens me."

"It's not the thunder you have to be afraid of," he said, "If you can hear it, you've been spared."

Now that she lay on her back, the tears were pooling up in the crevices at the bridge of her nose. She squeezed her eyes shut and the tears were forced out until they ran from the sides of her eyes and wet the hair at her temples.

"I still love you," Harry said.

"Oh, don't, Harry," she whispered, her eyes squeezed shut. "Please."

He didn't say anything more, and they lay there silently on their backs like two statues as the rain continued to beat against the windows.

"Do we have to go to this wedding tomorrow, Harry?" she asked. "Weddings are always so depressing."

"Not always," he said, "Ours wasn't, was it?" He turned on his side and held her.

"What happened, Harry?"

The lightning flashed again and she flinched, burying her head in his arms. Her tears felt first hot then cold as they fell on his pajamas.

"It's okay," he said, "It's just a storm."

His mind wandered backwards, and he felt as though he were up high looking at dawn over a fog-filled valley or hollow, from peak to peak over a long, stretched out mountain range. A familiar promontory showed itself in the distance, defiantly green above the shroud of fog settled at its feet. He remembered the time fifteen years before when the foreign desk fell to him because the man the *Free Press* first assigned to it had a heart attack. They went to Collioure, on a short vacation, walking from town to town in the Pyrenees near the Spanish border.

They had only been married a few years. He remembered lying in bed after making love on one of a series of perfectly warm, dry mornings along the coast. The room was three floors above the street, with a view of the Mediterranean out over the white curving arms of the harbor. From where they lay, they could only see the tips of the masts of the fishing boats bobbing back and forth slightly. Beyond the boats, on the rough Rousillon hillside, white houses with orange roofs lay scattered like broken tiles. The sun poured into their room and the whole world seemed bleached white as bones. They lay there exhausted, entwined, their tanned bodies slightly damp with sweat against the cool sheets, as if they had both just washed in on the tide. Pauline's black hair, even longer then, tumbled over on to his pillow like a sea growth of some kind and he buried his nose in it. It smelled like the ocean, like the white beaches of sand and salt and wind, like brine and the lives of shellfish deep in the mysterious blue of the sea.

On the cobblestones below, at a small fish stand on the quay, two old Catalan women were still haggling in the local dialect over the price of fresh mussels as they had all during the time he and Pauline had been making love. They heard the women's voices before they made love and they heard them again after, but in between there had been only silence like the roaring sea.

They listened for a moment, then Pauline smiled and whispered right into his ear, her lips so close they brushed his skin, "They're like birds, don't you think, Harry? Whenever I hear birds I'll think of those women down there and the sun and this and you like this." And then they had kissed again and the old women's voices receded once more like the tide.

The storm outside passed fairly quickly. The long loud thunder was replaced by softer chain lightning which passed, too, leaving only the soothing sound of the rain. It was like a mother comforting a child; shhhh, it said. The rain would be gone in time for the wedding. The newlyweds would begin in a world washed clean, Harry reflected; everybody had a right to that at least, to a fresh beginning. The room was still lit in pale green from the face of the clock, and in the distance he could hear the chuff of freighters out on Lake St. Clair, struggling down the shipping lanes with their full freights of ore.

DIANA CLOAKS HERSELF IN MOONLIGHT

Diana held a handful of Placidyl tablets in her palm. The orange pills reminded her of M&M's as she chose yet another one with her fingertips and pushed it through her lips. She pressed it against the roof of her mouth with her tongue and tasted the hard smooth shell. It was neither bitter nor sweet but something in between, a natural taste, like the oddly replusive yet sweet tang of Roger's tongue after he'd been smoking and drinking beer. She rinsed the taste away with a swig of champagne and swallowed the pill.

"To Roger," she said as pushed another pill in.

Roger Price was the reason she was there in that room of the Westin Hotel at the Renaissance Center committing either fiscal or literal suicide. She had checked in a few hours earlier, armed only with her charge cards and an overnight bag with the sleeping pills in it. When he'd told her that their affair was over, she decided there were basically two things she could do. She could either kill herself–that would be messy but final–or she could spend a lot of money stupidly to make herself feel less stupid about having fallen in love with Roger. And unlike death, which was sudden, going deep into debt would spread the remorse out over several monthly payments. She still hadn't decided which alternative to take, although she had already spent a lot of money.

A couple of hours after she arrived, she had ordered up a ninety dollar bottle of Mumm's Cordon Rouge, but after two glasses she realized that even that was not phenomenally wasteful enough to make her feel that she had done something less wasteful in falling in love with Roger, so she also spent fifteen dollars for a room service corned beef sandwich. That made it a little better, though the pickle gave her gas. Should she also order up an antacid, she wondered, or, in view of her possible death by overdose, would that be superfluous? Counterproductive even?

In a sense, counting the room, the champagne, and the room service, she was already on the road to financial death. That was bad. On the other hand, she reflected, if she literally killed herself she would not have to pay the VISA bill she had just run up. Then again, she thought, what if interest charges continue to accumulate posthumously? This clearly needed further thought.

The room seemed to hang high above the city. It had a view over the Detroit River into the flat black farmlands east of Windsor, and flashes of lightning lit the quilted landscape of fields and trees. From the thirty-fifth floor of the hotel the geometric pattern of the earth below reminded her of a Mondrian composition: stark, minimal, thoroughly rational.

Hot white forks spit from the sky and were quickly swallowed by the darkness. Lightning was like love. Sometimes those who are killed by it show no sign on their bodies; other times they're horribly mutilated.

"I sing the body electric," she toasted as she picked up the champagne and pressed another pill between her lips. The Physician's Desk Reference said that Placidyl should not be given to people who are suicidal. Well, she hadn't been suicidal when the doctor gave them to her to help her sleep. It took Roger, dear sweet Roger, to make her feel that bad about herself.

From the thirty-fifth floor, she watched as the storm approached her. It was giddy, sitting there in the air, seeing it come at her that way. The thunderhead was piled up like a mound of dark hair, like Roger's pile of black curly hair that he let grow in a wild Celtic forelock that tumbled over his forehead. The storm would fly in her face with brute male power, and she would swallow it as she swallowed Roger.

The first calm wave of the drug washed through her, and she put the rest of the pills into an ashtray on the end table next to her. She had taken how many? Five? Six? Ten? They made a sound like bullets as they fell against the glass. She pulled her chair closer to the window and settled into it as raindrops began to patter against the glass of the windowpane. Her reflection seemed to hang in space outside the window, thirty-five stories above the street. The raindrops on the window made her reflection look like an Impressionist painting, a Renoir, perhaps, a melancholic bather. No, she thought, not a Renoir, just a slightly overweight woman doing something stupid to help her forget. A genre scene, after all.

Her mouth began to feel dry and sticky, as if a thick paste were forming on her tongue and the insides of her cheeks. When she swallowed, her teeth stuck to her lips. If she stopped taking pills now, she guessed, she would only sleep a very long time. She picked a pill out of the ashtray, brought it near her lips, sniffed it and set it down again. She had not yet decided how final this sleep needed to be.

Outside, the fullness of the storm had reached the building. Her reflection became distorted as the wind bowed the window inwards. She looked like something from a funhouse mirror now, with an elongated head and squat body, then a round head and thin model's figure, like glimpsing herself in water, all in flux as the storm shook the glass. The tower vibrated with a sudden peal of thunder and Diana, though she was filled with a drug called Placydil, grew afraid. If the wind blew in the window, her shadowy reflected self riding out there in the sky would disappear, and the slivers of glass flying inward would solve her dilemma.

She took another sip of champagne and sat back in her chair to await the outcome. She had never drunk champagne this expensive before. It broke against her palate like silver beads. If living is a long thirst (where had she read that?) then loving Roger had been like crawling across the desert.

The first night she saw him, she was sitting on the steps of the Cranbrook Art Academy between the museum and library. She was a new student, just arrived to work on her MFA in silversmithing. A couple of others were there with her, late at night, leaning against the tan sandstone pillars, passing a bottle of cool white wine among them. The wine was sweet and ran down her throat easily. Someone had put a candle on a steppingstone in the middle of the reflecting pool that extended between the columns of the portico and the iron gates that separated the art academy from the rest of the world. The flame fluttered there like a yellow butterfly in the darkness. Another butterfly flickered in the water below. The classical bronze sculptures in the long reflecting pool were dark forms in the moonlight: men riding on the backs of dolphins and maidens trailing ribands. At the bottom of the steps, just in front of her and the others, stood a larger than life sculpture of Europa and the bull by Millais. The girl, half naked in a flowing chiton, sat astride the great bronze bull, her full thighs stretched over its bulk as it reached the long point of its tongue back to her. The tongue was long enough to pierce her heart, and Europa held it fearfully, but not without excitement, between her forefinger and her thumb.

Diana had heard about Roger Price already but had never seen him. He was all anyone talked about. He walked about the grounds like a Renaissance prince, bestowing the gift of his presence on whatever students were in his favor at the moment. Funded entirely by the school's endowment, he had no teaching duties, no lectures to give, only endless work in his studio. Life was a continuous grant for him, and over the past fifteen years Detroit area foundations and corporations had been tripping over each other to give him commissions. He had reached artists' nirvana. He was what they all dreamed of being, and they loved him and hated him for it at the same time. It was the kind of feeling, she realized later, you had for a snake: it was beautiful to look at and you found your hand wavering out to touch it, but at the same time you were mortally afraid.

That night, Roger came out of the sculpture building and walked towards them slowly beneath the shadows of the chestnut trees that lined the pool. The conversation centered on him. It always did. Earlier, his welding arc had flashed his shadow against the translucent glass of the studio windows. The brilliant flickers of blue light made him look like Haephestus at work in the bowels of his volcano. Now, he came up and sat down beside Diana and shook a cigarette out of her pack without even asking.

"Thanks," he said, lighting up the cigarette with her Cricket. He smiled. "You're new around here, aren't you?" She nodded. He had crinkles around his intense blue eyes. As he laid her lighter back down, the thick blunt fingers of his hand briefly brushed the leg of her jeans at the thigh and she felt her flesh tighten.

They were lovers for the whole year. It didn't bother her that he had a wife and a son who lived on the grounds, too. The wife had her own lover. They went their way. Diana and Roger were seen everywhere together. She hung on him at openings. She was in the audience when he spoke at Wayne State or the Birmingham-Bloomfield Art Association. They made love on the tattered green couch in his studio that smelled of metal and electricity.

It was a wonderful year, fill of gallery-hopping, shows, living for days on only cocktail snacks and free drinks, feeding on Roger mainly. Was it too much to ask it to last?

The inevitable finally happened when the new class of students arrived. She didn't know it was going to happen, but she should have been able to read the signs. They started in late July, the messages from friends who wanted to shield her. People began to treat her more nicely, with more sympathy. It was odd. Linda, who never drank tea, asked her in for a cup. Miriam, who was anorexic, took her to lunch, and Diana never suspected a thing, not even when they asked her odd questions. Was she feeling strong? Did she know of a good therapist? Had she packed a parachute? She didn't realize then they were only trying to cushion the fall.

One Sunday night in August she felt the bottom drop out. The old students had gathered to welcome the new students, as they had the year before, at the portico overlooking the reflecting pool. A riser had been set up for a stage, and one of the students, a post-modernist performance artist, had rigged a light and sound system. Roger had formed a rag-tag country-western band called The Bozart Mountain Boys, and they were in the middle of a set of Willie Nelson tunes. That night Diana learned what the others had known all along, that Roger cut one girl out of the herd each year, took her as his ducal privilege, an uncontracted fringe benefit. Not always the prettiest one, but usually the most vulnerable. He kept them for a year, then replaced them when a new flock arrived fresh from undergraduate school, their sheep's eyes wide with adoration. That was all he really wanted, after all, adoration, and it was easier for younger girls to give.

Diana sat on the steps watching as the concert began. She was sipping sweet mountain chablis from a Dixie cup, lounging there, confident, still unkowing, surrounded by several other women artists. She felt for a moment like a figure from a bas-relief, "Naiads after the Bath" or something, posed beneath the tall pillars.

She watched Roger's fingers pull at the thick strings of the electric bass. His voice was cracked and whiskey soaked like Kenny Rogers'. It seemed odd to her to hear that voice, so familiar from his whispers in her ear, strained through the jerry-rigged sound system. Hadn't they made love that very afternoon?

So confident was she that she watched only indifferently as one of the first year girls got up from her seat on the steps and strolled down to the stage. She was wearing faded jeans, very tight, and clogs that made too much noise as she walked. Her loose chemise, with V-neck and open-holed smocking, was cinched tight at the waist with a brightly colored scarf. Her long blond hair was braided to one side, the braid intertwined with leather lacing. She said something to Roger and he laughed and nodded as he returned to the mike.

"We've got a request from . . . What did you say your name was again, dear?"

"Tiffany," she said.

"Yeah, for Tiffany," he repeated. His voice echoed off the high walls of the art museum and library behind them. The Bozart Mountain Boys began to play and Diana noticed how Roger's eyes eyes followed Tiffany all the way back to her place on the steps, her clogs clicking like castinets. And it was then, all of sudden, that Diana felt the earth fall away beneath her. She knew the look. It had been the same one Roger had given her the year before. She pulled her gypsy shawl tighter around her shoulders and knew that everything had suddenly changed.

What had she loved, and hated, about him anyway, she wondered. Was it the smell of sweat and steel and ozone as he lay on top of her and forced his tongue into her mouth? Was it the way his veins bulged on his arms?

When she watched him work, the light from his arc assaulted her eyes so much she had to squeeze them shut and look away. Was it just his brute masculinity, so stupid and unfeeling? His art was so different from hers. It was brutal. He used cranes to lift sheets of inch-thick metal into place. He bolted and rivetted and welded, and the blood pulsed beneath the skin of his arms and neck as he worked. You weren't supposed to fall in love with men like that, not anymore. That was something that women *used* to do, and yet when he made love to her, her body shook and when he stopped she felt dead, and though she hated herself for it, she didn't want to lose him.

"What am I supposed to do now, Roger?" she had asked when it was clear to her that he had already made love to Tiffany on the studio couch. She had to shout over the loud crackle of the welding arc with which he was joining together two sheets of rusting steel. He didn't answer.

"You shit!" she shouted, throwing a heavy leather welder's glove at him.

He shut off the arc and stood up. In his heavy black apron and welder's helmet, he looked like a dark knight from a medieval romance. He lifted the visor and his light blue eyes were hard now like new-forged steel.

"Grow up," he said, "people fuck around here all the time and nobody gets hung up this way. We had a good year and now it's over. It doesn't mean anything."

"You shit!" she shouted again. She suddenly realized she felt like an addict must feel when the supply runs out cold. You hate the thing that fills your veins with something hot and then suddenly leaves you wanting more of it and more. The next thing she knew, she was beating him with her fists, hurling her hands against the thick leather apron he wore to protect himself against hot metal fragments and sparks. As she grabbed his shoulder, he simply shrugged and the force threw her half-way across the room. He turned his back on her then, yanked his visor down roughly and began to weld again. His arc exploded in a shower of red hot sparks.

The blue smoke and the smell of sweat and heated metal was like rat's breath to her now. In the winter, it had kept her warm there in the studio, in his arms. Now it seemed to beat against her. She ran from his studio, and grabbed her purse. She only wanted to be someplace cool and high, above the world, far away from him.

Now her whole life felt far away. The storm continued outside the hotel. Lightning, bolt after bolt, illuminated the city below making it look garish, like a city of the dead. The hotel tower shook and swayed in the gusts of wind.

Diana felt her eyes getting heavy, her mind closing out more and more of the world. She felt as though she were inside a paperweight, suspended in cool clear glass. She tried to lift her arms but couldn't. She was turning inward, becoming aware of a slow, careful plodding sound which she eventually realized was her heartbeat. She could feel its pulse in her neck and felt her head swell with each beat. Had she taken enough Placidyl to kill her? she wondered. She tried to count between the dull heartbeats the way you count between lightning and thunder to see how far away the storm is. The subtly increasing distance between beats told her how far it was between life and death. She forced her eyes open a moment. In the window in front of her, she seemed to hang above the city like a piece of sculpture, immobile, cast in pale blue metal, lit by the flashes of the storm, too heavy to move anymore.

And then, suddenly, she saw herself disappear. Everything else went, too: the lights in the towers below her, the glittering crab of streetlights that extended outwards over the city, the dull roar of the elevator and the hiss of the room's climate control system. Everything vanished, and as far as she could see or hear everything was dark and silent. It was all gone, all of it, as if a giant hand had wiped it away, and she felt as though she had been dropped into a deep black bag.

"Oh, shit," she heard herself mumble, "Am I dead? Have I killed myself for that asshole?"

She strained to hear something, anything. She heard nothing. Yet, she could still feel the chair's upholstery pressing against her arms and legs and back as if she remained in the hotel room. Is this all death is? she wondered. A hotel room? Dante, at least, had imagination. He put people head down in small cubicles in the ground. He had them chewing the flesh off each others skulls. Perhaps the modern hell is just a dark room in a seventy story hotel.

"Is this the price you pay for being addicted to men," she wondered, "eternity in a hotel room?"

Then she heard a dull thud. A heartbeat. Then silence. Then another. She searched inside, and though she could not move, she found some pain still lurking there in a dark place, proof enough she was alive. "Well," she thought, "It isn't death. It's only a power blackout. Now what?"

Lightning flashed. The long bolts of the storm over the blacked out city reminded her of the silver she beat on her anvil. Her necklace and the bracelets she wore felt cool, and when the lightning flashed they flashed, too, and showed her reflection still hanging there in the window, high above the city.

"Too close for comfort that time," she thought.

The champagne bottle was empty. She heard it thud on the carpet beside her as she managed to push herself out of the chair and fumble through the dark towards where she thought the bathroom was. She heard a noise, flesh banging into a dresser edge, and a few seconds later she felt pain swelling like a flower in her thigh. She swore. Would there be a bruise? she wondered. If so, she would create something to cover it. She would go down into her studio and bend and mold a lump of silver with her tools. Then she would incise it with sharp instruments and set jewels in it. And over each bruise she ever received, she would make a case of silver until finally she would be covered with armor, her body encased in cool metal to hide the wounds, and the largest piece of all would be a reliquary in the shape of a heart to hold whatever pieces of her own heart Roger had left. She would preserve the fragments carefully, parse them out only rarely, if ever, like slivers of the true cross.

As she made her way back to the bed from the bathroom, the inside of her mouth was sour and something clung to the back of her throat. She had vomitted all of it up, all of it. The pills, the champagne, the too-expensive corned beef and Roger. "God, I hate hotels," she said as she felt around with her hands and found the bed. She collapsed into it and saw a glint of metal on the pillow case.

The maid had left a mint when she turned down the bed. Diana undid the wrapper and slipped the mint into her mouth. There would be no getting out until morning. The elevator was out of service and she was too tired to walk. The mint tasted sweet on her tongue, and so, at last, she slept.

THE MERMAID'S SONG

Turning to the yard, Laura brushed the single patch of gray hair back from her forehead with the back of her hand. Just that one spot had turned white, as though someone had touched her there with a paint brush and created a white forelock that kept falling down. It seemed separate from her, something that ought to belong to someone else, someone older.

Behind her, Sam rustled in his sleep. The room was still filled with the yeasty smell of their lovemaking. It hung on the air waiting for the wind to blow it away. She sat on the chest by the window looking down at the yard where the garden light threw a fuzzy circle on the lawn and over her small garden. In the middle of the garden stood a rusting statue of a man riding on a wheel, something Sam had picked because it belonged to a famous architect. She had never liked it, but there it stood, pointing off to the horizon. The garden around it, however, was her own. She stared out at the garden blankly, her knees drawn up to her chin. A car drove past in front of the house, and she resettled herself on the hope chest, pulling her silk kimono tighter around her. It was a souvenir of their trip to Japan with the Chamber of Commerce group. The coolness of the material made her skin feel like marble in the hot night.

Perhaps she was turning into stone, she thought. Maybe the rest of her would slowly turn white, like her hair, and one day they'd find her bent over her garden like a classic statue.

It was unimaginable to her that anyone her age could be graying, have a seven-year-old child, still be so far from where she had hoped to be when she and Sam were married. That happened to other people, she had always thought, old people, like the tired gray couple at church who trailed behind them an air of wasted years every time they passed on their way to communion. The idea that she and Sam could ever become that couple had never occurred to her until recently.

Sam turned on his side toward her on his half of the bed. Unconsciously they had staked out their territory long before, an invisible line down the middle of the mattress, like a ridge off which they'd roll if they got too close or failed to sleep back-to-back. Now he lay on his back, one hand dangling languidly from the edge of the bed like the gesture of Adam on the ceiling of the Sistine Chapel. He was well tanned from working outdoors supervising the construction of the new office tower he was building in Troy. He had distinct lines where the white skin met the brown, making him piebald where the different lengths of his shirts and shorts ended. In the dark places most exposed to the sun, his skin had the look of smooth leather, covered with a fine sweat in the heat of the night. The tip of his penis, still slightly swollen and damp, looked like a large strawberry.

She had been dreaming of something before they had made love. Her moaning and tossing had wakened them both. She didn't remember the dream, but it must have been a bad one because she had crossed the forbidden ridge and rolled against him for what she remembered as comfort. He had turned groggily, perhaps in the middle of his own dream, and had slid his large hand along her calf and thigh, up her entire side and came around behind holding her close and tight for the first time in a long time. Not quite awake in the hot stillness preceding the storm, they had made love, clinging to each other, as if they were drowning.

Everything was confused for a moment. She didn't know where she was or who was handling her, and she only woke fully after he came, but by then he had rolled off and fallen asleep again without saying anything. She still felt pain and heat inside her where he had entered her. The uncertainty of what would happen in the morning kept her awake now. What would he say over breakfast? What would she? Would he even remember? Or would he rush off to work as usual, embarrassed because they had briefly broken down a barrier they'd erected some time before? She was sure he was sound asleep already. Perhaps he had never really woken up.

Before they married, she had never expected him to be a sound sleeper. He was always energetic and bright when they were together. Before they ever spent the night together, she had pictured him as a restless sleeper like herself, a mumbler who tossed and turned on the waves of bad dreams. But he wasn't. When he fell asleep, especially after sex, he was like a dead man. Sometimes he wouldn't roll over all night and would wake up in the morning with a stiff shoulder. She sometimes wished he would wake when she did in the night. It wouldn't seem so bad if they could be awake together sometimes.

Thunder rumbled in the distance. The storm the newscaster had predicted was coming right on schedule. Now the wind began to blow through the Japanese maple in the backyard. They had planted it as a sapling when they first bought the house, and eventually it had grown tall enough to shade the corner of the deck. The thin top branches began to swirl, and the copper colored leaves reached up like palms to catch the rain. The storm which had seemed so far away descended swiftly, but Sam did not move. Nothing could wake him. Laura ran through the house on tiptoe, checking the windows. The house was buttoned tight, but on her way toward the kitchen for a cup of herbal tea, she heard a noise from her daughter's room.

Missy was in bed huddled tightly against the wall, her arms wrapped tight around Lumpy, her bear.

"Did the storm scare you?" Laura asked, sitting beside her on the bed and reaching out to the hard tight ball of fear her daughter had become. She flicked on the small nightstand lamp, and the room was lit with a yellow glow. A pair of ceramic ballerina slippers hung from a ribbon on the wall. When Missy was born, Sam designed the room decor himself, from wallpaper to the Techline toy cupboards. He believed that children raised in an environment that showed good taste would grow up trouble free, but Missy eventually triumphed with her own careless design, scattering Barbie clothes across the carpet, leaving piles of her own wardrobe on the rocking chair. Already the room was like an archeological site, with layers of her childhood piled atop one another. Now she lay rigid, and Laura had to unpeel her legs and arms to get her to turn toward her.

"It's only a storm," Laura said, "You're safe here."

"But didn't the mermaid *ever* come back?" Missy asked in a whimpering voice.

It took Laura a few moments to make the connection. They had been reading a children's book a few weeks before, a retelling of an old Welsh story. Laura thought the book was harmless enough when she bought it at Borders. The story began innocently. *Once upon a time there lived a poor fisherman in a poor village by the sea.* The illustrations were full of bright blue seas and golden haired mermaids, and so she had bought it without reading the end. In spite of its fairy tale trappings, it turned out to be one of those modern neo-realist children's stories. In this story, the fisherman and mermaid married, of course, but that was not the end of it. The mermaid was the daughter of the mermaid queen, and the fisherman got the mermaid's treasure as dowry, but the mermaid, in marrying a human, lost her freedom. She agreed to take off her lower skin and appear with legs like a human woman, but she soon discovered she was not happy without her tail and scales. Soon her discontent began to show. At night the villagers were sometimes awakened by a haunting song coming from the fisherman's hut. It was terribly sad, full of longing for the sea, and quickly the neighbors began to suspect all was not well in the fisherman's house. On more than one moonlit night, the fisherman was seen rowing his beautiful wife out to sea in his skiff, a large wooden box between them. He would return alone at dawn, and the wife would be gone for a few days, a whole week once, before she reappeared looking fresh and new. Needless to say, rumors flew around the small village about where the fisherman's wife went on her journeys. After she had human children, the mermaid would still go off on her own, causing much comment in the village. The fisherman's face grew sad, but he would never explain to his children or anyone else where his wife went on her secret travels. And then one day, inevitably, her eldest child discovered her secret. Peering into the mysterious wooden box, he saw his mother's mermaid skin, shimmering green and gold, folded neatly in the bottom.

"Oh no," the mermaid cried, "you have discovered my secret and I shall have to leave forever now." And that night, by the full moon's light, the fisherman rowed his wife out to sea for the last time. When the boat was right above her mother's kingdom, the mermaid opened the chest, donned her fish skin for the last time and dove over the side, never to return to her husband and children. And so it ended.

When Laura turned the page of the storybook to find more, there was nothing. She smiled weakly at Missy, feeling the bottom go out of bedtime.

"You mean the mer-mother never came back again?" Missy had asked, terrified.

Laura fumbled for an answer. She supposed the story was meant to be some sort of feminist parable, but it made her uncomfortable just the same. She could imagine no other fear greater for a child than to be abandoned by her parents, but the author had apparently not thought of that reading of the tale. Laura said, "Maybe the mer-mother came back to swim with her children on the beach," but it was cold comfort to the child and to her. For the next few days, usually at bedtime, Missy asked again and again why the mer-mother had to swim away, and Laura could feel her daughter's fear as the child clung tightly to her, afraid to go to sleep lest her mother not be there in the morning.

"Maybe the author just made a mistake," Laura said. "Maybe she forgot to write the ending; authors do that sometimes." Finally, in her most reassuring voice she had put an end to it, she thought, by saying, "Honey, I'm sure the mer-mommy came back very soon, and she taught her children how to swim like merboys and mergirls and they spent the summer swimming along the shore and they were very happy." It had been a week or more since Missy had asked about the mermaid but now, perhaps because of the storm or a dream, the question came up again.

"I'll never leave you, honey," Laura said, finally sensing what Missy's question was really about. After a few more reassurances, Missy seemed convinced and was ready to sleep again. Laura turned out the bedstand light, tucked her daughter in beneath her light sheet and rubbed her back for a while until her breathing changed. But Laura herself could not go back to bed. She found the idea of sleeping beside Sam repulsive. It seemed impossible to her that she could ever sleep next to him. So why did she continue to do it night after night? She tried to push that question away as she wandered into the living room. She felt she needed to sit a moment in the Eames chair. She found herself hoping its large wings would fold over her like angels' wings and protect her. She wished her own doubts and fears could be calmed as easily as Missy's, with a simple lie, but it wasn't that simple. She curled down into the soft leather belly of the chair and felt the second wave of the storm coming. The lightning illuminated everything in the room and changed the colors to odd shades of blue. She felt the weight of too much history to the things she saw. Everything the lightning illuminated was covered with memories that clung like a thick layer of dust. Not that there would ever be dust in this house. Sam wouldn't allow it. Sam wouldn't allow a lot of things. How much did they have to sacrifice early in his career so they could buy the Barcelona chairs no one could sit in because the backs dug into your kidneys? Why did they have to send back the blinds she picked out because he didn't think they were the right shade of mauve? As the storm shook the plaster, she realized she hated the house he made her live in. It was the container into which he had put her the way he had pedestals built for the Brancusis and the display case for his antique pistols. She was contained inside "his" marriage even when they made love. How odd, she thought, that a woman can have her legs and arms wrapped around a man and yet still be inside him.

As the rain beat against the house, she wanted to travel again. To Europe, Japan, Hong Kong, the Upper Peninsula even. Anyplace. She would love to be sitting out this storm in a hotel room somewhere. She always found hotel rooms comforting. They had no past. They seemed cut off from time because no one really lived in them. Each day maids would come and make them exactly the way they were before. They followed handbooks that told them exactly where to leave the ashtrays and where to put the extra roll of toilet paper so if you traveled from hotel to hotel you would always know where things were. If you didn't look in mirrors, you would never have the sense your life was just ticking away. At least there was still possibility in hotel rooms, she thought, a sense of being able to step out the door into something new.

A great smash of thunder rocked the house like an explosion and she wrapped her arms around herself in the deep chair. She wanted things to be new again, when she didn't have to live with his art and his furniture, when she had something of her own, when it was just enough to lie together with Sam and look at him, to explore one another with eyes and fingers. Sam used to have a way of running his finger over her cheek as if he were petting a bird, and they would simply lie there and wordlessly touch each other and it was enough. She had loved it once, but then she had begun to realize it was his way of shaping her the way he shaped everything else until it looked the way he wanted it.

She did not want to be his canary any more. Lately, they made love only in the dark as a way of avoiding having to look into one another's eyes. Then they wouldn't have to read the disappointment there, knowing how loveless it had all become. In the darkness, or when they were only half awake, they could push all the uncomfortable thoughts into the dark closets of their minds.

When Missy was born, possibility, or something like it, came in through a window, but Sam contained her, too, until Laura realized she had no allies, no one who understood. After that brief hope was gone, there was only the growing sadness of distance from something. Outside, the thunder had stopped, but the rain still beat on the roof, and in her head, she could hear, plain as a bell on a moonlit night, the mermaid's haunting song.

Soon the rain was hissing softly and the thunder ceased. She went back upstairs to the bedroom, sat again by the window and began to cry. Sam had pulled the sheet up to protect himself from the sudden cool the rain had brought, but had apparently not noticed, or cared, that she had gone out. She sat on the chest and composed herself. There were worse things that happened to people's lives, she supposed, as she turned to the window and looked out.

The rain had become a light sprinkle. She hoped her plants would be all right. The storm might have washed the dirt away from the roots. Luckily it was late in the season. In spring a storm like this could have devastated the whole garden, torn the seedlings from their beds and killed them. She half-wished she had run out in the rain and thrown something over the plants to protect them, but there would have been no point. There was nothing she could have put over the flowers that wouldn't have crushed them worse than the rain. In the light below the window, she could see a bare spot where runoff from the downspout had washed a hole in the grass. What was left of the storm dripped slowly from the lip of the tube onto the exposed mud. In the morning, she would go out early, get her wheelbarrow and put pea gravel beneath the mouth. She should have fixed the earth beneath the downspout years before. That would have helped.

A slight breeze blew through the Japanese maple. Falling drops made a noise like a ticking clock. She recalled that the chest she sat on was her own. It had been her hope chest before they got married. She had filled it with things she thought she would need. Some of them had never been taken out in all those years. Sam would not have liked them, and she had never shown them to him. They were hers alone. Somehow, that thought made her feel better, and she pulled the silk butterfly kimono around her, wrapping herself tightly against the cool of the room.

CHIAROSCURO

"I think I've got a bottle of *rioja* in here somewhere," Peter Mason said, fumbling for the light switch. "Mandy gave it to me for my seventieth, but I decided to let myself age a little more before I drank it. Wine's better aged."

His fingers found the switch.

"Christ, what horrible light," he moaned as he walked across the bare wood floor of his studio. "You stay here, Esther, and when I turn on the lamp, turn this thing off. I never bothered to take out the factory lighting after I moved up here. It makes us look dead." He laughed lightly at the grim joke.

He moved agilely for a man of his years, quietly padding on the rope soles of the espadrilles he had favored ever since his trip to Catalonia after the war. He switched on the old floor lamp that he kept in the studio when he was working late and nodded to Esther who turned off the fluorescent tubes. The large open room was bathed in orange light, and he turned to watch Esther as she came across the darkened loft. In fact, he didn't want to be seen in the grim fluorescent light. It brought out the worst in everybody, every flaw, every blotch. At their age, he thought, they didn't need every liver spot and wrinkle emphasized. Maybe his eye was too sensitive to what light did to things, but that was how he had made his living for the past forty years.

"I still can't believe it," Esther said walking up to him and stretching out her hands to his. "I saw her name, Amanda Mason and the picture in the paper, but I never thought. Well, it's been over forty years, Peter! Yet, there you were."

"Yes, Mandy's getting a bit of a reputation now. Three books so far."

"She has your face. I knew she was yours, even before I saw you there. Why weren't you sitting right up front?"

"It makes Mandy nervous if I'm up front when she reads. I try to lose myself in the pack," Peter said, going to a small metal cabinet in what he called the 'living room' of the studio. It was actually just a corner where he had set an old wooden table, two chairs, a day bed, and some other odds and ends of paint-splattered furniture on a faded rug for when he needed to stay in the studio overnight. "I think that *rioja's* in the back here somewhere," he said, squatting down in front of the cabinet and reaching behind his emergency cache of canned spaghetti. "Here it is."

He pulled the bottle out by the neck and stood up, after two tries, with the help of a push on the cabinet. He felt lightheaded for a moment and the room seemed to spin a bit. He leaned against the cabinet and put his hand to his brow.

"Are you all right, Pedro?" she asked.

"Hmmm? Yes, yes," he said weakly. "Blood pressure pills. They make me dizzy sometimes when I stand up too fast."

He felt embarrassed to have her see him this way. Usually he didn't feel self-conscious about his age. In fact, he had fared better than most of his friends. He was alive at least. But to be with someone with whom you had been young almost fifty years before, it made you feel every ache and pain.

"Ha! *Pedro*. Nobody's called me that for forty years." He looked at Esther and realized he had changed far more than she had. She was still thin, not like most of the women he had known years before who had gone to fat after menopause. Perhaps living on kibbutz all those years did that to her. She didn't have the time to lounge around like American women. She had always been athletic, but not overly muscled. Her flesh still looked firm and elastic.

"You haven't changed a bit," he exclaimed, "it's amazing!"

She blushed and shook her head. "Don't be a fool," she said.

He shrugged and felt a blush go up his face. "All right, I admit it took me a moment or two to recognize you, but. . ."

"It's all right," she said. "I had an unfair advantage. I saw you first and you had no way to know I'd be in town for the benefit at the synagogue."

"Almost forty years," he said, shaking his head.

They stood silently for a moment as if to savor that expanse of time, then Peter pulled himself out of it and opened the drawer of the cabinet where the corkscrew was. In a moment, he had the foil off the neck and the screw into the cork, but he had difficulty pulling it out. Finally he put the bottle between his legs for better leverage and the cork emerged with a few squeaks and a resounding pop. He felt a little winded.

"Everything takes so long to do now, have you noticed? Up, eat, wash your teeth, paint a little. Suddenly the whole damned day is gone, and you've got nothing to show for it."

He took two mismatched glasses from the shelf above the sink and, turning them upside down for a moment to shake any bugs out (the old factory was infested with roaches) he set them on the bare top of the wooden table. There was a rumble above them and the lamp flickered for a moment.

"Storm," he said. "We're due. It's been so dry."

She nodded. "It's good to hear thunder again. We don't hear much living in the desert. Only guns, rockets exploding from time to time. I like thunder."

He poured the red wine into the glasses and handed one to Esther. They touched the rims together and drank. The first sip of wine had a bite to it, a sharp taste beneath the red that reminded him of *retsina*. He noticed Esther set her glass down on the table.

"The second sip is better," he said. "Go on."

She smiled, lifted the glass and took a small sip, just enough to wet her lips.

"You're right," she said.

Peter felt something move in his chest, a light thump, like a finger tickling his heart. His hand went to his chest, but there was no pain.

"Is something wrong?" she asked.

"Damned arrhythmia," he said, tapping his breast at his shirt pocket. "Plup-blup, like my heart stops for a second or skips a beat. Maybe I'm just so surprised to see you again my heart wants to jump right out of my shirt and fly around the room like one of those hearts you get on Valentine's cards. What do you think of that?"

He laughed, and she smiled, and then Peter poured more of the red wine into their glasses. He noticed that her eyes had not got filmy the way his had. They were still dark as stained walnut wood with the large black pupils floating in the middle. For a moment it seemed as if her eyes were the only things in the room, and he stared at them, remembering the way she used to be before the war and then after.

"Is this your work?" she asked, turning to the stack of canvases leaning against the wall of the studio.

"Yes, of course, it's what I've been doing for the last twenty years or so. This is the stuff that didn't sell yet. Some of it's good, some bad."

She flipped through a few of the paintings.

"You were so poor before the war," she said.

"Who wasn't? With the depression and all. But . . ." He stopped and took a long drink of wine. He noticed his hand was shaking a bit as the glass came to his lips, and he was glad she wasn't looking.

"But what?" she turned from the paintings.

"Oh, never mind," he said with a gesture that made him feel like a bashful boy. He was going to say, "But we had each other." Rain began spattering on the large glass skylight above them. At first it came in irregular patterns, but it quickly grew more steady. Thunder and lightning came again and the lights flickered once more.

"Do you remember the summer at Higgins Lake?" he asked. "Listening to the rain all night?"

"Of course. That storm in July?"

"I thought we'd lose the roof. I was scared. Jesus."

"You didn't act scared."

"How could I?" he asked, "With you there."

"I was whimpering like a spaniel."

"At first," he said, "only at first."

Suddenly there was a sharp crack of lightning nearby and the lamp in the corner went dark. The studio was black and smelled of paint and turpentine.

"Damn this place," Peter mumbled, "Every time there's a storm. Hold on, I've got a candle somewhere."

He waited for another flash of lightning and saw where the furniture was, then he started making his way across the room. For a moment, the studio was illuminated by the flicker of another bolt of lightning which turned the room a cold blue, like the color of a blind cat's eye. He tried to move carefully, to avoid banging into things. He changed direction only when the next flash of lightning came.

"Here, here somewhere," he muttered, walking in the darkness with his arms outstretched like a blind man. "Christ, you know I shouldn't even drive at night. Night vision goes first, but at least I can still see. You remember Lawrence? No, I think I met him after you left for Israel. He was a painter, went blind, had to turn to sculpture, you know, but he never got good at it. Ah, here. He's dead now, too."

The lightning had guided him back to the metal cabinet and he pulled open the drawer, fumbled through it in the darkness for a moment until he found what felt like the candle. He pulled it out and reached in his shirt pocket for a match.

A second later the studio was lit again with the warm yellow of a candle. It and the lightning threw shadows on the blank walls. He shielded it with his hand as he walked towards Esther.

"We're stuck now, Es," he said, "We can't get out until the elevator starts working again. There'll be a scandal, like there was back then."

He meant the remark to be a little joke. He had long since gotten over the shame he felt when Esther's husband discovered they were lovers. But he sensed Esther herself still felt the pain.

"I'm sorry."

"It's all right," she replied. She had turned her face away slightly, as if embarrassed. Though her hair had long since turned gray, she had not had it blued and curled the way American women did when they grew old. It was as silver as the moon and still straight and thick.

He looked at her now in the candlelight, and the features of her face seemed to disappear and leave only her profile which was remarkably the same as it had been forty years before. She still had the same strong jawline and high forehead he had sketched years before at Higgins Lake, with her lounging on the end of the dock.

"May as well relax," he said "There's no way out till the power comes back on."

The storm rolled on above them, washing across the glass in waves when the wind blew. The skylight seemed to rattle with each gust of wind, and torrents of water splashed down the outside walls like waterfalls.

He felt isolated and cut off from the rest of the world. Storms do that, he thought, force you into corners where you huddle against their power, praying for deliverance. They remind you of how fragile it all is. With Esther there, he felt strangely safe, maybe because her presence forced him to act as though the fierce lightning and thunder outside did not bother him. Just like Higgins Lake.

He took her hand and led her to the table where he tipped the candle so that a little pool of wax dripped down on a dirty plate he had left there. He turned the candle upright and set it in the wax, holding it there a moment until the wax was set. Then he poured more wine for himself. Esther's glass was still full and she had set it in front of her on the table.

Peter shook his head. "It amazes me to see you here," he said, taking a drink of the wine which had now lost its bite and was beginning to mellow as it breathed in the damp air of the loft. The wine warmed him. Even though it had been hot outside all day, his circulation was not as good as it should have been and the storm brought a sudden drop in temperature that made him feel cool. He sensed the warmth from the wine creeping up to his head.

"That summer there was a storm as bad as this, wasn't there?" he asked, "I remember that night. We were waiting for Harry to give you a divorce, the bastard."

"Times were different then," Esther said. "People didn't divorce the way they do now."

"Mandy's been divorced four years now. She's living with a guy, a stockbroker, and they don't care who knows. Jesus, how I envy them. If we had been born later it could have been so different, couldn't it?"

The candle sputtered for a moment and a curl of blue smoke went up into the room. A small dribble of wax ran down the side of the candle into the plate below. Outside, the rain continued to beat on the roof. They listened to it for a moment in silence.

Esther broke the quiet. "Tonight when I saw Mandy, I thought, 'She could have been ours.' It was silly of me, but I thought it nonetheless."

"Did you and Herschel . . . ?"

"Three," she replied, nodding. "They're all grown now, and grandchildren, five of them. Too late to go back now."

Peter nodded, too, and felt sad for a moment, as though something were being drained out of him. Then he shook his head clear and shrugged.

"What the hell," he said, "That's life for you, too short sometimes, too damned long others." He tossed back the glass of wine, drained it, set the empty glass back down on the table and filled it again from the bottle. "Remember before the war when we were single we used to drink *rioja* and when we'd get good and looped we'd talk about joining the Lincoln Brigade and going off to fight the fascists? And then some of us did and got used as cannon fodder and some didn't come back and then the real war started and we all went, and it was awful except that you and I had that summer at the lake afterwards."

He knew he was getting drunk, but he didn't care. He hadn't been drunk in a long time, but being with Esther again reminded him of those days forty years before when he was young and just out of the service and he had met her again and found out that while he was gone she had married Herschel, an idealistic young Zionist who had lofty ideas but who didn't understand her. In those days, they would drink beer and wine and gin, mixing it all up until they were silly, and drive out to a road house outside Detroit where they would drink some more. Since Herschel was always gone somewhere talking about making Palestine into Israel, Peter and Esther had fallen together as the tight crowd of art students at Wayne State had paired up two by two, and so they fell in love again as they had before the war.

He stared at her for a long time, amazed how after the passing of forty years there was still something there that had been there before, some thread of continuity. Somehow that thing we call personality remains after the hair turns gray and age spots appear on your once young hands.

His head began to feel heavy from the wine, and he rested it on his hand as he looked at her sitting across from him at the plain wooden table in his studio. She stared back with her deep brown eyes. They said nothing. The rain drummed on the roof and hissed in the streets below the old factory. Thunder rolled and crashed overhead like the surf, and they sat together listening to it. Peter took another sip of wine. It tasted thick now and felt like velvet on his tongue. He grew sleepy.

The candle threw their shadows large on the studio walls. The flickering light hurt his eyes, and he moved the candle from between them, pushing it to the side of the table. The moving light changed the way the shadows played across Esther's face and somehow, he felt, made her look younger. Perhaps it was because more of her face was now in the darkness, like a Rembrandt, where the outlines were only visible as darker spaces in the *chiaroscuro*.

But it was more than that, he thought, feeling the heaviness of his head upon his hand. He felt himself slipping into a pleasant somnolence, as if he were sinking into the soft featherbed in the cottage at Higgins Lake. The rain hissed on the roof and lulled him further.

"Peter?"

It was Esther's voice. He blinked and looked across the table. He could hardly believe what he saw. Esther appeared to be no more than thirty years old, dressed as she had been dressed at Higgins Lake. Her gray hair was again as black as ebony, and the opened top buttons of her blouse showed the tops of round full breasts.

"What's the matter?" she asked. Her voice, too, was younger.

He shook his head trying to clear his vision.

"I must be drunker than I thought," he said, pushing his wine glass away from him. "God, you're beautiful, Esther!"

She laughed. Her teeth were white as pearls between her lips, and her laughter was the cascading laughter of a young woman. A sudden flash of lightning lit the room and Peter felt cold. He felt the hairs on his arm and the back of his neck stand up straight. Esther's eyes seemed to flash with the lightning, as if they were gemstones of the sort they worshiped in India, the ones reputed to have captured moonlight or the cold light of a star.

"What **are** you?" he asked, terrified, "A ghost or a memory or what? Or am *I* dying?" He had heard that when you died the spirits of those you'd loved came for you. He tried to push away from the table, but his chair wouldn't move. It seemed nailed to the floor. He stared at the apparition across from him, at her face, her neck, the arm she had rested on the table. Her skin was firm and smooth, the flesh beneath it fresh, the down-like hair on her forearm delicate and dark, not gray.

"Who are you?" he asked again.

"Don't you remember?" the figure replied.

He stammered, searching his memory for something he could not place. "Yes, I remember, I remember. . . ." He could not say what. He put his hand against his forehead and squeezed his eyes shut.

"What, say what you remember."

"Swimming!" he said desperately. Nothing else occurred to him.

"By moonlight?"

"Yes!" And then the memories came to him with extraordinary clarity, in a rush, things he had not thought of for years. "And the pines, yes, brushing our bare skin as we ran from the lake when the moon disappeared!"

"And then?" she asked. Her hair was darker and fuller now, rising up like a dark cloud and swirling above her head like smoke. Her eyes flashed in the dark and she spread her arms, and he remembered.

"Then falling for a thousand years into the featherbed," he cried, "deeper and deeper and our naked arms and legs, cold and blue from moonlight and water, tangling, weaving, and your tongue gliding in and out, your nipples up and firm from the cool. And you, what do you remember?"

Esther, the young transformed Esther, threw back her head and ran her fingers through her dark hair. "The bed, soft against my back and you above me like the sky, heaving like the waves and above us both, above the whole world, the rain that fell that night, the lightning that flashed outside the window and your hands and arms tight around me until I cried!"

"And then the rain."

"On the roof. All night."

He looked across the table, but his eyes were tricking him now. Was she there or not? He squeezed his eyelids closed and felt tears run down his face, two lines, cool as silver. He opened his eyes again. The bottle of wine was empty. His arm knocked it over as he groped across the table for her hand, but he took hold of nothing.

"Christ, I loved you!" he sighed.

"Dad?"

A touch on his arm. He awoke with a start and felt a horrible crick in his neck. The studio was light with daylight and he stared around confusedly for a moment before he heard his daughter's voice again. She was standing behind him, a green rain slicker on, her hair wet with drizzle.

"I got worried when I didn't see you after the reading last night. I tried to call you at home but couldn't get through. I should have known you were here. I had a hard time getting home last night myself. The freeway was flooded all to hell."

Peter blinked in the bright morning light, still disoriented. For a moment, it seemed as though he had never been there before.

"What time is it?" he asked. "Was anybody here when you came in?"

"It's about nine," Mandy said, smiling as she righted the empty wine bottle. "Have a good time last night?"

"I've got a hell of a stiff neck," he said.

"You should have if you slept that way. Why didn't you use the cot?"

"I came here with Esther," he said.

"Who?" Mandy asked.

"Esther Lefkowitz, uh Schnee, that was her married name. She married Herschel Schnee, forty years ago or more. You must have seen me talking to her after the reading last night. You did see me talking to someone, didn't you?"

"There were so many people, and they all closed in on me. What did she look like?"

"She looked, well, beautiful."

"What's this?" Mandy asked, picking up a piece of drawing paper that lay on the table in front of the full glass of wine that sat across the table from her father. It was the picture of a young woman with teeming, thick black hair and eyes that glowed. The face was obscured in shadows. The lines were uneven here and there and she knew he had drawn it when drunk.

"That's her," he said, looking at the drawing. He recognized the style but didn't remember doing it. "I must have drawn that," he said, "last night. I was drinking Spanish wine, you know how that screws me up." The pencil lay there, too, yet he had no memory of ever picking it up.

"Maybe we should go, dad," she said.

"Yes," he replied, then said, "No, no. You go ahead. I want to work a little. I've got that thing over there on the easel half done. I'll be all right." His hand automatically reached for a brush and pulled it out of the old coffee can. He wiped the turpentine from it with a rag and looked at a canvas mounted on an easel in the corner. He used only oils. It was old-fashioned, he knew, but he liked being able to push the paint around before it dried.

"Are you sure you'll be all right?"

"Yes, sure, I'll be fine, Mandy," he snapped. She started to make him some coffee on the hotplate. He would never admit it, but he liked the way she mothered him sometimes, bustling around the studio, dropping in on the spur of the moment, pretending she just happened to be in the neighborhood. He really knew she had come to see if he was all right up there alone in the old factory loft. He found it oddly reassuring, even thought he knew that somewhere in the back of her mind, she must have thought she would come up there someday and find him dead. The way Amanda moved, she reminded him of her mother, especially as she got closer to middle age herself and had children of her own. He had married Amanda's mother two years after Esther left for Israel. In time, he had almost forgotten Esther, though occasionally over the years, when searching for something to paint he would run across sketches of her in old notebooks and be shocked again at the depth of feeling he still carried for her.

Amanda brought him a mug of coffee, strong and black the way he always liked it. She had been doing that since she was a child and used to hang around his studio and watch him work. He had always hoped she would turn out to be a painter, but she turned to writing instead. In the corner, he had stacked some canvases he had let her paint when she was little.

"Listen, Mandy, are you happy to be here?"

"Hmm?" she asked, not understanding the question.

"To be *here*," he said, "on the planet, I mean."

She wrinkled up her nose in the way she had done since she was a child whenever she thought he was being funny. "That's a strange question. Are you in one of your moods again?"

He shrugged. "It just could have been so different, that's all. I could have married someone else besides your mother once, but I didn't. But if I hadn't married her then there wouldn't be you and this and all. I mean, my life could have been so different, but it wasn't, and *your* life, well, your life wouldn't have been at all." He waved his hand as if to chase the thought away.

"What's this all about?" Amanda asked.

"Oh, nothing. Say, are you happy with Jim, your stockbroker man, I mean really happy?"

"Yes, sure. For now. Why? What do you mean?"

"Oh, nothing, just hold on to him, that's all. Hold on."

"Are you sure you're okay, dad?"

He glanced up at the skylight. The light filtering through it was slightly paler than a robin's egg. He could tell from the light that it was still overcast outside and was likely to remain so all day. He knew about light and what kinds of light threw what kinds of shadow.

"Yeah, sure, I'm fine," he said, "Just old. Hand me that sketch I made last night on your way out, okay?"

"Come for lunch today?" Amanda asked.

"Yes, I'd like that," he said turning to the canvas. "I'd like that a lot."

MISTAKEN
IDENTITIES

"The orbit of any one planet depends on the combined motion of all the planets, not to mention the action of all these on each other. But to consider simultaneously all these causes of motion and to define these motions by exact laws allowing of calculations exceeds, unless I am mistaken, the force of the entire human intellect."

Isaac Newton, *Principia Mathematica*, 1687

"Shit happens."

Anon. Late 20th century bumper sticker

THE ART OF THE FUGUE

The memory of a darkened physics lab entered Dr. Spencer McLaughlin's mind as he sat in the cathedral trying to listen to Bach's "Fugue in A Minor." The scene was fifteen years before. He could picture Dr. Bluffton leaning against the blackboard at the front of the dimmed room in his tattered lab coat.

"Observe the crystal I have placed between the fixed plate and the piston head in this hydraulic press," he said, lecturing with the tired enthusiasm of a magician who's performed the same trick too many times. "As the pressure increases gram by gram, the internal stresses build within the crystal. Soon, the structure of the crystal will no longer be able to withstand the stress, and then the molecular web will collapse releasing a blue-white flash of light. After the event, only a pile of dust will remain." It happened exactly as Bluffton had said it would. There were no surprises in Bluffton's class.

Spencer now sat up in his chair and wondered why this particular scene appeared so clearly in his mind as he listened to the Bach fugue. He had come to Washington to deliver a paper on experimental psychology, not physics. He certainly didn't have physics on his mind as the fugue's prelude began. True, he had trouble following the variations without a score, and his mind had wandered, but why did it land on an afternoon fifteen years before when he and a small group of other undergrads sat around a glassed-in hydraulic press to watch that piece of crystal explode?

Spencer liked to believe no accidents occurred in the world of the psyche. He firmly believed an underlying order connected everything together, even when thoughts seemed random. All events, thoughts and mental images are related, he told his students. Though the connection among them might be obscure at first, one simply had to achieve the proper perspective in order to see the inevitable pattern. Psychic life was like the apparent wandering of the fugue. The *arpeggios* and variations of the Baroque masters were arranged around well-defined themes that were always there; you simply had to identify them and all the rest would fall into place. Now he sought to do that with his own thoughts, his palms pressed together, his eyes closed, fingertips poised meditatively on his lips.

He had intended to spend that Sunday afternoon walking around the Mall, but a cold March rain was falling, so he changed his plans. In the *Post*'s arts calendar, he saw a notice for a three o'clock concert of Buxtehude and Bach at the National Cathedral. He grabbed a cab from the Capitol Holiday Inn where he was staying, but arrived late because the taxi got stalled in traffic on Massachusetts Avenue.

Rushing into the cathedral, he hastily grabbed a program and walked up the side aisle, past the statue of George Washington, his rubber galoshes squeaking on the stone floor like honking geese. He finally took a seat from where, he realized too late, he could not see the organist. He did not dare move, however, because he had made so much commotion coming in late. Still, why this particular memory?

Closing his eyes, he pictured the darkened physics lab again. In the center, dimly lit by a green light, was the hydraulic press, the piece of white crystal poised between the pressure plate and piston head. There was no perceptible motion, only a low-pitched hum from the mechanism and an occasional click as the pressure gauge recorded the increasing stress. The students sat in a semi-circle, and he tried to picture them now and sort through them methodically.

Only one face stood out in his mind. It was pale, almost white, standing out like a flower among the dim shadows of the others. Whose face was it? He could not remember. Spencer opened his eyes and flipped his program over. The organist's name startled him. Martha Kronhausen.

Bang. The crystal exploded with a flash. The girl with the lily-white face was named Martha Grogan. As he had rushed up the aisle, he quickly glanced at the program, and the name of the organist, printed in boldface on the back, had subliminally reminded him of Martha Grogan, the pianist he had known when he was in college. This triggered the memory after fifteen years.

He relaxed in his seat, once again admiring the crystalline perfection of Bach's composition and the human mind. The pattern always became clear. He enjoyed the mathematical clarity of Bach, as cool and intricate as the calculus in its own way. He immersed himself for a moment in the purity of the music, but then a strange idea began to nag at him: could Martha Grogan and Martha Kronhausen possibly be the same person? Was this more than the subconscious mind nibbling on a pun? Kronhausen could be her married name, he thought, and the brief program note verified his hypothesis that she was not single. "Mrs. Kronhausen currently resides in Arlington with her husband and two children." It said she had earned her Masters degree in organ performance from the University of Michigan. That was not far from Detroit where he and Martha Grogan had been in school together. And the thought began to torment him. Could it possibly be *his* Martha up there?

He stretched his neck to see around the pillar blocking his view of the organ console, but it was no use. As he wiggled in his seat, the woman next to him shot him a cold stare, so he was forced to retreat into his thoughts. It would be much too coincidental, impossible, he told himself, if he and Martha should meet again all these years and hundreds of miles later. He quickly lost track of the fugue and became obsessed with the idea. The permutations to achieve the probability figures would be nearly incalculable, and yet if one assumed there were no accidents in the universe, what else could explain the strange series of events that had put him in the cathedral that day? Perhaps it was something like Jung's synchronicity, not that he was a Jungian, heavens no, but consider: his partner Rollins, not himself, was supposed to be addressing the APA that evening on their joint research on the peripheral perception process in Norway rats, but Rollins had broken his leg three days before when he slipped after a late Spring ice storm. Then the rain spoiled his walking plans, then he'd read the *Post* and ended up at the cathedral where a concert was being performed by a married keyboardist named Martha. It was as if a controlling intelligence had brought him to the cathedral at that precise time and place for some purpose.

True, he had a bad seat, but the accuracy of the pattern was remarkable anyway, somewhat akin to a variance of a few meters in a moon shot. After fifteen years, the ineluctable laws of the universe had brought him close to her again as if at last to finish the business he had left unfinished with Martha Grogan, *if,* of course, it was Martha Grogan up there in the wooden embrace of the great organ console.

It had to be, he thought, as he again stretched to see around the large pillar. It was no use. The woman on his left stoutly refused to budge, and two more latecomers had taken seats on his right. He was penned in, and all his rustling was causing people to turn, so he could only sit back in his chair and listen to the music. However, he now listened more closely for he was trying to recognize in the organist's style some indication whether, in fact, this Martha Kronhausen might really be, or have been, his Martha Grogan.

The touch seemed sure, and the difficult coordination of the hands and feet as they played on three different keyboards was handled deftly. Too deftly? he wondered, and then felt ashamed for doubting that fifteen years of training and experience could have changed Martha Grogan from the way she had been when they'd last met. After all, he had not seen her since the morning of her senior piano recital fifteen years before.

He cringed at the memory. He had fallen asleep on her couch the night before waiting for her to come back to the flat she shared with a roommate. They had met in the physics class and started dating when he discovered she shared his interest in Baroque music, though she was less in love with its formal precision than with its technical challenge. He was worried about her. She was practicing until there were black circles under her eyes, and in between rehearsals she would bite her fingernails almost down to nothing. When no nails were left to bite, she began tearing at the scarf skin around her cuticles until her fingers looked like half-peeled carrots. As the concert date approached, she grew ever more distracted and upset. She would burst into tears at the slightest provocation. She had virtually stopped eating.

The day of her senior recital, she didn't return to her apartment until dawn. The sound of the front door opening woke him slightly. It took him a moment to remember where he was. A pale blue light filtered through the thin curtains of the living room.

She lay down beside him on the threadbare couch and put her arms around him. Her body was warm and he tucked his head into the soft curve of her neck and nuzzled there. She held him tight, and he raised his head up and kissed her on the lips. He tasted salt, but in his half-awake state he didn't realize she was crying. He held his lips to hers and stuck his tongue out to taste the salt again. Half asleep as he was, he started to become aroused and his hand went up her back, moved around and began to caress her breast. That was when she pushed him away and sat up on the sofa edge.

"Not now," she said.

That was when he opened his eyes and realized it was dawn.

"Where have you been?" he asked.

"I'm not sure," she said. Her eyes looked incredibly tired. "I just want to be held."

"You're not sure where you were all night?"

She shook her head. Her hands were trembling a little, and he noticed there was dirt beneath what was left of her fingernails. Her left knee had a red abrasion on it, as if she had fallen down. Her shoes were wet and muddied.

"Good grief, what happened to you?" he asked.

"I don't know. Everything's fuzzy, like it happened in a movie."

"You must be able to remember something," he said. He was frightened by the uncertainty in her voice. He always liked to know exactly where he was, and he kept a journal to record his daily comings and goings so he wouldn't forget. "What's the last thing you remember clearly?" he asked.

"Just hold me, can't you?" she asked, and he put an arm stiffly over her shoulder, but he couldn't just sit there.

"Tell me what happened," he said.

Martha closed her eyes and concentrated. The deep circles of black beneath her eyes were accentuated by the paleness of her skin. Her nostrils were pinched and she pressed her lips together until they were almost white. He felt awkward and useless.

"Well, I was sitting in the practice room about eleven and I was practicing the Rachmaninoff piece for the recital," Martha said. "I was right in the middle, you know the part where it goes ta-dum-de-dum, when suddenly I felt as though someone was in the rehearsal room with me."

"Was there?"

"No," she said, "but it felt cold, like I was inside a refrigerator. I kept on playing but I couldn't shake that feeling, then all these memories started to come back as I played."

Performance anxiety, he thought.

"What sorts of memories?" he asked.

"Oh, you know, things, just stuff from the past, you know."

"What sort of stuff?" he asked. Though he was a confirmed behaviorist, he nonetheless felt some comfort as Freud's spirit began to fill the room and Martha began to open up.

"Stupid stuff," she said. "It seems stupid now anyway." She pushed her hair back from her forehead and gave half a laugh. "I just started remembering all sorts of things. Like my father . . ."

"Ah," he said.

"My father hated the way I played the piano. I could never play well enough and . . .well, what the hell, it seems silly now it's morning. I pushed too hard, that's all. I need some sleep." She shrugged and got up and walked towards the bathroom. "I just need to crash for a while, then I'll be all right."

"Martha!" he said, "You can't just say it'll be all right. We're dealing with a five or six hour blackout. What happened next?"

She returned to the sofa.

"Oh, all right," she sighed, as if she had to complete a distasteful homework assignment. She closed her eyes and continued quickly, "The next thing I knew it was five hours later. I was in Ted's on the Park drinking a cup of coffee. I don't know what happened in between. The waitress was talking to me like we had been talking a long time. Now can I take my bath?"

"What were you talking about?"

"The weather, I think," said Martha, a little irritated. "I don't know. Nothing, I guess. You know how it is with waitresses."

"In other words, you just blanked out and woke up at Ted's?"

She shrugged and grinned, half-embarrassed, "I guess so.

He suggested she go through her pockets to see if she could find any clues to where she might have been. She pulled out her keys, some change and a movie ticket stub.

"Here's a ticket from the multiplex. Isn't that weird? Maybe I went there. I don't remember. It's like the whole night didn't happen."

Suddenly it flashed into his mind.

"Wow! Of course!" he exclaimed, "psychogenic fugue! We were just talking about it the other day in Abnormal Psych. Sometimes people wake up hundreds of miles away, days or weeks later, and in the meantime they've taken on whole new identities and names."

"Spencer!" she said, turning to the movie guide of the *Free Press*, "I'm not crazy. I'm *not*." She ran down the list of theaters until she came to the multi. Suddenly she tossed her head back and laughed. She threw the open paper at him. "This is too much," she said, "Well, this explains it. Look! Isn't that rich?"

He glanced down the list of movies and saw the midnight art theater was showing a revival of an old movie called *The Five Thousand Fingers of Dr. T.*

"So?"

"So, don't you see? It's a flick about this weird doctor, Hans Conreid, who imprisons kids and makes them play piano. I must have flipped out and gone to see it. I saw it before when I was a kid." She laughed at herself. "Too much."

Suddenly she seemed relaxed and flopped down beside him on the sofa, as if the mystery had been solved. Spencer, however, was still concerned. For the first time since he had begun studying psychology, he was in the presence of something he had only read about in textbooks and he didn't want to let it go by.

"What about all the dirt and your knee?" he said.

Martha shook her head as if it wasn't important.

"Oh, I'll be all right once I get through this recital tonight. I've been working too hard. I just need a bath and a nap, a bubble bath, no, maybe bath oil, I've got some *heuile de bain* left. Then I'll sleep until three and get ready for the recital. I borrowed Charlotte's old prom dress. It looks great."

She rose again to go to the bathroom.

"Wait a minute," he said, his voice growing shrill as he tried to follow her, "You were just wandering around Detroit all night in a psychic blackout, Martha. You were fuguing! You can't just brush that off. You ought at least to try to figure out what caused it."

"I know what caused it, Spencer," she said, "I've been pushing too hard. I freaked out, that's all."

"That's denial, that's what that is," he said, "We learned about that last week in class. You can't just walk away from this and take a bath."

"I can, too," she said wearily, closing the door to the bathroom. The bolt slid to with a sharp final click. "I just don't want to deal with it anymore, Spencer."

"Martha!" he called as he followed her to the bathroom door. He heard the water splash into the tub. There was no answer. He grew more concerned and noticed his heart was pounding violently. Psychogenic fugue was a serious symptom, he knew that, but he didn't know what to do about it. He wished a qualified professional were in the house with them. Someone had to do something. He thought briefly of calling Dr. Headley at the university's Clinic for Abnormal Behavior but the clinic didn't open until nine.

Then he heard the medicine chest open and suddenly, though he didn't know why, he thought, "Razor blades!" He got down on his hands and knees and tried to peer through the keyhole into the bathroom. She had hung her skirt over the doorknob and he couldn't see. She's going to kill herself, he thought. She's too calm, given what's just happened. She's checking out. He started to panic. He grabbed the handle of the locked door and rattled it. "Open the door," he shouted.

"Go away," Martha said.

"You've got to deal with this."

"I am dealing with it," she said.

"What do you mean?" he asked. No reply. "What do you mean?"

He heard her body slide into the water then a few seconds later a wincing cry, "Ow!"

"Martha, what's the matter?"

"I cut myself," she said.

"Cut?"

"With a razor."

Panicked, Spencer stood up, backed up a few feet and got a running start. His shoulder hit the door, and he felt the frame splintering as the lock gave way. Martha screamed as he came through the door frame.

"Don't do this to yourself," he cried, rushing towards the tub blindly. "Don't do it."

"Do what?" she asked.

He looked, expecting to see pink-tinged water, but he only saw Martha sitting bolt upright with her injector razor held up in front of her the way people in movies hold up crucifixes when they're surprised by vampires.

"What the hell are you doing, Spencer?"

His chest was heaving and he looked at her wrists. There were no marks.

"I thought . . . I thought," he gasped.

She rolled her eyes and used a washcloth to daub at a spot of blood where she'd nicked her calf. He fell to his knees on the cold tile.

"I love you, Martha!" he said. He blinked his eyes, amazed at what had just come out of his mouth. He tried to figure out if it was true or not. He wasn't sure. He wasn't sure of anything at the moment except he felt things now in a rush he had never felt before, a mixture of pain, humiliation, confusion and inadequacy he thought might be love.

"Can we talk about this later?" she sighed. "I'm really stressed."

"I love you," he said again, as if testing the words to see if they had come out of his mouth the first time. "I mean, I think I love you and . . . and, I mean, I've studied this stuff, Martha, and I can help you. I want to help you, do you understand?"

"Spencer, please, I can't deal with this now. I've been up all night. I'm exhausted."

"I'm here to help," he said, "That's why I'm a psych major. I want to dedicate my life to helping people. How can I help you?"

She held out the razor. "Shave my legs," she said.

At that, he reeled out of the bathroom and fell limply on to the cushions of the sofa in the living room. His hands were cold and when he held them out, they were shaking. He felt, for the first time, overwhelmed by things he didn't understand. Everything he had learned meant nothing to him. None of it had taught him how a person could recover from psychogenic fugue by shaving her legs. Maybe he would learn that in graduate school.

After half an hour, he got up and knocked softly at the bathroom door that she had kicked closed again. There was no answer, so he left a note and went to the Psych Department's animal lab where he had to complete the final run of his semester-long project in genetic learning. Would mice, he wondered, who were descendants of other mice who knew how to run a complicated maze be better able to run the maze than mice who were descended from an untrained control group? Over four generations so far the results were inconclusive. Sometimes a thoroughbred mouse both of whose parents had earned mouse PhD's in maze running would just sit there, while another mouse, out of nowhere, would streak through the maze as if a map of it were imprinted on its brain. That day he ran the fifth and final generation of mice through the maze, and the results showed nothing. He felt like a failure.

When he returned to Martha's apartment, her roommate said she was dead asleep and said that she, the roommate, had orders to murder anyone who tried to wake her. He never talked to or heard from her again. He was so mortified he couldn't bring himself to go the recital that night. He saw her at graduation, across the crowded field house, she with the music majors, he with the bachelors of science.

When he got to graduate school, he did indeed learn more about psychogenic fugue. It was listed in the *Diagnostic and Statistical Manual* under dissociative disorders. He memorized the symptoms and passed the exam, and it was around then he decided he would rather do research than practice therapy. He realized he would never understand the human mind, and how could he hope to help anyone until his understanding was complete? The best he could hope for was to push science forward a bit, studying peripheral perception in rats, teaching those who would come next and throw themselves against the indefatigable mystery.

Bach's A-minor motif presented itself now in a haunting echo which announced the conclusion of the fugue. The melody was full of hesitation, half-stated motifs and fragments of theme that Martha Kronhausen performed flawlessly. He was now convinced that Martha Kronhausen and Martha Grogan were one and the same. How could it be otherwise? It had to be her up there at the keyboard, he decided, and when the fugue was over he would go to her and explain. He would finally tell her he was sorry he hadn't known enough to really help her then, and at last the mess he had made when he was young would be cleaned up.

The *arpeggios* of the conclusion finally gave way to a strong double pulse of the A-minor chord and Spencer quickly got to his feet to go to her, but everyone else in the crowded cathedral rose at the same time and he found himself trapped by a standing ovation that rattled through the cathedral wildly.

Shouting, "Bravo, Martha!" he roughly shouldered his way past the people on the aisle. He looked toward the organ, but he couldn't see over the heads of the audience. He ran toward a place where he thought he might get a full view of her, but all he saw was a flash of black hair as she bowed. Martha Grogan's hair had been black, too, but when the organist rose, her hair fell across her face so he could not see her. Before he could get any closer, she turned and fled towards the sacristy. Like a flushed bird, he thought. Did she see me? he wondered. Is it really her? It has to be. He couldn't tell as she walked away. It looked like her, in a way, about the same height, but the hair was differently styled, yet there was something about the waist. Fifteen years had passed. It was impossible to tell for certain without seeing her face. She entered the sacristy and closed the heavy oak door behind her without turning around. Spencer dashed across the nave in front of the altar as the applause continued. He rushed towards the sacristy door, but just as he reached it an usher stopped him.

"I'm sorry, sir, no one is allowed."

"Please," said Spencer, "I think I'm an old friend of hers."

"Think?" the usher asked.

"I mean I used to know her and I haven't seen her in fifteen years."

The head usher, seeing a problem, came over. Spencer tried to explain.

"Mrs. Kronhausen left explicit instructions, sir," the old man said. He looked at Spencer as he might look at a madman or an assassin. "She has her own following here in the District, yes, but she's shy, you see, very shy. She never allows. . ."

"Oh, hell," said Spencer, pushing past the two into the sacristy. But the room was empty. A back entrance led out into the rear parking lot. He dashed through the door, but all he saw was a dark Mercedes with a Virginia license plate driving off. Rain covered the window, obscuring the face of the dark-haired woman who drove it. He shouted her name, but she did not stop, and he realized it was senseless to try to chase her on foot.

He sat in the cathedral for a while, listening to the thunder rumble outside. Someone coughed in the rear of the church. The sound hung in the air for a moment like the echo of the fugue, and then it was gone.

THE THEORY OF CHAOS

Martha Rumsfeld Kronhausen almost lost her fingering in the prelude, that's how surprised she was to see her ex-husband Geoffery come in. At least she thought it might be Geoff. She just caught a glimpse of a man coming in the front door of the cathedral as the audience was applauding her rendition of the Prelude and Fugue in D-minor. The large door flew open and a man in a rumpled raincoat, a man in a hurry and Geoff was always in a hurry though he never got anywhere, was briefly silhouetted against the pale light outside before he darted to the left and came up the ambulatory. She dove back into the wooden arms of the organ console and nervously set the stops for the great fugue in A-minor. Above the audience's hollow coughs and foot shuffling, she could hear the rhythmic squeak of his rubber galoshes reverberating through the nave. It had to be Geoffery.

She didn't want to look up, but when the squeaking stopped her eyes involuntarily left the score and looked over to where the sound had ceased. He was not there, unless, she thought, he ended up behind the large pillar. That would be just like her ex-husband, to show up again this way, after seven years, to magically step around a curve in the space-time continuum and then, like a dolt, to end up behind a pillar.

She blew out a deep breath and poised her fingers over the opening chord. She was surprised to see the tips trembling. She exhaled again, trying to focus calmly on the score in front of her. Its familiar arrangement of prelude, theme and variations calmed her somewhat.

She took refuge in the solidity of the notes, the same notes played by organists since Bach wrote it three hundred years before. The concert had gone well so far. Her playing had been relaxed. She felt loose, her muscles warm. Then out of the blue, no, out of the cold and rainy gray, had come Geoff. If it really was Geoff. No, she told herself, it *had* to be him. It would be like him to show up again, all these years after time zero.

That's what she called the day she walked out on him. It was the term physicists used for the beginning of the Big Bang, the day with no yesterday, the morning before which there had been no night. He was down in the basement of their apartment on the University of Michigan's North campus staring at the screen of his Apple II GS as it slowly drew out the diagram of a Mandelbrot set.

"I'm leaving, Geoff," she said.

He scratched his right eyebrow, his eyes never leaving the screen.

"Look at this!" he said punching a button. The screen seemed to move in like a camera on the image and gradually a tiny section of the screen became enlarged to reveal a pattern that looked exactly like the diagram it had replaced. "It's amazing," he said, shaking his head, "Each level of complexity resembles the whole set, like a camera panning in and out, worlds within worlds, the microcosm in the macrocosm."

She had seen all his chaos diagrams before, the seahorse tails, the butterflies, the island molecules, a million magnifications in each direction, all the same universe, all the same rules.

"I'm leaving, Geoffrey," she said again, but he just sat there like Archimedes who was too busy scratching geometry in the sand to notice the Romans had invaded Syracuse. A legionnaire, unable to distract him, had simply lopped off his head. Q.E.D. She wished she could do the same with Geoff.

"Can we talk about this later?" Geoff asked. "I'm in the middle of a run." He tapped on the keyboard. The computer made a sound like the "poing-poing-poing" of kids hitting baseballs with aluminum bats.

"This *is* later, Geoff," she said, "It's good-bye. It's time zero. The Big Bang has begun. It's over."

She was trying to talk his language. She hoped he would understand.

"I'm leaving, Geoffrey, and everything about our marriage is about to be sucked into a black hole, to be condensed into a white dwarf, to be wiped out, never again to be recalled, do you get it? Do you understand that yet?"

He held up his hand like a policeman, still staring at the screen.

"In a minute, in a minute. Jesus Christ, will you just *look* at these permutations?"

They had first met at a Beethoven's birthday party when they were undergraduates. Every campus has its small clutch of intellectual misfits, students who come to college in order to jump into the great intellectual debates of the ages instead of to get drunk and go to football games, and she had found herself thrown into this crowd. They were the bright kids who sit in the front of the classroom and eat alone in the darkened corners of the snack bar. Finding it impossible to learn what they really wanted to know in the classrooms, they banded together and tossed around theories on the origin of the universe. Their theories were all wrong, of course, but that wasn't the point. And they did things like throw Beethoven's birthday parties.

It was 1971. If Beethoven were alive, he would have been 201 years old. The air of the living room that night was thick with marijuana smoke. People sat tailor-style on the floor, eyes squeezed shut, listening to the Fifth Symphony's knock of doom, but she, having heard it too often before, wandered into Geoff's bedroom and found him spread out on the floor in *savasana*, the yogi's sponge position, wearing a set of fat gray Koss headphones, bulbous things like sailors on the decks of aircraft carriers wear to screen out noise. His eyes were shut. He had thick black hair that stood up in front like the swirl of a dairy freeze cone. It got this way because he compulsively grabbed his forelock whenever he got a new idea, which was almost constantly. At first glance she took him for one of those students, usually literature majors, whose ambition is to grow up to be doomed Welsh poets.

She brushed his foot with her boot and he shot up in a rather startled way, as if he had been somewhere else. She handed him the hemostat she was carrying and he took a deep drag from the lit joint in it.

"You've got to fucking hear this, man," he said lifting off the headphones and handing them to her. Those were the first words she ever heard him speak. He called her "man," as if he didn't notice.

She squatted on the floor and put the phones over her ears, but she heard only a persistent and not very pleasant hiss, like air escaping from a wet tire.

She popped the phones off.

"They're not working," she said, "All I'm getting is static."

"No, no, no," he said, "That's what it's supposed to sound like. This tape was made by a couple of guys from the Bell labs. They had this big earphone radio telescope and they kept getting this sound everywhere they turned it. Listen closer."

He abruptly yanked the headphone plug from the cassette player jack and the large speakers in the bedroom emitted the sound, a sharp crackling hiss that made white noise over the dull thump of Beethoven coming from the front room.

"Get it?" he asked like a wild-eyed maniac, "Get it? Listen."

She listened but she couldn't make sense of it. John Cage? she wondered. Geoff cranked the volume up louder and took another hit on the joint. She took one, too. Beneath the hiss she now made out a low rumble.

"Sound waves travel slower than light, remember that," he said.

She was confused, her head spinning. She hated it when she felt ignorant, when she couldn't get what someone else seemed to think she ought to know.

"All right," said Geoff finally, "I'll tell you. They finally figured out that this noise is the background noise of the universe. Get it? It's like the actual sound of the Big Bang, man."

She stared at him. He seemed to think it was very important that she get this, but between the dope and the physics, she was lost.

"*This is the very sound of the beginning of time, don't you see?*" he asked breathlessly.

She was beginning to comprehend. The idea began to work on her and she tried to translate it into her terms. A vast cosmic rumble out of which all else came. The opening chord of the universe. And the more she thought about it, the more she felt she was falling into a deep, exciting place. This strange Geoff was leading her somewhere she had not been before. She had never met anyone quite like him.

"The universe," he said, sitting on the edge of the mattress, waving a bottle of cheap wine in the smoke of the bedroom as if to encompass the whole cosmos, "is echoing off itself. The universe is unbounded yet finite, get it? I mean, everything we know about the universe is wrong, man, it's not infinite anymore."

She had smoked too much marijuana (though in those days there was no such thing as too much marijuana) and the thought of an unbounded yet finite universe took a hold on her frontal lobes only slowly, but when she began to get it, she started to grin and her head began to nod up and down like one of those souvenir dogs of Mexico that people put on the rear decks of their cars. "Wow!" she said, because she was bright enough to comprehend the enormity of what he was saying, but then, suddenly, a disturbing thought intervened. "But doesn't there have to be something *outside* the universe?"

"Yeah," Geoff said, coming close and staring at her nose to nose, "And I know what it is."

"You do?" she gulped. His eyes, green, had flecks of gold in the pupils.

"Yeah," he said, weaving over to his tape box, "I realized it one night while I was lying here stoned. I've got it on tape. You want to hear?"

She nodded.

He ejected the Bell lab cassette and popped another in its place.

"Outside the infinite yet bounded universe, and known only to me, Geoffrey T. Lannon," he announced, "there's this!"

And suddenly the jet-engine roar of Virgil Fox playing Bach's Toccata and Fugue in D-minor shattered the room from speakers big enough for an Iron Butterfly concert. She had heard the piece before performed by timid church organists, but she had never heard it this way. The huge speakers sent the vibrating waves of sound right through her flesh and seemed to make to make each cell spin round and round. The floorboards of the bedroom vibrated.

"That's it?" she shouted above the rumble as the sustained roar of the prelude exploded into the fugue itself.

He nodded, tears in his eyes.

"I knew it all along," she said, and they grabbed each other and held tight, both of them crying. Afterwards, when the music died away and there was only silence again, he told her that during the fugue he had seen rays of light shooting out of her head.

"The whole universe is music, man," he whispered in her ear as they lay on the mattress, "Pythagoras was right. The whole fucking cosmos vibrates and hums and sings, right from the subatomic level on up."

Now, almost twenty-five years later, sitting at the organ of the National Cathedral in Washington, she knew that Virgil Fox wasn't really that good and she had merely mistaken the chaos of Geoff's mind for something else and that's why she had married him. She allowed herself to get swept up into his imagination which she imagined to be like the inner core of a star blowing light out of itself. After all, no one else had ever seen rays of light shoot out of her head before. It was only later, much later, that she realized what a fool she'd been. The aura he saw coming out of her head was caused by the 60-watt Soft-glo bulb behind her.

As she lowered her fingers to the keyboard, she tried to reassure herself. All these thoughts and memories had gone through her head very quickly, like a fast cut montage in a movie. She sensed the audience waiting. Well, it probably wasn't him after all who had come up the side aisle, she told herself. The warm opening chord of the prelude swelled out of the pipes and filled the nave.

But then, as the notes reached her ears, she thought what if it *was* Geoff squeaking up the side aisle like a dork? And this is where her fingers faltered, though not enough, she hoped, that anyone noticed. He had shown up before like this, unannounced, at least three times that she knew of. She had spotted him in the dark corners of churches where she was giving recitals, lurking like Quasimodo, his black coxcomb floating above the white oval of his face. Nothing changed about him ever, not his hairstyle, not his clothes. Twenty years after the sixties had been officially pronounced dead, he was still wearing the same jeans and flannel shirts, still playing the same record albums, and still talking in that pained, alienated-young-white-male voice that made Paul Simon rich. Only now he was 45, and he still carried his adolescence around with him like a bubble. What did he want after all these years? Perhaps he came looking for her every few years the way Peter Pan kept coming back looking for his shadow. She was the only piece of his life from back then that had gone missing.

Then, the familiar green sickness came on her. Stage fright. She hated it and thought she was done with it after all these years of performing. Her fingers went gummy and her mouth went dry. Drops of flop sweat ran down her back, and the score, which she had rehearsed and performed without flaw many times before, began to swim in front of her, the sixteenth note arpeggios rising and rolling like waves, the crescendos like mount Everests which she had to scale without oxygen. Why could he still do this to her? She wanted to stop the performance right then, jump out of the seat, yank him from behind the pillar and stuff him into an organ pipe. But would the audience understand? They had come to listen to Bach, cold cool Bach, not to witness the end of the absurd Italian opera that was her marriage to Geoff. She tried to regain her composure. Bach was too intricate to get emotional about and in some ways the more you tried the worse it got.

She tried to force herself back to the music fundamentals: don't arch the fingers too high, play from the first knuckle. Her hands were stiffer now than they had been when she was a student. The fourth dimension, time, was doing its degenerative work since she had turned forty. Still, when she played that usually didn't matter. She found ways to compensate for not being twenty anymore. Before a performance she would put a little dab of hand cream in the web of skin between her knuckles on each hand and massage that in while stretching. When she was younger, she could just sit down and play.

Baroque music went better if you didn't think about it too much. You had to let your brains go to your fingers or something. She tried to wrap herself in the music, to get inside the fugue and let it play her. The fingers knew well enough what to do if the mind didn't interfere. The contagious pulse of Bach was something you had to give yourself to, unreservedly, like when you made love. The body knew how, the mind did not.

She took a deep breath and squeezed shut her eyes to make herself stop looking at the score. It was like leaping into a gorge at night. Two false notes squeaked out of a soprano pipe and she nearly panicked, but then her fingers took over. She felt the huge knot of muscles between her shoulder blades begin to loosen and her torso began to sway with the pulse of the fugue. She opened her eyes again. The score had stopped pitching about, the mountain ranges were again manageable.

Nonmusicians don't believe you can think about anything else while you play, but you can. You have to. Too much thinking about only the notes causes mis-steps, catastrophes. Best to let the fingers work and the mind wander, as long as it doesn't wander too far. The swaying pulse of the music would bridge you over the dangerous thoughts.

Now she could afford some "lookback time" while her fingers and feet made their way through the music without her. That was a term physicists used to talk about looking at light from stars. What we see in the night sky is not what is actually out there. The light twinkling above us may be seven hundred million years old, and the star that emitted it may have exploded before the first life on earth crawled out of the ocean. When we look up into space we are therefore peering into the well of the deep past. The light endures like memory, and so every once in a while a pulse of light from the supernova of their divorce reached her again. What surprised her was how much it still hurt, though the star of their marriage had exploded eons before.

He had never been able to say "I love you." In the beginning, it didn't bother her. His intellectual brilliance dazzled her. He would say things like, "I think we belong together, Martha. There aren't any accidents in the universe, you know. All matter, including us, has been organized and orchestrated since the Big Bang. Think of it. Billions of years, billions of permutations, combinations, apparently random but actually interconnected events, all leading up to this: that you and I have met and have, well, have met and . . .Well, it's all beyond us, beyond our control, you see because we're part of the life of the universe."

That was as close as he ever came to saying it, to saying, "I love you." That was supposed to be romantic, she supposed, and at the time it was. No one had ever caught her up in a cosmic drama before, and she was enough of an aesthete and intellectual to get swept up into the romance of it all, but eventually, after they got married, as years went by, she wanted just once to hear him say it. "I love you."

The fugue continued to unroll itself beneath her fingers all this while, unattended, on its own, she merely the vehicle for the music.

When they were in graduate school, they had tried a marriage counselor, a woman in Ann Arbor, not from the university, who wore chunky brass bracelets and decorated her office with Escher prints.

"He can't say it, he can't say, `I love you,'" Martha said.

"Can't say `I love you,'" the shrink echoed in her best Rogerian manner as she turned towards Geoff rather robot-like with raised eyebrows. The ball was in his court.

"Well, can't she infer from the evidence?" Geoff asked, stumbling over himself. "Nothing in the universe is laid straight out. You've got to look at the pieces and the pieces form an identifiable whole. I married her. People get married because they love one another, don't they? Therefore, she should be able to infer that I love her."

The therapist turned back to her, wordless, her eyebrows arched in an interrogative mode.

"But can't he *say* it once, for Christ's sake?" she'd stormed.

"Can't you say it?" the therapist asked.

He sat silent and sullen.

In the end she guessed that love, for him, was in the realm of the six invisible dimensions that he and his physicist friends talked about: inscrutable, impossible to see or prove or even experience, yet if you assumed their existence as a theoretical construct it made the mathematics of life easier. Perhaps in a parallel but invisible universe, the other six dimensions of Geoff were living a deep and rich emotional life. Perhaps over there, hidden by the mask of the space-time continuum, all of his emotions gave themselves free rein. Perhaps he, or some other dimension of him, was really over there, out of sight and sound, shouting "I love you, Martha! I love you madly!" but the message never made it through to the normal four dimensions in which the rest of him lived.

In the meantime, she had to quit school to work as a waitress while playing the organ at two churches in order to eke out the stipend Geoff got as a grad student while working on his dissertation on fractal geometry and chaos theory.

"You don't need to study the theory of chaos, Geoffrey, you've got the practice down perfect!" she found herself screaming one night when she returned from her waitress job and found him in the computer room hacking away, ankle-deep in crushed Fritos and pop cans. He was supposed to have gone to the store to buy things they needed for dinner that night with Tom and Marcia.

He simply looked up from the screen, blinked and said, "Huh?"

It was then, or shortly after, that she began noticing things about him she had never noticed in the early days: how his mouth never seemed quite closed, for instance, or how much his two front teeth resembled the teeth of a rat, how his eyes were slightly crossed and how pale he was from his hours in the basement. He was so pale that when he took off his shirt his stomach was the color of a fish's belly.

"You'll never finish, will you, Geoffrey?" she asked the day she told him she was leaving. She meant his dissertation. He thought she meant solve the riddle of the universe.

He turned from the computer and for a moment he looked almost pathetic. "We've nearly got it," he said, "Don't you understand? These equations can explain random events. If we can get it figured out, there will be no more chaos. At last we'll understand."

She began to sway now to the music, her eyes closed as her fingers played.

What was it men loved so about thinking they had it all figured out? she wondered. What does it mean, this attempt to draw order from what they thought was chaos? They seemed obsessed with it. Like Bach, to impose the order of the fugue on the persistent background hiss of the universe. What was so bad about chaos anyway, about letting go to it? The fugue with its variations and retrograde motions, its turning things upside down and inside out simply pulled a few threads up from the chaos for a while and when the music stopped they returned. Why couldn't men like Geoff accept that? Why did they want such mathematical clarity?

As she neared the three-quarter mark of the fugue, the cold sweat had stopped, and a warmth flowed through her. The line between her and the organ music faded and she entered a strange place performers know, a place of silence in the midst of noise. She felt as she had felt when she was giving birth to her two children. Adam, her second husband, was with her in the delivery room both times. The chaos took over and the world disappeared, just as it was disappearing now. All was vibration, humming sound, the atoms whirling and vibrating in her and the walls and the air as the contractions squeezed her, as if she had been taken over by the pumping jug-jug-jug of Stravinsky's *Rite of Spring*. In childbirth and sometimes in performance she felt it. The chaos was right for the whole universe was giving birth even as it exploded. She was the wind blown through the organ pipe. The chaos was nothing to be feared.

However, as the fugue neared its end, the structure began an apparent breakdown that would resolve itself only in the final chord, and she realized how tired she was. Her muscles felt long and drawn out. She felt damp between her shoulder blades and at the base of her neck where her hair fell down. She felt she was returning and she grew afraid. The double bar of the fugue was approaching. The delicious flow would cease. And then what? She had to decide what to do.

There was nothing she could do for Geoff. After the concert he would come up to her, his cheek hollow, his face haunted, looking like Manfred would have looked if Manfred had a computer, and his eyes would be accusing. "Why did you leave me?" he would ask, his shock of black hair curling up from his forehead like a question mark of smoke. She had no answer. She thought she could live without an answer. So why was she still afraid of seeing him?

She didn't want to see him, yet she knew that he would come up and lurk at the outer fringe of the small clutch of admirers who hung around after a performance. She decided she would leave. He had to know that it was over, to know she was done with him, that she wouldn't stand for him haunting her this way anymore. She had nothing more to do with him, nothing.

Her fingers formed the final chord, struck it twice, holding the *fermata* just a shade longer than she intended, stalling the inevitable, and then she let go. Silence for a moment, then applause. The audience was standing. She tried to smile. She slid off the organ bench and stood in the aisle. She bowed, once, twice. As she raised her head, she thought she saw, out of the corner of her eye, the man in the raincoat making his way up the side aisle. Was it Geoff? She still couldn't be sure. He was hidden by the crowd. She couldn't bear to see his face. If he looked at her with his lost boy look she would be finished, she would have to listen, and she was done with him. Forever.

She turned her back on the crowd and rushed across the sanctuary. A few shouts of "encore," but she did not stop.

"No visitors," she whispered to the young usher who opened the sacristy door for her. He nodded. Her heart was pounding as she frantically gathered up her purse and coat. She felt pursued. She heard voices on the other side of the sacristy door. Someone was trying to get in to see her, insisting. She slipped on her Totes and ran for the back door. She thought she heard the sacristy door open as she jumped across the puddles of the parking lot to her car in the rain.

The automatic locks of the Mercedes snapped shut with a reassuring click. She felt safer as she started the engine and quickly backed out of the reserved parking space. As she reached the end of the drive, she looked in the rearview and saw a man in a raincoat charge out of the back door after her. She thought she heard him call her name, but through the rain-spattered rear window she could not tell if it was Geoff or not. She tried to jam a cassette of herself playing Telemann into the tape deck but her hand was trembling and the cassette fell to the floor. She swore and was surprised to find herself crying as she drove towards the parkway for the long drive home.

FIRST PERSON, SINGULAR

HOLY TOLEDO

One hot, humid August afternoon Arthur Schreck doused his common-law wife with gasoline he'd brought home from the Bonded station on Lagrange Street and threatened to start her on fire unless the police could find a way to kill him first.

That same afternoon Sczeblewski and I were about a mile away, on the banks of a sluggish creek surrounded by stinkweed trees. The water in the creek was warm as spit and offered no real relief from the heat. Our game was to ride as fast as we could toward the drop-off overhanging this creek and slam on our brakes at the last instant. Our goal was to skid sideways through the mud and stones to see who could come closest to the edge without falling in. We did this over and over again the day Arthur decided to kill his wife and whoever else chose to go along with her.

We didn't even hear the first shots Arthur fired at the police who had come when Mrs. Kozlowski, who lived next door, couldn't take Arthur's wife's screaming anymore. As we rode up Lagrange Street, we saw small knots of neighbors gathered on street corners looking the way people look in tornado weather, gazing nervously off into the sky in the direction of Schreck's house, as if expecting a menacing pillar of wind and cloud to rise up from it.

"They say Artie Schreck's got himself holed up," someone told us when we stopped at the corner, "Three squad cars of cops down front can't get a shot at him. Don't you boys go no further."

"Shot his wife," said another.

"They say a cop's dead," someone added, "I heard he shot a cop already, the one who showed up first thing."

"Shot a cop?" I asked, nervous. I had three uncles on the Toledo force and knew a lot of cops my uncle Ned played football with.

"All them Schreck's is trash," someone said. Another man nodded and spat into the gutter.

Then I heard the gunfire: staccato pops in twos and threes. I felt the concussion of the shots poke me in the chest like a finger a split second before the sound hit my ears. Then we heard the deep roar of a police shotgun and after it nothing. All of us on the corner sucked in our breath. We stood there for a moment in the flat, slick silence.

"They must have killed him," somebody whispered hopefully, "He must be dead."

"It's all over!" somebody in the block ahead shouted and the knot of people on our corner began to move towards the Schreck house like a wave. But then the cap-like crackle of Arthur's pistol started again. "Get back, everybody get back, he's still alive!" And everybody retreated to the corners again.

Without thinking, my legs pumped furiously at the bike pedals and I rode past the frightened knots of people until I came to the police barricade on Lagrange Street. A cop I didn't recognize was keeping people out and was rerouting traffic up a secure side street. The cordon was far enough away to be out of the range of gunfire and some of my neighbors from Baker Street had managed to get out when the shooting started and were gathered by the yellow sawhorse wringing their hands and looking over the houses in the direction the shots were coming from.

"You can't go in there," the cop said.

"My house is in there," I said, "That white one by the alley."

"That doesn't make any difference," he said, his hand firmly on the sawhorse, "You just wait outside here." I went back on to the sidewalk.

A few men in sweaty T-shirts had drifted out of the Alamo Bar on the corner and stood against the wall with half-empty beer bottles. Safely out of range, they philosophized on the situation between the gunshots.

"She give him cause," said one, "Been bumping some truck driver works for Roadway."

"She's his *ex*-wife, ding-dong," said another, "They's estranged or something. An ex-wife can bump anybody she pleases, and you can't say shit about it."

"You should know," said the first man with a mean snigger.

"Screw you," said the second.

"Still, it bothers a man," said the first, taking a reflective swig from his beer bottle, "Don't matter if it's his real wife or ex-wife or whatever bumpin' around like that. It bothers a man just about the same."

"'Cept Artie Schreck ain't no man," said a third man, who up to that time had been fully occupied peeling the wet label off his sweating beer bottle with his thumbnail. Then he added, "God knows what he *is*, but he ain't hardly human, that's for damn sure."

And the three of them laughed at the joke and spat until another huge shotgun roar sobered their mood. The young cop at the barricade tensed up as the small arms fire started again, now louder, now softer as Arthur ran from window to window shooting.

Just then my uncle Ned and his partner Cal Fugate pulled up to the barricade in their squad car. They usually worked the Old West End, up near the cathedral, but they had been monitoring the shoot-out on their radios and came over to give back up. I was almost disappointed to see them because I had visions of them inside the barricades trading shots with Artie Schreck. At family gatherings, when the women were in the kitchen, uncle Ned told stories of what he did on the job, of arrests he had made, of shootouts he had been in. He had a way of making everything sound funny and, because of that and because of his football days, he was always being asked to speak at Knights of Columbus dinners and Rotary Club lunches. He could make a room full of men laugh until their sides hurt. When Uncle Ned was scheduled to talk, they didn't even need an NFL highlights film to bring people out.

That day, however, he wasn't smiling. His face was set hard. So was Cal Fugate's whose dark eyes were like knife points, and whose chocolate brown skin burned a shade darker than normal. Uncle Ned's hands were gripping the wheel of the squad car so tightly that the flesh around his knuckles was turning white. He squeezed and released the wheel again and again.

"They can't get a shot at him?" uncle Ned asked the cop at the barricade. The young cop shook his head.

"Artie Schreck's the white one, ain't he, Kayo?" my uncle asked me. I nodded, trying to look as grave as the young cop at the sawhorse.

There were three Schreck brothers, and people in the neighborhood used a shorthand to tell them apart. Roman was "the dark one." Vincent was "the handsome one." And Arthur they called "the white one" because he was an albino, the only one I had ever seen, though, if the truth be told, his skin wasn't so much white as it was nearly colorless, semi-transparent, like the strip of fat along the side of a steak. Even his lips gave the impression of having no color to them. They were white as grease. It was his eyes that scared people the most. They looked blue at first, but up close you could see there was no color to them at all. They were glassy disks, as cold and clear as dead fish eyes. Even when he was little, people would cross the street rather than have to look at him. Everybody agreed it was only a matter of time before they'd have to put a bullet in Artie Schreck the way you have to do to a foaming dog.

"Must be *some* way to get a shot at him," Fugate said to no one in particular.

I swallowed hard, to keep my heart down in my chest. "I know a way," I said.

Just then I felt a hard slap on the back of my head that crossed my eyes for a second. I turned and saw my mother standing there.

"You get yourself right home, mister," she shouted as if *I* were the one holding somebody hostage somewhere. "I was worried sick." Slap. Slap. "You could be shot or dead or lying in the gutter for all I know." Slap. "When we get home you're never leaving the house again, you hear me, mister?"

"What do you mean you know a way, Kayo?" my uncle Ned asked calmly. He was used to my mother's screaming and knew it didn't mean anything.

"You keep him out of this, you hear me, Ned?" my mother said, slapping the back of my head again for emphasis.

"I know a way you can do it," I said, "get a shot, I mean." My mother started pulling me away from the squad car by the tail of my shirt but I was clinging to the door handle. My bicycle slipped from between my legs and clanged on the street. "You can sneak right behind the house and see right in," I said, "I know the way."

Suddenly I felt a searing pain on the side of my head. My mother had grabbed me by the top of my ear.

"Did you hear me, young man?" she yelled, swatting me with her free hand until I thought my ear would pull loose.

"Lighten up on the boy, Edna," uncle Ned said, "If Artie Schreck's got his ex-wife held hostage and Kayo knows a way, we ought to hear about it."

"She's not his *ex*-wife," my mother interrupted, "She's his common-law wife, the trash."

"That doesn't help any, Edna," uncle Ned said.

"Well, she can't be an ex-wife if she's common-law, you know that. I swear to God, if we don't get out of this damned neighborhood pretty soon . . ."

And then she started to cry. She was good at that. In fact, she was famous throughout that part of Toledo for crying. She had an aunt or something back in Ireland who was a professional at it and Mom inherited the gift. Every time there was a funeral, people made sure she was invited.

"Can we really get back there without being seen, Kayo?" Fugate asked.

"There's a way through the alley," I said, "through Baxter's old garage, through the bushes behind Bone's, then you slide through an old piece of sewer pipe the city left there last year."

I knew this because Scrub and I had found a way to sneak behind Mrs. Kozlowski's to a place where we could watch her daughter Marcie taking a shower on hot summer nights. Marcie was Woodward High's homecoming queen, and on sticky nights, when all the windows were open, we could climb unseen into an apricot tree after dark and eat fruit and watch Marcie. We could also see into Artie Schreck's house. But if the police were caught in front of Schreck's, there was no way to get back there because the houses were sandwiched together and Artie could see them coming every way except the way I knew.

"Don't you be shittin' us now, Kayo," Fugate said, his voice so soft and intense I had to stop and think again whether it would work, but I knew it would.

The radio in the squad car crackled with garbled voices as the gunshots continued. You could hear the shots through the radio and from the house a block and a half away.

Ned sat there a moment staring toward the middle of the block of closely placed houses then he looked over at Fugate. The two of them had been together so long they didn't need to talk anymore. They were like an old married couple that way. Fugate nodded, a short quick shake of his head, just enough to tip his chin and Ned picked up his radio handset. The whistle and static stopped for a moment as he pushed the transmitter button.

"Yeah, this is twenty-three," he said, "We think we got a way behind him, over."

He released the button and there was a burst of static. We could hear the gunfire in the air and an eerie echo of it on the radio. The voice that came back sounded like it emanated from behind a waterfall. "He's got us pinned, twenty-three," said the voice, the chopped words filtering through the static, "I'd say go if you can."

It was the voice of Commander Sessions who was supervising. I knew him from church. He was in charge of the Knights of Columbus Friday night fish fry at St. Benedict's, the most successful one in the whole diocese. He ran it like a field marshal, and you should have seen those fish fly.

Uncle Ned repeated what I had told him. There was a pause during which we heard the roar of a shotgun that made the radio shriek with feedback. The reverberation of the blast was followed by a moment of calm and then the sharp crack of Artie firing again.

Sessions' voice came out of the black box beneath the dash. "Call when you go in," Commander Sessions said. "We'll give you seven minutes then we're going with gas. You be there behind when he comes out. We got to end this thing. We think he's gonna torch the wife."

Ned pulled the squad car through the barricade and up to the curb beside Kilgus market. I snuck in right behind them, but the young cop closed the barricade before my mother could get through.

"Ned, you are not taking that boy anywhere, do you hear me?" she shouted.

Ned stepped out of the police car and pulled his hat off. "Kayo's not going nowhere, Edna," he said. "He's just going to draw us a map and that's it."

"That better be all, Ned," my mother shouted, "You've had the devil in you since the minute you were born, Ned Boyle, but if you cross me now I'll nail your carcass to a tree. You keep that boy out of there."

Uncle Ned ignored her.

"You take this sheet of paper and draw me a simple map, Kayo, don't leave anything out, hear?"

Fugate got out of the car and opened the trunk. As I drew the map, using the warm hood for a desk, he came up with two bullet-proof vests in one hand and a shotgun in the other. The vests were large and bulky and looked like umpires' chest protectors. The sight of those vests made me go cold. I gripped the pencil tightly and stuck out my tongue. The map had to be exactly right, but my hand was shaking and my mouth was dry. Behind me I could hear the squeak of leather as Ned and Fugate pulled on the vests. I could smell the odor of the leather, like horse sweat, coming off their holsters and belts.

When I turned to them with the map, I hardly recognized them. They had unbuttoned the safety straps on their pistols and their guns hung heavy in their holsters, ready to be used. The six spare bullets in their belt loops shined now with a brittle and cold light.

I looked at Uncle Ned's face and could see the fear had made deep lines along his forehead and cheeks. No one thought Ned would ever become a cop, though I had never known him any other way. He had been in and out of scrapes with the law all the time when he was in high school. Nothing serious; he just liked to raise hell and come as close as he could to an imaginary line he had drawn for himself. Still, no one ever thought he'd become a cop until he came home one day shortly after he graduated from high school and announced he was going to the police academy and he hoped to the join the Toledo Police Force when he finished. The only thing that could have surprised the family more was if he had become a priest. Even that would not have been so surprising because our family, being Catholic, did believe in redemption, but we also knew it would not come without repentance and uncle Ned had never shown any signs of being sorry for what he'd done. But he had become a good cop, and others respected him, and no one complained when they were assigned to duty with Ned Boyle.

Fugate took off his cap and threw it on the front seat of the squad car. The hat left a line in the tight black curls of his hair and I saw a few beads of white sweat clinging to his hair the way raindrops bead up on a sweater. He, too, had a look on his face I had never seen before. I remembered the time when I was six or seven when I'd fallen asleep in his car on the way home from a football game he and uncle Ned had taken me to, and rather than wake me up he had scooped me up in his arms and carried me safely off to bed. But now I hardly recognized him either. He was like a dark cloud as he tightened the straps of the bulky vest. His mocha colored skin was a shade or two darker as the blood rushed to his face, and his large hands, big enough to palm a football easily, gripped the stock of the pump-action shotgun tightly.

I laid the crudely drawn map down on the trunk and swallowed hard.

"Here's the alley, here's Baxter's," I said, pointing with the pencil, "the door's off the hinge, here's the conduit . . ."

I showed them how to get through the bushes and into the conduit which lay right up against the trunk of the apricot tree. From the lip of the conduit or from behind the tree they could get a clear bead on the back windows of Schreck's house so if he was driven out by the gas they would have him.

When they were ready to go, uncle Ned radioed Commander Sessions and they walked quickly to the top of the T of the alley, the gravel crunching beneath their heavy black cop shoes, my small map gripped tightly in uncle Ned's hand.

I watched until they turned the corner of the T and then, looking back and seeing my mother was momentarily distracted, I went after them. I did not think about whether I should go or about the danger back there. I could hear the gunshots, but I didn't care. I had spent most of my life listening to uncle Ned's stories, sitting with the men after Thanksgiving Dinner, and now I could finally see one of those stories as it unfolded. I knew I could get safely into Baxter's garage and from there I could see whatever happened. I could be no more than twenty feet away, and I would not miss it for my life.

By the time I crawled into the half-open door of the Baxter's garage and edged up to the crack in the door, uncle Ned and Fugate were inside the old sewer pipe, crouched there like paratroopers ready to jump out of a plane. I tried to imagine how Ned would tell the story later.

"There we were, inside this big tube, see, waiting . . ." He'd build the suspense until everyone was on the edge of their seats. He'd find a way to make it hilarious. "I said to Fugate, `I hope there's no sewer rats in here . . ."

There were a few more gunshots from the front windows of the house then I heard a low sound, whump, followed immediately by the sound of tinkling glass. Then there was a muffled pop, like something exploding inside a pillow. I looked at the house and saw a few wisps of white smoke come drifting out of the gaping windows on the side like early morning fog. I could hear choking sounds now from inside the house. The teargas had gone in. Uncle Ned and Fugate hunched tighter inside the tube, then Uncle Ned slid out and hid himself behind the trunk of the apricot tree while Fugate moved to the lip of the conduit, lying down, his shotgun held ready, aimed at the rear kitchen window. I wiped the sweat dripping from my nose and pressed my eye to the crack in the door.

The gas was moving toward the back of the house, driving Schreck in front of it. Uncle Ned's hand tightened on the handle of his gun. He held it at the ready. And then the woman began to scream.

"Oh, God! Oh, God!"

Her screams rose up out of the gas smoke, and I could tell Arthur was pushing or pulling her toward the rear of the house, and then I finally got a whiff of the gas. It was the first time I had ever smelled it. The first whiff was vaguely sweet when it touched my nostrils, but the second made the back of my nose begin to burn and my eyes begin to water and it quickly felt as though the inside of my head would burn out. It was sour ammonia and rotten eggs. But I didn't move from the crack. There was enough air in the old garage that I could stand it.

"Come out, Schreck," uncle Ned shouted from behind the tree.

And suddenly Arthur appeared in the window. I saw uncle Ned's hand move to shoot but then stop, for Arthur had snaked his long white arm around his wife's neck and held a cigarette lighter near her head. Her hair was matted down to her skull with gasoline and her doused clothes clung to her thin body. The eyes of both of them were red and swollen and Arthur's pockmarked face was as pale and ravaged as a death's head. Whitish-yellow tear gas poured out of the shattered window framing the two of them.

"I'll light her!" he shrieked. His wife let out a cry like a spear-stuck pig and then closed her eyes and bit her lower lip hard, her head down in a posture that said she had resigned herself to dying in flames like a Halloween cat.

"Let her go, Schreck," uncle Ned said. His voice was cold as ice. Schreck now knew Ned was behind the tree, but he had not yet spotted Fugate in the conduit.

"Fuck you," said Schreck, "This is it, man!" I heard the flint strike and the lighter go on. He held the quavering flame next to his wife's head who whimpered now in a deep throaty murmur, "Oh Jesus, oh Jesus, oh Jesus." My mouth went dry as sand.

Uncle Ned didn't dare move and neither did Arthur or his wife. For a moment we all stood there, frozen, the flame of the lighter the only moving thing. I have no idea how long it was. It could have been two seconds, it could have been a million years. Then another tear gas canister broke through the front windows.

Schreck jumped. "They're coming in! They're coming in!" he cried.

"Oh, God, he'll kill me, he'll kill me for sure!" the woman screamed. "Won't somebody help me please God?"

Suddenly, uncle Ned burst from behind the tree and sprinted toward the house. Schreck saw him coming, dropped the lighter and threw his wife away from him. His gun hand came up fast as a snake and pumped off one shot. I don't even think I heard it. I only saw the window frame splinter crazily and my uncle Ned flew backwards and crumpled to the ground, a spurt of blood gushing from behind his left eye. He fell to the dirt spinning and screaming in pain.

I flung open the garage door and raced into the yard.

"Uncle Ned!" I shouted. And the next thing I knew I was staring down the barrel of Artie Schreck's gun. His colorless eyes met mine for an instant, and I felt a pain shoot through me like an ice pick. I knew he was going to kill me right there and then.

I closed my eyes, but suddenly Fugate's shotgun roared not more than two feet away from me and I opened my eyes and saw his massive black body hurtling out of the sewer conduit through the cloud of blue smoke left by the shotgun blast. He was screaming at the top of his lungs and he fired again. The shotgun pellets rattled against the siding of the old house and Schreck winced sideways but not before he turned his gun away from me and squeezed off a shot at Cal Fugate. The shot hit Fugate's bullet proof vest and made his shoulder jerk sideways as if somebody had punched him hard, but he kept charging at the house and then Schreck fired again and Fugate's uniform sleeve blew apart in an explosion of blood and fabric, but he didn't stop running. His legs spread wide, he dug up dirt with his feet and leapt right over uncle Ned. Schreck stood in the window, smoke pouring out around him, and raised his gun to fire again but before he could get off the shot, Fugate leaped head first through the broken window frame with a terrible cry. For a moment, the back half of his massive body hung out the window, those tremendous legs a foot above the ground below, and then he tumbled out backwards with Schreck's skinny frame squeezed between his arms.

Schreck was screaming, too, and Fugate slammed him to the ground so hard the pistol flew out of his hand. Schreck's colorless hair fell down over his face as he tried to scramble sideways on all fours like a wounded dog, whimpering the whole time, but he couldn't get away for Fugate then leapt on top of him and straddled him with his massive legs. With his good hand and arm he flipped Schreck over on his back and pressed the muzzle of his service revolver right against the middle of Arthur's forehead. Fugate's hands were shaking.

"Move!" Fugate shouted, "Gimme some cause to blow your fuckin' brains out, you hear? Just gimme cause!" He was shaking and furious, but Arthur did not move. He was so terrified that all he could manage was to lie on his back and dig his fingers into the dirt beneath him to anchor himself to the ground in hopes that the big black man who hovered over him would not blow the better part of his head away.

"Ned? You okay, Ned?" Fugate called.

There was no answer.

"He's still breathing," I said.

Fugate never took his eyes off Schreck. Arthur had shut his own eyes tight, not daring to look at what was happening to him.

"You get your ass out of here, Kayo, now," Fugate ordered. "You hear me?"

"But Uncle Ned."

"Now," he repeated, but I didn't move. I watched and waited for primal justice to be done. I considered it my right after what Arthur had done to my uncle. I pleaded with Fugate to blow Arthur Schreck's head off. I wanted to see that albino die right there for what he had done to Uncle Ned.

But Fugate didn't do anything like that. He just started nodding, his head bobbing up and down and he held his fire. The blood from his wound ran down his sleeve and covered Arthur's face. I could tell that every muscle in the black man's body wanted to pull the trigger and blow the front of Arthur Schreck's head away, but he didn't do it. He held his fire and trembled. There was a dark beauty to what this man was doing and I could not bear to look any longer.

Finally he mumbled through his tears, "You get your ass back in that garage, Kayo, and you never saw none of this."

Then he called out to the others, "I got him, it's over, it's over," and no sooner had I gotten myself back into the garage, than the yard was filled with men with guns who formed a circle around Schreck and Fugate the way dogs will surround a rat in the alley. I watched as two medics rushed in and moved uncle Ned to a stretcher and rushed out of the yard with him. I heard the siren start and fade away.

Fugate still had his gun pressed against Arthur's head. None of the men in the circle around him moved. It was Fugate's kill if he wanted it, they seemed to say, and they were just there to witness, but I knew he would not fire, though I didn't then know why.

Finally, Commander Sessions broke through the line of men. He laid a hand on Fugate's shoulder.

"Good work, Cal," he said, and Fugate's body relaxed and the gun went limp in his hand. He got up off Schreck, who lay there with his transparent eyes flicking from cop to cop in the circle around him.

Schreck seemed to sense that things were over. He tentatively opened his mouth and turned his head aside. He spit into the grass to get rid of the taste of tear gas, and then he lay still, all the rage gone from him. He looked small and unimportant to me.

"Take Cal to Mercy with Ned Boyle," Sessions said to one of the officers standing there, and Fugate left, his hand over his bleeding arm, without looking back at the ring of men closing around Arthur like a tightening rope.

Within minutes everyone in the neighborhood knew it was over. The people who had stood in tight little knots on the street corners flooded into Bancroft street in front of Schreck's house. I snuck through Kozlowski's yard and joined them, as if I, too, were a distant witness only. A police woman brought Arthur's wife, wrapped in a blanket and smelling of gasoline, out of the house and led her to an ambulance. The crowd parted like the Red Sea to let her through, then they jeered and threw things as Arthur was led into the police car like a stumbling bear on a chain.

"Shoot the bastard, fry him," people were shouting.

Arthur lifted both handcuffed hands and flung his middle fingers up defiantly, but it was a futile gesture.

Nobody but I had seen all that happened behind the house that day and no one but I had seen just how much it took for Fugate not to kill Artie Schreck. Any of a dozen men, in the smoke and fire and confusion, would have killed him, but Fugate had not.

After the police left that day, the kids in the neighborhood wandered around collecting spent shell casings from the gutters. Gordon McCarthy found a piece of glass with blood on it. We put these things in special boxes or wrapped them in cloth as if they were relics. When my father came home from work, he drilled a hole in a shell casing I had found and I tied it on a boondoggle thong and I wore it around my neck for two years before I put it away in a drawer.

My Uncle Ned lived. The bullet had fragmented, having hit the window frame as it left Schreck's hastily fired gun, and so it had not hit him with full force. They weren't able to save his eye, however. They gave him a commendation and then moved him off the street to a desk job he never really got used to. At first he wore an eye patch, and made much of it, as if he had been a Barbary pirate, but eventually he got fitted for a glass eye which was so lifelike that people thought it was real. He and Fugate made quite a career after that in the local bars. They would go into a place and pretend they didn't know each other. After a while, Ned would bet Fugate he could pop out his eyeball and wash it in a glass of whiskey. Fugate would bet he couldn't and they'd argue and call each other names until pretty soon everybody else in the bar got involved and Fugate collected the money from them and pretended to be as astonished as everybody else when uncle Ned took out his eye and plopped it in a shot glass. They got great laughs out of it, and, as far as I know, they never paid for a drink again, ever.

MILK

My father returned from Europe in the great tidal wave of GI's who had survived World War II, and, like most of them, he quickly set about getting everything he had missed thanks to the Depression and Adolf Hitler. By 1951 he had a job, a house, a car, a wife, and a family which included me as its oldest son. My father had no reason to think his life would not be happy forever. Eisenhower was in the White House, and golf was what you did for excitement.

On Sunday afternoons, he and his former Army buddies, their hands wrapped around beer bottles, would sit in the garage on old milk crates and tell stories about how they had cheated death.

"Remember the time Tommy Flanagan was sleeping in his foxhole and that Kraut mortar round came whistling in and almost blew his ass off?" Everybody would laugh and nod. "Blew him ten feet in the air and when he landed he just rubbed his eyes and said, `Who farted?'"

From the time I could walk, I would hide in the bushes outside the garage and listen, gathering information about life. By the time I was ten, I had learned to sneak into the garage and sit on the outer edge of this charmed circle inhaling whatever wisps of story and cigar smoke came my way. My father and the others pretended not to notice I was there.

They loved to tell their stories. It didn't seem to matter that they'd told them before, and I didn't care that I had heard them before. I was fascinated by how the stories were always the same, yet were also always changing, evolving, moving farther from the truth until at last they acquired a mythic polish so that in the end poor Tommy Flanagan had been blown sixty yards, not ten feet, into the air, and had turned at least three complete somersaults before finally crashing down on the major's, then the colonel's, then the general's mess table and saying, to Ike himself in the later versions of the story, "Was it *you* who farted, uh, sir?"

Then the men laughed long and loud, and coughed and spewed cigar smoke at the ceiling and slapped one another on the back.

And so I sat there week after week for years until one Sunday I became aware of yet another change. It was subtle but definite. Gales of laughter still followed the stories. That much remained. But now and then the laughter gave way to a hollow silence which held them suspended until someone, usually my uncle Ned would say, "Geez that was a time, wasn't it?" And the others would nod, and a solemn shadow would cross their eyes as if they realized, at age 36 or 37, that something significant had happened to them once and compared to it the rest of their lives were turning out as flat and unchanging as the farmland around Toledo.

As middle age crept up on my father, his dreams seemed to flatten out before my eyes, and his ambition seemed capable of nothing more than mad weekend drives into the flatlands of northwest Ohio where we'd push the rim of the horizon around in front of our Plymouth without ever getting any closer to it. When we returned home tired late at night, my father would be muttering beneath his breath and my mother sat sullen in the passenger seat.

In those days he turned from his desperation and boredom to the open and welcoming arms of Mrs. Ida McMurtry, a housewife on his milk route who lived on Utica Street in a white clapboard house with hydrangea bushes out front. Perhaps he felt the danger of a love affair would take him back to his war days when life and death seemed charged with an electricity that had faded over the years. I know about this affair only because his method of carrying it on involved me in a minor but crucial role. I was a mere spear carrier, but enough of a plot device to insure that my mother would never suspect anything, for who could imagine that a man would carry on an affair practically under the eyes of his own young son?

It worked this way: about once a week that summer, my father would yank back my covers, and rudely haul me up by my shoulders before daylight. Gasping, my heart pounding, I'd come to, and he'd say, loud enough for my mother, who was still in bed in the next room, to hear, "Up already, son? Well, good, I need some help today."

"It's five a.m.," my mother would mumble, "Leave the boy sleep."

"Got a cottage cheese special today, Edna," he'd say, "I need help hauling all them cartons. Besides, he wants to go, don't you, K. O.?"

And before I could protest, he'd swing my legs out of the bed and put my feet on the cold floor and shove me toward the brightly lit bathroom where he'd splash cold water all over my face. "He's wide awake anyway, aren't you, son?"

By 5:30 we'd be at the yard, hauling the milk and egg crates on to the truck. The combined smell of sour milk and of the lit cigar he always kept in the corner of his mouth made me ill, but I was almost awake by the time we got to Utica street. The sky would be barely gray over the oil refineries on the East Side, but the men on Utica street would already have left their houses for their jobs at the Chevy plants or the scrap iron yards that made up the cityscape of that part of town.

Utica Street was full of cats at that hour, hundreds of them, and as the milk truck rounded the corner, they appeared and disappeared like animals in a magic show, oozing from beneath parked cars and leaking out of cracks no bigger than my hand, and as my father's truck rattled up the street, they followed it with their eyes, lusting after that great metal cow full of milk. Two beeps of my father's horn and they vanished like water into sand, and there, in her front window, behind the hydrangea bushes, appeared Mrs. Ida McMurtry, her cloud of red frizzy hair floating above a flower-print house dress. Some days she just stood there, and my father drove up the street looking disappointed. On other days, however, she would tuck her fists into her armpits as soon as she saw us coming and she'd waggle her elbows like a chicken trying to fly. This was her signal, so my father said, that she needed eggs that day. In fact, it meant her husband was not home.

"Mrs. M needs some cackle-fruit this morning," my father would say with a definite lift in his voice, but he wouldn't stop the truck right in front of the McMurtry's house. Instead, he'd drive up the block and park in front of an old house near the corner. He'd crush out his cigar in the ashtray, check his hair in the side view mirror, grab a carton of eggs from the egg box and head up the alley, never the sidewalk, back to the McMurtry's. He'd leave me a quart of chocolate milk for breakfast and tell me my job was to guard the truck. After about three-quarters of an hour, he'd come back down the alley, whistling, a freshly lit cigar crooked between his fingers, his Eisenhower-style creamery jacket slung over his shoulder carelessly. I knew nothing of delivering eggs and assumed this was how it was done all the time.

But one day that summer my father was gone longer than usual. It was one of those hot August mornings when the world feels like it's been stuffed inside an old gym shoe. The sun had just come up, and the hopeful freshness of dawn was giving way to the inevitable heat of day. An hour passed, and he did not return. For a while, I sat on the high driver's seat and fiddled with the pedals, then I poured a bit of chocolate milk on the curb and watched as thousands of ants crawled all over it, but still he did not come back. The sun rose higher, and the water from the melting ice on the milk crates began to run, and still he did not return, and when the waxed cartons of cottage cheese began to sweat, I began to worry that something might have happened to him. Even I knew that too much time had passed for merely delivering eggs. I wanted to go looking for him, but my father had given me strict orders not to go to the McMurtry's house under any circumstances.

And then I noticed something, or someone, moving behind the yellowed curtains of the old house my father had parked in front of which was not McMurtry's house but another of the asphalt shingled cubes people lived in over there. A hand had pulled the curtain back and, in the triangle of open space, I saw the face of the man who lived there. I looked up his name in my father's leather bound route book. Peter Janovich. He took three half gallons of milk two times a week. I had no idea why an old man living alone in a tiny house on Utica Street needed that much milk, but, in order to help make up for the time we'd lost while my father was delivering eggs to Mrs. McMurtry, I put a checkmark in the book and loaded the wire bottle carrier with Peter Janovich's three half gallons.

The door was open before I got there.

"Give to me my milk!" the old man said. He snatched the bottles from the carrier and pulled himself back into the house like a turtle drawing into its shell. His heavy foreign accent turned milk into a two syllable word. I stood there a moment waiting for him to give me the empties from the previous week's delivery, but he did not come.

I knocked and heard a sharp voice. "What?"

I explained I needed the empties.

Nothing in reply. I knocked again. "Piss in your empties!" he shouted angrily. And then I heard some kissing noises and the scuffing of plastic against the floor.

I knocked again.

"What?" came the shout from inside.

"I have to get the empties," I replied. "My father said."

I had to shout to be heard, for even though it was turning into an unbearably hot day, the old man had sealed the house as tight as a tuna can. Plastic from winter still covered the windows of the small house.

"Come get them yourself!" he called out.

I hesitated for a moment, frightened by the old man's angry tone, then I opened the door and was assaulted by a horrible smell, something vaguely familiar, but a thousand times more powerful than I had ever smelled it before: concentrated cat urine, so sour and strong it brought tears to my eyes and burned my lungs. The small house was jammed full of cats, thousands of them, it seemed. They were everywhere: on the refrigerator, on chairs and tables, on bookshelves. They were rolled into balls in corners and lounged on the window sills licking and grooming themselves with a loud wet clatter. At least twelve played inside empty paper bags strewn on the floor, and another dozen cat-shaped lumps loomed beneath opened newspapers. As far as I could see, in the kitchen, the living room, the small bathroom, and even the bedroom of the tiny house, the house held nothing but cats, all colors, shapes and sizes of them, as if Nature, abhorring vacuums, had dictated that in this one weird spot all emptiness was to be filled with cats to the nth power of catdom. At last I knew why this old man needed three half gallons of milk twice a week. The stench hit me in the face like a baseball bat.

"Come in," the old man said. "You like cats?"

I guessed that a lot hinged on my answer to the old man's question, for as soon as he asked it every cat in the house stared at me warily, backs arched, eyes narrowed to dangerous slits, nostrils flared, and claws half-unsheathed as if they knew already how I felt about them and were only waiting for confirmation.

"You like cats?" the old man repeated. I looked in the direction the voice came from (for until then I had seen only cats), and to my amazement I saw that Peter Janovich was down on his hands and knees on the kitchen floor, drinking milk from a pink plastic bowl just like a cat. He had lifted his face from the bowl and he, too, stared at me waiting for an answer. He had combed the long end hairs of his white mustache out to either side of his nose like a cat's whiskers, and a few white drops of milk still glistened on the hairs.

"I said you like cats?" he asked again, more insistently, his large emerald eyes staring at me over his bowl of milk. Under the circumstances, it was clearly a loaded question.

"Yeah, sure," I lied looking at all the half-bared claws and fangs around me, my mouth and the back of my nostrils stinging with the yellow tang of cat pee. "Cats are okay."

"Okay!?" he said indignantly, rising from the floor, "Why cats are best animals in world. Not like dogs. What good are dogs? Pissing and shitting all over sidewalk, not enough sense even to bury it. Dogs, hah!" He rubbed the drops of milk from his whiskers with the rounded backs of his hands. The cats around me, sensing his agitation, did not relax their guard one bit, but seemed ready to pounce, waiting only his signal. I had a vision of my body on the floor, my life's blood pouring from thousands of bloody scratches.

The old man lifted his milk bowl from the linoleum and motioned for me to come into the kitchen. He shoved a cat off a chair, pulled it back from the wooden table and directed me to sit. "You will have some milk, yes?" He poured more milk into his plastic bowl and slid it in front of me.

"Uh, I think I need to get back to the truck, sir," I said weakly.

"What for?" he asked. "Your papa no come back soon." Then he winked and added, *sotto voce,* "When tom cat's with lady cat he don't watch clocks."

I didn't have any idea what he was talking about. I looked down at the bowl of milk he had put on the table before me. The pink plastic had been scratched beyond cleaning. The smell of hundreds of cats was raging in my nostrils, and the milk itself seemed to have brown swirls in it where dirt or old cat food had dislodged itself from the side of the bowl.

"Drink," he said.

"Thanks anyway," I replied, inching back in my seat. "I just finished a quart. I don't think I can drink anymore."

The old man shrugged and pulled the bowl back across the table to himself, lowered his head and began to lap at it.

"I used to been a cat, you know," he said between sips.

"Yes, sir," I agreed, feeling a cool sweat break out over my body. I had never been in the presence of an insane person before. I tried to get out of the chair.

"Where you go?" he said sharply, looking up with his back slightly arched. All the cats in the house seemed to tense as well. I had noticed long before that these were not gentle house cats. More than one had an eye or ear missing, and several had big open sores from battles in the alleys and scrap iron yards surrounding Utica street. "You no believe I was a cat? You think I'm crazy or something?"

"Dunno" I shrugged, trying to smile as politely and non-threateningly as possible. This was not the sort of conversation one normally had in Toledo.

"You think is impossible cat can turn into man? Well, why not? Men turn into animals all the time, why not other way around?"

I cleared my throat and mumbled, "I guess I never thought about it that way."

"American boys no think of nothing. You think plenty later, I tell you, when you not a boy no more, when you turn into man yourself. Is true: one night I go to bed as cat in corner by nice warm stove; next morning, I wake up and I am human being. Worst thing ever happen to me."

He paused, as if waiting for me to confirm him in his belief. I had to admit he did look like a cat. His face was triangular with the inverted pyramid shape of a cat's head, and his large green eyes seemed to look at things that weren't there as a cat does when it tracks sounds beyond the pitch of human hearing. He kept a few long hairs of his white mustache brushed out to the side like cat whiskers and the corners of his mouth were curved up in an enigmatic smile which suggested that, like a cat, he knew things no one else did.

Finally, he broke eye contact with me and stared down at the table sadly.

"Pah," he said, waving his hand, "Never mind what I say."

He muttered a few words in a language I didn't understand then shook his head and continued to stare down at the table top. The house was filled with the sounds of cats licking themselves.

"I was happy as a cat, you know," he said, tears welling in his eyes, "but being happy ain't never good enough, is it?"

His thoughts were broken by the shrill blast of a rag man's tin horn. Peter Janovich looked up, grinned strangely and spoke aloud to his cats.

"Our friend brings us mouses!" he shouted, jumping up from the table. All the cats converged on the back door of the house waiting for the old man to open it. Thirsty for a breath of fresh air, I joined them. Cats swirled around my ankles, clawing excitedly halfway up the door as the old man yanked it open. Cats flowing all around me, I tumbled out into the light of the alley and nearly ran right into the sweaty flank of the ragman's horse. Compared to the smell of cats inside the house, the horse gave off a pleasant humid odor, and I drank it in deeply.

"You have something for me today?" Peter Janovich asked, his eyes intensely searching every corner of the wagon.

The rag man, an ancient man whose skin was as dark and greasy as the leather traces connecting his cart to his lean and lank horse, picked up a small wire cage from the seat of his wagon and tossed it down to Peter Janovich. The old man quickly counted the mice in the shoebox-sized cage. There were about a dozen of them, squealing and clawing at the wires. Some were bloodied from biting at each other. Peter Janovich reached in his pocket and gave the black man fifty cents.

"Ah, beautiful mouses," he said, holding the cage up in front of him, "Beautiful mouses!"

The cats, meanwhile, leapt into the air around him, straining for the cage and what was in it. They took frenzied runs up the old man's pants legs, and crawled over one another's backs to get at the mice. Finally Peter Janovich opened the cage and shook the bloodied mice on to the stones of the alley. The cats boiled over them in an explosion of fur and blood and noise. It was chaos, but soon the mad cluster broke into smaller eddies as cats batted the bloodied mice in all directions with their claws. Peter Janovich watched all this with a calm look, as if it confirmed something he believed deeply about life.

The whirl of activity moved around front of the cart and spooked the rag man's horse which jolted forward suddenly. The rag man hauled back on the reins to stop the horse from bolting, and then from the back of the old wagon, piled high with all the jetsam of the neighborhood, I heard a low moan. I looked back and saw a pair of spindly legs dangling down and at the end of them were my father's work boots.

I ran around to the tailgate and found my father sprawled out on top of an old ironing board. His left eye had a small cut beneath it that was beginning to puff up like a prize fighter's eye. Blood trickled from his nose and was crusting on his upper lip as it dried. When he saw me standing at the foot of the junk man's wagon, staring at him atop the pile of neighborhood junk, he muttered, "Oh, shit," and let his head drop back down again.

"You never know what'll turn up in folks' trash these days," the rag man said to no one in particular. "Found this behind McMurtry's, yep."

My father moaned again and said to me, "Go get me a piece of ice from the truck, K.O."

By the time I returned, the rag man and Peter Janovich had helped my father down from the wagon. The cats and mice were gone, and the alley seemed oddly calm.

"A man ain't got but one life, mister," the junk man said as they led him limping through the back door into Peter Janovich's kitchen, "You gots to be more careful when you mess around."

My father sat at the battered kitchen table and put the ice up to his cut eye, letting loose a few words I had never heard him use before. The knuckles of his right hand were scraped and bloody, and the melting ice made the blood pink and watery. Peter Janovich opened a cupboard and fetched down a half-empty bottle with a silvery label.

"Take some slivovitz," he said, pouring a shot of the thick liquid into a coffee mug for my father. The old man poured a shot for himself and the rag man, too. My father winced as the alcohol stung his cut lip. He seemed intensely uncomfortable. As he pressed the ice chunk to his cut eye, he looked up on top of the refrigerator and noticed a pot-bellied mandolin sitting there.

"You play that potato bug?" he asked Peter Janovich nodding towards the instrument. He seemed to want to get the attention off himself.

"I don't know what you call potato bug," Janovich said, setting down his slivovitz and wiping his hands on his pants, "but this I play, yes."

He lifted the instrument down and brushed the fingers of his right hand over the strings. They made a high pitched ringing sound, like someone saying "zing" between clenched teeth.

"My father used to play one of those," my own father said. It was the first I'd ever heard of any artistic leanings in our family. Peter Janovich held the instrument out toward my father like an offering.

"Naw, never caught the knack myself," he said, "but you go on and play. Take my mind off things."

Peter Janovich took a moment to tune the mandolin then he strummed the strings a few times with a plectrum he had taken from a small wooden box in a drawer. The tone was high pitched and clear, and he began to pluck out a melody in a minor key. It must have been something he brought with him from wherever he came from. Gradually his fingers loosened, and the stiff awkward picking of the right hand became a smooth tremolo. As he played, a faraway look came into his eyes and into the eyes of my father and the rag man, a lost abstracted gaze as if their minds were gone elsewhere while their bodies remained in the room. I know now that "sad" is too simple a word for the expression on their faces which reminded me a little of the hollowness that came into the eyes of my father and his friends sometimes in the garage when uncle Ned would say, "geez, wasn't that a time?" But it was even more intense and haunted than that, without any trace of the young men they might once have been in another time or place. There also seemed to be something in the melody that absorbed the sadness of these men and changed it into something else I cannot describe to this day except to say that as the slivovitz both stung and eased the pain in my father's cut lip, this melody seemed to be both an astringent and an anodyne to some pain that was not suffered by the three of them alone but belonged to many others and even to all the ages. The melody still haunts me though I cannot now hum or whistle the tune.

The old man's right arm crossed the face of the mandolin as he played, and the edge of the instrument pushed his unbuttoned shirt cuff up to his elbow. There was a line of numbers tattooed across his forearm. At the time it made no sense at all to me why this old man would have numbers tattooed there. Many years later, having seen numbers on the arms of other old European Jews, I realized Peter Janovich, like my father and many others, had endured the madness of their times.

The song ended, and we all sat there silently for some time, staring at the floor or the table top. There was nothing we could say about his playing that wouldn't diminish it, so we sat dumbly for some time until Peter Janovich finally rose and put the old instrument back on its perch.

"I do not play much anymore," the old man said, apologetically.

My father absently put the ice to his lip and made a sucking noise, then winced.

"That McMurtry, he a tough old bird," the rag man said breaking the silence.

"Aw, I coulda took him," my father mumbled, sucking on the ice a bit to ease the swelling of his lip.

"Not with your pants down 'round your legs, you couldn't," the rag man said, stifling a laugh.

My father flashed angrily for a moment, but then, seeing the rag man only meant to tease him in a friendly way, he joined the others in a burst of rueful laughter that seemed to go on for some time. I didn't understand until much later what was funny about the whole situation, about life itself, maybe, but I laughed, too, and my father lifted his slivovitz and they all drank off their cups and shook hands and said farewell.

Later, back in the truck, my father grew grave again. After we had driven a short way he said, "Listen, son, if your mother asks anything about what happened today, we'll make something up, all right?"

"You mean lie?" I asked.

"No, no, not lie," he said hurriedly. "Tell a story, that's all, we'll make up a story."

"What's the difference?" I asked.

"Well," he said, thinking that one over, "lies hurt people, but stories, well, stories protect them. You know. Oh, you know what I mean." He pulled a cigar from his work shirt pocket and peeled off the cellophane. He wedged the cigar between his sore lips and, when we were stopped at a red light, he lit it. "We'll have to make something up, K.O.," he said, pathetically. "That's all there is to it. It would kill your mother if she knew. We could say I tripped over the curb and fell or something, all right?" He sucked desperately on the cigar, then blew a plume of smoke into the cab of the truck. And I realized that my father, one of the men who had defeated Hitler in his youth, was afraid, and for the first time in my life I felt sorry for him.

I thought about his proposal for a moment. I thought about all the stories my father and his friends told over their beers on Sunday afternoons, and I thought about Peter Janovich telling me he was a cat, and I heard in my head the song the old man had played, and I know now that even at that age, I must have already had a growing sense that what people normally called "reality" had to be an overrated concept. In reality, I realized, cats tear mice limb from limb, and all our stories are just the gut and alum and lint we use to staunch the bleeding and pull together the ragged edges of our wounds. And so in the end I agreed to make up a story with my father. The made up version of things is all we ever remember anyway. Told often enough, with the right intonation, it would eventually become true.

"Sure," I said finally, "We can tell mom you slipped on a step and broke a couple of bottles but you could have been cut up a whole lot worse."

"Yeah, that's the ticket," my father said, "Because she really doesn't need to know." His voice drifted off as he puffed reflectively on the cigar then began adding more details, "It was on those slick steps over on Peck Street, you know that house on the hill there. Those steps are a mess anyway. Yeah." He nodded once or twice, as if setting it in his head and then looked at me admiringly, "That's pretty good, K.O. Pretty damned good. I like that bit about the bottle breaking." He blew a self-satisfied puff of smoke out his nose and lips and added, "That way we can make her glad I wasn't hurt worse than I was. You're all right, boy. Someday you might be a good story teller."

As we drove to the next stop, his worries seemed to go away. The story settled, he began whistling a wandering melody between his teeth. The song was vaguely Irish, as he was, and I could tell by his slight smile he was already forgetting what had really happened to him that morning and he was forming yet another story. This would be a story he would not tell either my mother or me. It would be a story he would tell to his friends in the garage when he thought I wasn't listening. It was going to be the tale of how he had cuckolded (though he wouldn't use that word) this guy named McMurtry, and I knew as I watched him formulate it in his head that every time he told it down the endless years of Sunday afternoons to come the red-haired Ida McMurtry would grow more voluptuous and love-starved than she had ever really been and my father's victory over her husband (for it would become that in time) would grow ever more decisive and brutal.

Over the years after that, I crouched outside the garage and heard the story grow just that way. And as I listened, my father and his friends grew older and sadder, and they traveled farther from their once-perfect youth until finally I could take it no more and went forth to find my own way in the world.

ORGAN WORKS

A Story in Four Movements

I. Prelude

The first time I fell deeply and stupidly in love, I was in the choir loft of St. Benedict's cathedral, sitting in front of the big, awkwardly placed organ. The juxtaposition of the church's huge musical organ and the first arousal of my own small pipe should come as no surprise. Church organs and those that govern sex and venery are notoriously unpredictable, temperamental, and inconveniently positioned. The organ at St. Benedict's was especially so. Most big churches are designed around their organs, but at St. Benedict's the organ seems to have come last, as if it suddenly occurred to the church's architect one day that the cavernous basilica required a large instrument to fill it with sound.

Similarly, I suppose, the Master Architect, having created all from a few well-chosen words, and Adam from mud and Eve from Adam, seems never to have planned for sexual reproduction. One assumes that if children were needed before the fall, one could simply call them forth and thus populate Eden with a few words made flesh. It would have saved a lot of fooling around with biology, morning sickness, strange food cravings, blood, water and post-partum depression. But then human beings, not for the last time, proved unpredictable, and God was suddenly faced with an engineering problem. Be fruitful and multiply, he had said. He apparently hadn't figured out exactly *how*. Perhaps in the manner of persimmons. In a world where there was no death, there didn't seem to be any pressing need to work out the details of reproduction. But then came the troublesome business with the tree, and, well, how could God overlook something like that, so he said woman would multiply her pains in childbirth. He had to be quick about this pronouncement because punishment is no good unless meted out soon after the act. But what did that mean, exactly? He had to think fast, so he routed the whole business through an area where there was already a good deal of plumbing and threw the ancestral couple out of the garden whereupon, immediately, they decided to try out their new organs and fell on each other passionately and produced Cain, the world's first murderer. (Cf. Genesis for fuller treatment.) Little more needs to be said about the further consequences of the over-hasty plumbing of the human reproduction system. One only needs to examine the testimony of four thousand years of dirty jokes, bathroom humor, erotic literature, romances, tragedies, the *Carmina Catulli,* Dido and Aeneas, Puccini operas, wars, rape, pillage, massacres, bride thefts, fine arts, bar room brawls over cheap women, the *Iliad* and the *Odyssey,* crimes of passion, psycho-sexual serial killers, the troubadour songs of the doomed 13th century Cathars of Provence, jealousy, top-40 hits, the *Commedia Divina,* and the personals section of any big city daily, to see the trouble organs cause if they are afterthoughts rather than part of the master plan from the morning of the first day.

As for the other kind of organ, the one commonly called the King of Instruments, I can only speak knowledgeably about the one at St. Benedict's, the one from whose loft I fell so deeply and stupidly in love when I was about fourteen.

It was an absolute plumber's nightmare. Driven by a massive, wheezy bellows, its four thousand pipes were jammed behind the choir loft into a space so small that some of the ranks had to be laid down sideways while others were hung upside down from the ceiling like families of bats. To enter the loft, the choir had to duck between the ranks being careful not to bump any pipes out of tune. The whole mess was so unsightly the designers hid it from the congregation by a grille of ornamental, but soundless, pipes that shielded the sensibilities of those who cherished the illusion that beautiful music could come only from beautiful instruments. In the same way, we postlapsarian humans have covered our other organs with flies, pleats, thongs, loincloths, codpieces, stomachers, kilts and various other garments that both ornament and conceal those other organs whose musical possibilities I had not yet begun to explore.

For over fifty years since its first erection, so to speak, St. Benedict's organ stood back there, big, lumbering, and awkwardly positioned. By the time I arrived in the boys' choir, the parishioners had gotten used to it, and, as Catholics did with fate, time, death, sex and all the other unpleasant but unavoidable difficulties of life, they learned to work around it without referring to it very often.

By the time I started singing in the boy's choir there, in fact, the parishioners had actually come to love the old gargantua, even though it was already fifty years old and had never been adequately overhauled. Not that no one tried, of course. My best friend Richard's father, the cathedral's organist, strove mightily with string and wax and duct tape to keep it going long beyond the point where it would have expired of natural causes. There was talk of replacing it even, but every time the church started a save-the-organ fund, either the roof leaked or the boiler in the school blew out, and the money collected for the organ work was spent on something else. Musical purists, however, were relieved whenever a new organ project fell through, for even though the old organ was temperamental and unpredictable, the sound the ancient wheezer gave out when it was up and working was astonishing, unequaled by anything a newer or more sophisticated organ could produce. It was actually beyond sound. It was pure energy, power, maybe God Himself. It overwhelmed the ear, bypassed it completely and penetrated the entire body. In the choir loft, we could actually feel the notes going right through us. The vibrations ruffled our surplices and passed through our lungs, kidneys, hearts and intestines like an atomic blast.

It was no wonder, therefore, that I first fell in love, deeply in love, from that perch high above the congregation, when my own awkwardly placed and troublesome organ works first rumbled to life.

It was on Holy Saturday night, during Easter vigil in the ancient Latin rite, when all the statues were covered with purple palls and the liturgical year was poised between the waves of death and resurrection like a ship becalmed on an uncertain sea. The nave was thick with the sweet smell of incense, and the Easter fire threw sharp shadows on the high walls and pillars. From up in the choir, we could see monsignors hovering around the bishop like bees. We watched as his eminence solemnly carved the year into the paschal candle and set grains of incense in it for the wounds of Christ. Then, lighting a taper from the tall candle, he passed the fire to the congregation. Little by little, light the color of honey filled the church as the flame passed from hand to hand. Soon hundreds of candles were lit below, and the nave glimmered in the cloud of incense like a misty valley filled with glowworms.

Then I saw her hair. I only noticed the hair at first. It was a subtle flash of gold off to the side of the dark mystery, something bright that caught my eye. I forgot about the service. I watched that hair, gazed at it intently until it seemed to become something almost alive, an exotic animal with a life of its own swimming like a jellyfish in the smoky nave.

I stood deep in meditation on that golden hair for I don't know how long, my revery only interrupted when the bishop intoned the *Gloria in excelsis Deo*. It was time to sing the triumphant Easter song. Richard's father pressed down on the keys of the old organ, but, with a dying sough, the ancient bellows took one last gasp and deflated like a bad tire. Richard's father pressed the keys again, but nothing came out, not a peep.

Nobody in the vast cathedral moved. They were frozen by the silence. The altar boys stood immobilized, unable to fling the covers off the statues until the music sounded. Richard's father pushed the keys once more, then beat on them with his fists, but still no sound came out. The silence thundered through the nave. We stood there mute, tense, waiting, biting our lips to keep from tittering in nervousness. The bishop's eyes bored angrily upward. As if expecting a miracle, he intoned the opening antiphon again: *Gloria in excelsis Deo*, louder than before, as if his singing could order the organ back to life. Richard's father pressed the keys but there was still no response. The organ was dead. The bishop's face went red and his eyes bulged. Richard's father muttered a florid curse in Dutch and pulled madly at the organ stops, kicked pedals and hit switches, but all to no avail.

And then, just then, the girl with the long blond hair turned and looked back up at the loft to see what was happening, and, at that very same moment, miraculously, inexplicably, the old bellows lurched back to life. Resurrection! Richard's father pressed down the opening chord and the four thousand pipes of the no-longer-silent organ burst into brilliant noise just as my eyes met the ever-blue eyes of Melissa Pettibone who was gazing up at me, or at least in my direction, longingly, yearningly, her lips aglow with the supernal orange of Tangee lipstick. And then she smiled and just like that I fell, tumbled, plummeted into love. My heart leaped up and darted through the nave of the cathedral above her head like a happy dragonfly and as the organ notes blazed through me I sang at the top of my lungs: *"Gratias agimus tibi propter magnam gloriam tuam!"* We give you thanks for your great glory!

What amazed me most about all this, once I had breath and time to think about it, was that in my dullness I had never really thought much of Melissa Pettibone before. I had known her for years. On the playground, we used to call her Missy Packrat. The last time I had noticed her, when we were in sixth grade together, she was a not-very-bright little girl with dull rodent-colored hair, with a nose too long for her face, and knees that knocked together like the spindly joints of a fawn. But somehow, in the intervening years, as my voice changed from soprano to a broken, unreliable baritone, Melissa had changed too, though I had not noticed it until that very night.

For starters, she bulged in places she had not bulged in before. I could see the outline of her bra beneath the pale blue Easter dress she wore. As the words of the *Gloria* came out of me, I examined that mysterious piece of underwear with telescopic eyes, studied the palimpsest of the straps, cups, hooks and eyes whose cantilevered suspension and subtle architectonics upheld Melissa Pettibone's emerging womanhood.

Grinning like an idiot, I nudged my friend Richard who stood next to me and I nodded downwards towards the sea of heads below us, certain that if he even glanced in her general direction he could not fail to see her, so much did she stand out from the otherwise lackluster crowd in the nave below.

Richard looked and saw Melissa gazing back at the choir and suddenly he stopped singing as though something hard had lodged in his throat. His eyes glared at me. Richard's father missed the baritone part and hissed in our direction from the organ console, and Richard's eyes flitted back to the page. He blushed, buried his face deep in his hymnal and continued to sing—*Qui tollis peccata mundi, suscipe deprecationem nostram*—not looking up again until the music was completely done. But when he did look up again, it was in a sidelong way, as if I had wounded him somehow.

Immediately, I experienced all the insane jealousy of a lover. Was he in love with her first? I wondered. Had he, sometime before that night, also seen the honey-light of Melissa Pettibone's hair and begun to flutter around it like a doomed moth? If so, he had just become my blood enemy.

By the time the Mass was over, I had convinced myself it was true, and before leaving the cathedral I knelt before the altar and made a solemn vow to kill Richard, my best friend, if he had any feelings at all towards Melissa Pettibone, my own true love.

II. Partita

The following Wednesday, Richard's Aunt Anja met me at the door of the big old half-timbered house that Richard and his father lived in. Every Wednesday afternoon, we would meet there after school to practice Latin for our Thursday morning class with Father Burckhardt who had somewhere got the idea that Richard and I were destined for the priesthood. I had no leanings that way myself, but I didn't complain because the Latin lessons liberated us from one day of Sister Torquemada's math class.

"*Tak*," Aunt Anja said, as she let me in. She already had the tea on a tray. Every week at exactly four o'clock, Aunt Anja would supply us with a pot of dark bitter tea in a Delftware pot and a stack of sugar cubes. At our house, nobody drank tea unless they were at death's door, and then it was laced with honey, lemon and a shot of Irish whiskey, so this little European ritual usually struck me as pretty exotic. That particular Wednesday, however, I wasn't thinking of tea.

I had my ball cap pulled low over my eyes, and I could feel smoke gathering behind my forehead. I had spent three whole days watching them. Richard and Melissa talked to each other on the playground four times and she had laughed at one of his jokes twice, the same joke. Did I need further grounds for suspicion? I was going to ask him, point blank, "Do you have the hots for Melissa Pettibone?"

Of course, I still hadn't figured out what exactly I would do if he said yes. I was a voracious reader in those days. Our local library had a shelf of Sir Walter Scott and the less salacious novels of Rafael Sabatini. I therefore had a vague idea that you were supposed to duel to the death in these cases, but I had no idea where, in the old neighborhood around the cathedral, I could lay my hands on a pair of finely tooled single-shot pistols. Perhaps swords, I thought, as I followed Aunt Anja's wide skirt up the stairs.

The stairwell was filled with woodblock prints by Dürer, or imitations of them, hung in dark frames on the dim walls. Twisted figures of the crucifixion and saints lives, mostly, cold and oddly cruel in a way. The whole house had always reminded me of a funeral parlor for a sort of sadness hung in the air like the odor of stale chrysanthemums, and it was as quiet in the house as if the walls were lined with black velvet or some other buffer against light and sudden sound. Not that it bothered Aunt Anja, however. As we climbed the stairs, she managed to keep up a constant chatter, I don't remember about what, in her heavily accented voice.

At the top of the first landing was a painting that was different from the others in the stairwell. It hung in an alcove set in the plaster. One day, Aunt Anja had told me that it was a painting of Richard's mother who had died when he was only five. The resemblance was striking. Richard and his mother shared the same long, sharp bones in the nose and jaw, though his mother's neck was longer. In the painting it curved slightly like a lily's stem as it came up to meet her head, which seemed to float separate from her body, as if it had only some artificial connection. I would later recognize the style as Modigliani's. The flowered dress she wore was the fleshy pink and white of magnolia blossoms in the spring. She was quite beautiful.

"What did Richard's mother die of?" I had asked one day.

"Shot herself in the head, k-poo, like so," Aunt Anja said, almost cheerfully, as if it were some slight eccentricity the mother had. "Luff," she added, shaking her head, "What are you going to do, eh?" and then she shrugged and continued up the stairs with the tea.

At first I thought "luff" was a strange Dutch disease that made you insane, then I realized she had said love. It made no sense to me when she first told me, but the Wednesday after I'd seen Melissa Pettibone from the organ loft, I thought I understood. I was beginning to realize that love, or luff, could make you think and do all sorts of strange things.

Richard was at his work table with one of the thin drawers from his butterfly box in front of him. He had a special wooden case built in which he kept his collection. It had very shallow drawers with glass covers on them. The bottoms of the drawers were lined with cork and Richard kept his butterflies in them by pinning them in place with bead-headed pins so they seemed to float, wings outspread, perfectly level, only one-sixteenth of an inch above the bottom. Below each specimen he had glued a neatly typed label with the Latin and English name of the bug.

"Look," he said as Aunt Anja laid the tea tray on the table and left us alone, "This is the one I told you about."

I threw my baseball glove and Latin book on the bed and looked. The butterfly Richard wanted me to see was as big as my hand and so stunningly blue that it hurt my eyes. On each of the upper lobes of the wings was a yellow spot fringed with a deep red ring the color of cranberries.

"It's from South America," he said, "I just got it in the mail last week, what do you think?"

I was in no mood for butterflies. He had shown me all of them before, his *Satyridae* and *Nymphalidae*, his *Danaidae* and tropical *Heliconeans*. The only butterfly I would have been interested in right then was his *Polygonia interrogationis*, the one that had a silver question-mark shape emblazoned on its under hind wing, for I had a question, too, and I was going to ask it right out.

"Do you love Melissa Pettibone?" I blurted, my fists jammed into my hips aggressively, as if I already knew the answer.

Richard looked at me strangely for a moment, then shrugged.

"She's nice," he said. His voice was noncommittal, wavering, like he was deciding. Maybe yes, maybe no.

In my mind, I cocked a dueling pistol. He tilted the butterfly box up slightly so the cool light coming in from the window would not glare off the glass cover. He stared at the new butterfly.

"Yeah, but you don't, like, *love* her or anything, do you?" I asked, "Because if you do . . ."

I let that sentence hang for a moment so he could imagine whatever dire consequences he wanted, then I said, pleading more than I wanted to, "Just tell me, all right? That's all."

Richard got up and walked over to the cabinet where he kept his butterflies. He slid the drawer with the new butterfly back in. It glided smoothly, like it was riding on felt, until it locked into place with a soft metallic click.

"No, I don't love her," he said. The backs of his ears were red and he did not turn around.

"You're sure?" I asked.

He turned to me and then laughed, like it was a stupid question. "Yeah, I'm sure," he said.

I don't remember what we did after that. Probably we studied Latin as if it were a normal Wednesday. But nothing was normal about it at all. With Richard out of the way, I thought, Melissa Pettibone could be all mine.

III. Passacaglia

What followed were the longest two months of my life. This all took place before the so-called sexual revolution, before the mass media taught every twelve year old the intricacies of French kissing and casual bed hopping. It was the tail-end of the Age of Repression, the last moment, culturally speaking, when anticipation, imagination and expectation made up a significant part of one's sexual coming of age.

Not knowing what else to do, I spent hours staring at the back of Melissa Pettibone's head in class. I walked four blocks out of the way twice a day just to pass her house. I grew faint and nearly passed out once when her living room curtain flickered as I walked by. I made elaborate excuses to find myself somewhere I knew she would be, but then was too scared to talk to her. I courted her by proxy. I went to Woolworth's and sniffed sample bottles of perfume that smelled like the perfume she wore. If she threw a piece of paper away, I watched to see which piece it was and later, surreptitiously, fished it out of the wastebasket, unfolded it and pressed it flat in a book. If the paper happened to have gum that she chewed in it, I unwrapped the gum and put it in plastic wrap to keep it fresh and once in a while would take it out and inhale the odor. I treated these things like third class relics. In a word, I made a fool of myself.

And why not? Melissa Pettibone was no longer an ordinary girl. She had appeared and seized my heart in a theophany of incense and gold, in the holy of holies, the cathedral itself, with the bishop and all his minions in attendance. She had first shined forth on Holy Saturday, in the blessing of the waters and the burning of the light, enshrined in the mystery of the alpha and the omega. In my mind, Melissa Pettibone came freighted with all the weight and authority of the Holy Roman Catholic and Apostolic Church. Getting my greedy hands on her swelling breasts would take some doing.

"All you have to do is talk to her," Richard said one day when he got tired of my endless groaning, but that was easier said than done.

How could I even begin? I wracked my brain for days and finally hit on a way.

Like a well-planned murder, I would make it look like an accident. I figured out that by running through an alley as soon as school got out, I could hide in the big lilac bush next to the bus stop in front of St. Vincent's hospital. Melissa had to walk by it on her way home and if I could leap out of it at the just right moment, I would be face to face with her at last. It would look fated, or at least the result of an unavoidable accident. The rest, I thought, would take care of itself.

"It won't work," Richard said.

"Why not?" I asked

"For starters, people don't, as a rule, fall out of lilac bushes."

I decided to go through with it anyway, in spite of all the arguments Richard could muster. As soon as the school bell rang the next day, I fled the building and tore through the alley behind the hospital. I got to the bush early and crawled into it, broke off a few blossoms to hand to her and crouched there waiting, panting, for what seemed a long time. Finally I saw her coming, a block away. My grip tightened on the lilac stems. My nose filled with the sweet scent of the bush that hid me. I could see Melissa's face slightly tilted up to the spring sunshine, a dreamy half-smile playing over her lips as she approached. She cradled her books and binder in her arms, clasping them to her breasts. Was she, perhaps, thinking of me? As she came closer, my fist closed tighter around the lilacs and my mouth went dry. I closed my eyes and listened to the wooden heels of her pumps clack like castanets on the pavement, louder and louder as she came closer. My heart began to thud to the same rhythm until finally I could stand the suspense no more and burst out of the bush, landing on the sidewalk smack in front of her, lilacs thrust forward as I babbled incoherently, "Melissa, I publahahahahahahah you."

She shrieked. She jumped. She dropped her books, scattering them all over the sidewalk. She shouted, more in surprise than anger, I hoped, "You moron you idiot you scared the ever-living life out of me are you out of your mind or what?"

And before I could explain (how could I ever explain?) she scooped up her books and was gone in a huff, the hem of her school uniform skirt snapping around her knees as she stormed away, leaving me kneeling on the pavement with a fistful of flowers.

I felt a hand on my shoulder. "I told you it wouldn't work." It was Richard. "Come on, man, I'll buy you a Coke."

I had no idea where he had come from. I felt humiliated. I guessed he had witnessed the whole spectacle. He didn't laugh, however. He just reached out his hand and helped me up. I started to toss the now-worthless flowers into the bus stop trash bin, but Richard grabbed them from me.

"For Aunt Anja," he said, "She loves fresh cut flowers. In the Netherlands, she says she had them every day. Maybe she'll give me extra dessert."

He inhaled the flowers' sweet scent. I had the smell all over me from crawling in the bush and I tried to air out my shirt before I got home.

"I think I'm going to die," I said, mortified as I looked back at the spot where I'd leapt out of the bushes.

"You won't die," Richard said, and he smiled in the wry sort of way he sometimes did when I made a fool of myself.

IV. Fugue

I never recovered from that fall, though God knows I tried. I thought of groveling, I moaned incessantly to Richard, who was patient. I wrote long letters that I never sent. I thought of learning to play the guitar so I could serenade Melissa beneath her window. But I actually got around to doing nothing at all. And then, quite suddenly, time ran out. Before I knew it, it was graduation day and I would never see her again. She was on her way to the all-girls Ursuline Academy, and I was going to the all-boys St. John's High. These were Catholic prep schools, but what were they prepping us for? I wondered. Life without girls, life without Melissa? What would be the point of that? I was miserable.

Graduation day was the hottest June afternoon anyone could remember. Up in the choir loft Richard and I sat side by side. As the only baritones, we had to sit in the choir to fill out the parts of the Mass. We were sweating through the cheap acetate graduation gowns we were wearing, but I didn't care about the heat. Throughout the Mass all I could see was Melissa Pettibone, down in the nave with the other graduates. I anatomized her throughout the service. It was Melissa (who else?) who walked the bouquet of spring flowers to the Mary altar accompanied by the syrupy goo of Schubert's *Ave Maria*. The bouquet, a ball of carnations on a stick, quivered slightly in her hands and she even sniffled once or twice as she laid it down, gently, reverently on the altar. Her feet, I was sure, never even touched the floor.

After Mass, all the graduates raced out the door and gathered on the lawn outside the church, hugging, kissing, screaming. The girls had thrown off their black gowns and the bright pastel colors of their graduation dresses looked like an explosion of flowers on the grass. The boys, in black and white, stood on the edges in small groups. Autograph books went quickly from hand to hand. I signed some and passed mine around and stood on the church steps for a moment until I located Melissa in the midst of the swirling crowd. She was way off in the middle of the church lawn and I decided it was time to play a last desperate card.

Leaping from the step, I managed to elbow my way through the tangle, pushing aside books that were thrust at me, throwing myself forward until at last I stood nose to nose with Melissa, her lovely eyes still red-rimmed from the tears she had shed at the Mary altar.

"P-p-please," I stammered like an orphan begging for gruel as I thrust my autograph book out in front of her.

And without looking at me much at all, she took the book and signed it with her pink pen. (It was a pink Papermate, I noted, with the hopeful logo on the clip of two hearts intertwined.) Breathlessly, I pulled the book back to see what she had written, what message, what secret longing from her heart. I read the words with my heart in my mouth.

"To a nice guy, from Missy P." She had dotted the i with a smily face.

That's all? I blinked. I looked at the mostly white page again. She hadn't even written my name, and it only occurred to me then that perhaps, after eight years of school together, she didn't even know it. In spite of all, however, as if to show the lengths of idiocy to which the first stirrings of hormones drive us, I still harbored a shred of hope. She had not yet handed me her book to sign, but when she did I would finally get my chance. On that virgin white sheet of paper, I could finally pour out the months-long yearning of my heart. I reached out for it, but she had disappeared, run away. Where had she gone?

I heard a car honking and, looking up, I saw Melissa and five or six other girls giggling, shoving, and elbowing each other out of the way for the chance to get a ride in Jesse Salinas's car. It was a '57 Chevy Belaire convertible with a raccoon tail wired to the antenna, and I knew then that I was doomed for not only was Jesse a Mexican, which made him cool, but he had been held back twice so he was the only one in eighth grade who had a mustache and, even more important, a car. I stood there helplessly with my autograph book limp in my hand.

"Whoa, girls, one at a time, one at a time," Jesse said, pushing his shades down his nose to see them better. He shifted his toothpick to the other corner of his mouth and nodded to Melissa, "How 'bout you first, babe?" She giggled with delight and eagerly jumped into the passenger seat and off they roared in a squeal of blue tire smoke.

I admitted I was finished. It was over. Kaput. Ended. Completely done, or undone. *Consummatum est.*

I couldn't have felt worse if I'd taken a fast ball right between my eyes. I stumbled blindly back into the church. The dim air felt welcoming and cool as I collapsed into the last pew and stared down at the pathetic autograph she'd written. "To a nice guy," it said. Why didn't she just rip my heart out and be done with it?

The faint smell of incense hung in the air. I closed my eyes, and contemplated praying to St. Jude, patron of lost causes, but before I could summon up a prayer, I heard a noise above me in the choir loft. Just a peep, one note that flew out of the organ pipes like a bird. I turned and looked. Richard was just crawling into the console. His foot must have bumped one of the pedals. In all the rush of the crowd outside, I had forgotten about him.

"What are you doing up there?" I called out. "Why aren't you outside with the others?"

"Why aren't you?" he asked back.

I had no answer to that, so I climbed up the crooked back stairs to the choir, crawled between the organ pipes and joined him. Richard's autograph book, unopened, lay on top of the console.

"Aren't you getting any autographs?"

He shook his head. He looked sad, though I couldn't imagine why. Nobody was sad to leave St. Benedict's. Even I, except for Melissa, was ready to move on to high school.

"This is for you," Richard said suddenly, reaching beneath his graduation gown. He pulled out a carefully wrapped package about the size of a small book. It was wrapped simply, in a foil paper, with no bow or anything, but it was clearly a present. I didn't know quite what to say. I felt embarrassed, of course, because I hadn't even thought to buy him anything, but then nobody did. Graduation from St. Benedict's was such a shared release that it would have been like prisoners buying each other things on a day of general amnesty. Everyone was equal so no gifts were expected.

"Well, go ahead, open it," Richard said.

The sound of tearing paper filled the whole church. I peeled back the wrapping and saw that Richard had mounted and framed one of his prized butterflies. The frame was a simple black wooden one, and the bright butterfly had been pinned to a piece of black cardboard to show up the colors more.

"It's a silverwashed fritillary," he said.

I sat there staring at it, feeling an odd sympathy with the bug that had been mounted to the board with a pin through its heart.

"You could say thanks," Richard said, flashing me that brief smile of his. "Do you like it?"

"Yeah, sure," I said, "I just feel bad I didn't get you . . ." I let the apology finish itself. Richard turned and looked out over the nave. The church was empty except for the altar boys who were finishing the last chores of putting away the candles and the empty ciboria. Richard's eyes were focused somewhere above the central aisle.

"I suppose we won't see each other much anymore," he said. He was on his way to Catholic Central for high school.

"What do you mean?" I said, "Don't be stupid."

"I'm not being stupid," he said, "People go away and never come back."

"It's not like I'm going to Mars or something."

I grabbed Richard's autograph book from the top of the organ console where he'd laid it.

"Here," I said, "I'll sign your book and you sign mine."

I handed him my book and opened his. To my surprise, it was completely blank. One perfectly white page after another fluttered through my fingers.

"Richard, you didn't get any . . ."

"Who cares," he said.

"What's the matter?"

He shrugged. Over the past few months, I had thought he was getting more depressed or something. He had slid into it gradually, but I had been so preoccupied with Melissa I never asked him why. He never said just what was making him unhappy, but sometimes he seemed to have all the air pumped out of him, and sometimes when we were studying together or I was moaning about Melissa, I'd notice him just staring off into space as if he were seeing something no one else could see, no one could understand, even if he could find the words to talk about it. I'd never asked him about it because I figured that anybody whose mother killed herself when he was five probably had enough to be sad about without my poking into it, but now he was worse than I had ever seen him before.

Hoping to cheer him up, I turned back to the very first page in his autograph book and wrote, in letters that I knew immediately were too large and happy, "To Richard, my best friend! (Really!) Good Luck in High School!" and then I signed my name with a big joking flourish.

I showed it to him and he tried to smile but didn't do a very good job of it. He opened my book, and, on his way to the empty pages in the back, he thumbed through the signatures I'd collected outside, some of them sloppy, hastily written, some obscene. He paused ever so briefly at Melissa's signature, read what she'd written and smiled his half smile and shook his head. Then he held his pen over the opposite page. He closed his eyes, looking for a moment like a diver might look before he jumps off the edge of a cliff. Then, taking a deep breath, he opened his eyes, pursed his lips and scrawled something quickly across the page. That done, he slapped my book closed.

"Well?" I asked after a moment, "Come on." I held out my hand.

"No," he replied, holding the book so tightly his fingers clenched white around the cover. I reached for it, but he pulled it away. I reached again; he yanked it back. I finally got a grip on it, but he still held it tight, fiercely even.

"C'mon, it's *my* book," I said, twisting it in his hand until I finally wrenched it free. "What did you write in here anyway, peckwood?" I flipped through the book to the page he'd signed. The black scrawl seemed illegible until I realized it wasn't written in English. In a quick nervous hand, he had written "*Amo te*, Richard." I looked up at him, then down again at the page and read the words again, *Amo te*, in a dead language.

"It's not a joke," Richard said, his voice flat.

I suddenly felt a sort of rushing sound in my ears, as if somebody had grabbed me by the feet and was holding me upside down over the edge of the choir loft. I stood there staring at the page, trying desperately to construe some other meaning of the word *amo* such as "I like" or "I feel fond of," but it was no use. Father Burckhardt's lessons had been good, and Richard and I had conjugated it often enough together, making up bawdy jokes about the *pueri* and *puellae* who went off *in sylvam* together in such numbers. I looked up at Richard. He stared palely over the nave, like a man facing the wall, and didn't say a word.

"Jesus, Richard, you ruined my book," I said without thinking and from the way he sucked in his breath so sharply, you'd have thought I had slapped him. I guess I may as well have.

"I'm sorry," I stammered, but it was too late.

He turned towards me angrily. "Never mind, you'll never have to see me anymore anyway, will you?" And before I could stop him, he jumped up from the organ seat where he'd been sitting and bolted out of the instrument. His feet and hands hit the pedals and keys and set off a harsh dissonant chord. One pipe got stuck and its single note continued to sound, like the cry of a wounded bird.

"Richard, wait!" I called, but I could hear him clattering down the choir steps already, and the next thing I knew he shot out from beneath the loft, running as fast as he could right up the center aisle of the church with his fists clenched.

"Come back," I called. "Wait." But he was gone out the transept door and my words echoed uneasily through the empty church.

I sat there for a long time listening to the shrill note of the stupid organ pipe that had gotten stuck. The shrill whistle would stay stuck until the bellows died or someone crawled into the inner workings of the organ and pulled the pipe out and fixed it.

For the first time in my life I became aware I had inflicted an involuntary and stupid gash on someone. I knew even then it would make my spine twist for the rest of my life whenever I thought of it for I realized that even if he could have heard me, and even if Richard would have come back, it was already too late to reverse things. In fact, I admitted to myself, I was even grateful that he had already disappeared because I couldn't have faced him if he had started coming back up the aisle. What could I say?

Slowly I tore Richard's page out of my autograph book, folded it up and put it in my shirt pocket. I wouldn't throw it away, but I didn't want anyone to see it either. It seemed like a message in a bottle that I'd found, a desperate note from someone far away and unknown. I stared once again at Melissa's impersonal note and tore it out, too, and one by one I tore all the other pages out and let them, with their hastily scrawled autographs and schoolboy humor, flutter to the floor.

Had Richard been imagining me the way I had been imagining Melissa Pettibone? At different times of the day did he stop and wonder where I was? Did he secretly follow me home? Pick up pieces of paper I had dropped? What was he feeling, I wondered, as he hid somewhere that day and watched me leap from the lilac bush and grovel at Melissa's feet? Had I hurt him the way she had hurt me, stupidly, unconsciously, like a kid stomping on ants?

I closed the empty covers of my autograph book and looked at the mounted fritillary he had given me. On the backside of the frame, in his careful way, he had glued a neatly typed piece of paper on which he had put the butterfly's Latin name, its English name, its range and habitat, and the story of its too short life copied from a book:

> An elaborate flight display serves to synchronize the courtship cycle of the silverwashed fritillary. Once they've located each other, usually through sight, the potential mates circle each other and perform a spectacular joint flight, never touching, never meeting. The male glides below and darts in front, circles, dashes into and out of view, but the sought-after mate flies on as if unaware. Once alighted, however, the two insects posture, exchange scents, and if mutually receptive, they conjugate in a careful sequence of seven acts, after which the eggs are laid and the parents depart and die.

The one shrill note of the stuck organ pipe kept shrieking above the deep roar of the bellows until it finally drove me crazy. I got up and tried to turn it off, but, as might be expected, the on-off switch on the organ console wasn't working. I let the shrill pipe play on and descended from the loft. Blessing myself with holy water, I went back out into the bright daylight. I supposed I would have to see Richard again someday and tell him I understood, but I also knew that nothing between us would ever again be the same. The organ works were too confusing, too difficult to get around. As I walked down the church steps, Jesse Salinas pulled up to the curb in his hot Chevy. Melissa jumped out and another girl jumped in. Jesse revved his engine loudly and peeled away, and all the girls in their bright graduation dresses shouted after him, "Take me next, Jesse, please take *me*!"

ALTERNATE LIVES

TRAJECTORY

Out of nowhere, a small yellow missile fell at Dave's feet. He did not see where it had come from. Anticipating his meeting with Hank McTaggart, he had not been aware of anything around him. Then he heard something clatter along the pavement, and felt a tap against his shoe. He stopped and looked down. There, resting against his wingtip was a small rocket. He looked up, expecting to find some child a few feet away following it, but no one was there besides the usual lunchtime assortment of people on the mall: a few bankers and lawyers, a few business types, the Chinese schizophrenic who occasionally shouted at no one in particular, and street people collecting cans for return deposits. None of them was likely to have fired this toy missile.

He looked up toward the mostly-abandoned upper floors of the buildings along the mall. No kid up there with a missile launcher either. He looked down again at the rocket. The pedestrian traffic flowed around him like water around a rock in a stream.

He bent down and picked the toy up, holding it between his thumb and forefinger as if not wanting to claim it. Tilting his head back, he peered at it through his new bifocals. The missile had an archaic look to it, like a blunt cigar in shape, with large blue tail fins. The Air Force logo, white star inside a blue circle, was decaled on the side. Compared with the sleek modern missiles his grandson A.J. played with or chewed on, it seemed downright clunky. It had a Cold War feel about it. It was not a laser-guided smart bomb of the sort he had watched going down

Iraqi air shafts a few years ago on TV. This was an old dumb bomb of the kind we would have lobbed at the Russians back in the 1950's.

Then something flashed in his memory. A hot rush went from his feet to his forehead as he remembered something he had not thought of for years. Suddenly he knew for a fact where this rocket had come from. His hand trembled, and he could not catch his breath. He wanted to throw the thing away, but his fingers were frozen on it, and he looked at it again to reconfirm what he already knew.

Now he feared it might explode like a loaded cigar. After a moment, he realized people were starting to stare. He caught a glimpse of himself in a store window and realized how silly he looked to others, holding the thing at arms's length and staring at it dumbly. Yet how was he supposed to look? What is a grown man supposed to do when the toy rocket he had launched forty years before finally finished its trajectory and landed at his feet nearly two hundred miles from where it had left the launch pad?

There was no question about it. This was the very missile he had shot on a summer day forty years ago into the rose bush of his back yard in Toledo, Ohio. It was the very rocket he saw disappear into the thorns and that he never found again, though he searched for what seemed like hours in and around the bush, though his father, now long dead, also looked for it that day and again in the fall when he cut the rose canes down to their nubs. They searched in the grass behind the bush, in the cracks in the bricks in the foundation of the garage, even out into the alley, but they never found it. Dave's last view had been of it arcing up into the bush and then it was gone.

"It can't just have disappeared," his mother said, trying to console him, for it had been his favorite toy.

"It'll turn up some day, Dave," his father had said, laying his hand on his shoulder.

That autumn when the leaves fell and the weeds along the fence shriveled and died, Dave searched again. He searched among the cut-down rose nubs almost daily until the snow came and then in the spring he searched again, and then, one day he just gave up. Despite what his father said, it had not turned up again, at least not until now, and from its disappearance he learned something of irretrievable loss, and he carried that unfinished flight inside him until today when, apparently, the flight ended.

He felt a little faint, wanting to toss the thing away. It defied so much of what he had come to believe in. Things and people disappeared, time moved in one direction only, death was final. He felt the need for a strong drink, but opted instead for a coffee bar since it was closer.

"May I help you?" the girl behind the counter asked. She had silver rings piercing her nose, eyebrows, ears and lips, as if she had been attacked by an out of control grommet machine. He looked up at the bewildering array of choices on the menu board: lattes, espressos, cappuccinos, mocha javas, pure arabicas and Ethiopian harrar. How could he decide at a time like this? The espresso machine hissed and let off steam like a copper and chrome dragon.

"Decaf?" he said uncertainly.

The girl smiled at him. Was it a condescending smile? She couldn't have been more than nineteen. The silver rings in her lip, nose, and eyebrow stretched at her smile lines. Did she think he was foolish, standing there clutching a child's toy rocket?

He looked around the coffee shop. He had not been in the building since it was a diner some years before. He had appraised it once. Now it was unrecognizable. The Art Deco diner stools and booths had been taken out, the walls had been stripped down to brick. He was almost the only one over twenty-five. He cradled his toy rocket in his palm, felt its cool smooth plastic, tried to imagine what mysterious hole in time it had gone into forty years before and where it had been in between. His cup of decaf clattered on the saucer as he made his way through the crowded two-top tables filled with kids in Birkenstocks intensively journaling. What the hell did they have to write about yet, he wondered. As if their lives would make a book. Now *this*, he thought, holding the rocket in his free hand like a captured bird, this would make a book, or at least an episode of *The Twilight Zone*.

He found a small table behind a pillar and set the toy across from him, clearing away the cream and sugar containers between. He stared at it.

Where had it been all these years, and what trajectory had it followed to get here? Could its sudden reappearance be explained by the laws of physics, or would other laws be necessary, laws that had to do with the human heart and memory and longing and time? It had once been his favorite toy, but after it was lost, he nearly forgot it. He had forgotten much else besides. What had happened to the spring-loaded launcher? Useless after the missile was gone, that, too, had become part of the irretrievable past. And what had happened to the house he'd lived in when he fired the rocket? His family had moved out of it after his father died because his mother couldn't stand the memories, then someone else had lived there, and then someone else, and then someone else again, he supposed. His younger sister, who had been in the sandbox at the time he fired this rocket, was now twice-divorced, trying to raise a son whose main goal in life was to climb stairs on a skateboard. His mother, who had been in the kitchen listening to the radio and ironing when he'd launched it, was now retired from the job she had to take after his father died. And all the years in between, unseen, this little rocket had been following a perfect parabolic trajectory, ascending while he went to college, met Ruth, raised Cassie and Steve, tried to build a career in a roller-coaster economy, moved his mother to Florida where she retired. All the time, above him, this rocket streaked toward its apogee and then—when exactly?—it began its incredible descent. Was it about the time he had to switch from tennis to golf? When the house he and Ruth built was emptying out? When his doctor told him to switch to decaf? He now wore bifocals without shame.

Yet, considering its long journey, the rocket looked in fairly good shape. A few scratches along the sides, the color faded a bit, one of the fins a bit bent. The toy showed surprisingly little effect of the strain of liftoff. There were no scorch marks from what must have been a terribly hot re-entry. In fact, there was only a slight scuff on the nose where it had hit the pavement a few moments before.

"Nothing's ever gone for good," his father had said the day the rocket was lost, attempting to console him, "It'll turn up again." At first this gave him hope, then, after his father died, he thought it was a foolish thing to say. In all the intervening years, he had never known anything to come back. Now, however, with the rocket in his possession again, he thought his father must have been wiser than he had ever given him credit for.

Dave felt a tingling on his hip, pulled his pager off his belt and read the LCD. He recognized the number, a client he was supposed to meet. He picked up the rocket, curled his fingers around it lightly, then slipped it into his sport coat pocket as he made his way through the journaling Birkenstocks back to the street. Maybe they were scribbling in an attempt to keep their lives from falling away, he thought, to fix the memory so it could be retrieved some day in the future. Maybe they needn't bother.

HOUSE OF DREAMS

Maris was the most talented dreamer I ever met. She came to Bruce's House of Dreams every Thursday at one o'clock, regular as clockwork. Usually gifted dreamers are a little bit loose about time, like the drifters who fall into the House of Dreams wearing tie-dyed shirts and Tibetan lama hats from the Spirit Dream catalog. They wander in when they feel like it. Sometimes they make appointments; most times they don't. They come out of the dream cubes with a bright glow in their eyes and their pupils dilated, then they drift away again until the wind blows them back.

But Maris was different. No prayer wheels, no incense, no exotic clothes. When she first walked in, I thought she had come to the wrong place. She dressed like a straight arrow, full suburban: khaki slacks and loafers, always tasteful, even a little conservative. In the fall, she wore white turtlenecks with little mushrooms or autumn leaves on them, and she always smiled as if she didn't have a care in the world. She never talked much, either. In this, too, she was unlike the young Birkenstocks who came out of the cubes and insisted on telling me every detail of their dreams whether I wanted to listen or not. Though she said little, Maris ran deep. I knew that from the monitors. On a good day, she could reach REM in less than 12 minutes which was pretty extraordinary given the troubled times we live in dreamwise. She intuitively understood the discipline of dreams.

It isn't clear exactly when people lost the ability to dream on their own. Bruce thinks it was about 1972, or at least it started then and things got worse over the past thirty years. Bruce is not a trained dreamer, and he has no academic credentials to speak of, but he is one of the best natural dreamers around, and, in the years of running his House of Dreams, he has acquired as much knowledge of dreaming as psychoanalysts used to have before psychoanalysis went out of business because people's ability to dream by and large dried up. They don't even teach much about dreams in college psychology classes anymore because the talent has so atrophied. Dreaming is considered by most people to be a vestige, like an appendix, something antediluvian that we don't need anymore since we have TV and the Internet to dream for us and drugs to control mood swings.

Bruce and his House of Dreams, however, have been successful in spite of all this. There are still enough people out there who at least *want* to dream or to find out what dreaming used to be like that Bruce has been able to keep the House of Dreams going on a commercial strip dominated by muffler shops and fast food joints.

The House of Dreams is a simple concrete block building that used to be a discount furniture store. Bruce said it was sheer luck that he was able to buy a store already called House of Dreams. He didn't even have to change the large sign out front except to add, in small letters above the word House his own name and to blot out the word Furniture on the bottom.

Some customers still come in thinking it's a furniture store, of course, and they're taken back a little by the small white cubicles. Each cell is equipped with a low watt bulb controlled by a dimmer and has a small plain mattress without sheets. Instead of sheets, Bruce uses the sort of white paper on a roll that doctors use on their examination tables. He uses cloth covers for the small pillows, of course, but he says using real sheets would drive the cost up and then dreaming would be too expensive for many people. He also feels the white paper adds credibility, makes it seem less like checking into a cheap hotel in the middle of the day. And since people dream best on their backs, the white paper makes little difference in terms of comfort. He keeps a supply of light airline blankets for people to cover themselves if they want, for body temperature goes down even while taking short nap.

Other than that, each cubicle has only a small chair so people can sit down and take off their shoes.

He never had to spend a penny on advertising for the dream house. From the very start, word of mouth was enough. After twenty-five or more years of people not dreaming, there was a vast, untapped desire to dream out there and Bruce was catering to that. We have never been overwhelmed with customers, not like Computer City or the appliance store up the road, but business is steady enough to compete with the nail salon and tanning booths next door.

The first day Maris came in, I pegged her for someone who still thought the House of Dreams was a furniture store. When she stepped out of her mini-van, well, I assumed she was a soccer mom looking for a deal on a china hutch. It was unfair of me, of course, and I later kicked myself for judging dreamers so much by their outer appearance. I now know that dreaming is such an internal thing, buried so deep in the limbic system that there is no way to judge the dreamer by his or her exterior.

She was biting her lip nervously as she approached the counter and saw the small green monitors at the control desk.

"Is this where I can come to dream?" she asked tentatively.

As I said, I was a little surprised. I had taken her for a hutch-seeker. I saw her look nervously at the row of closed doors running the length of the store. Red lights were on above some of the doors, like the lights over confessionals in old Catholic churches. The lights showed which cubes were in use. It being one o'clock on a Thursday afternoon, dream traffic was light. We had a couple of Birkenstocks in room three and in room five a businessman who used to live in California. All of them were experiencing REM in waves of about twenty minutes.

"Yes," I replied, "you can dream here. Sure."

"I've never done this before," she said with a nervous smile.

"It's really simple," I said. She looked hesitant, and I assumed she would be a one-timer, if she even stayed at all to dream, but, not for the last time, I underestimated her. She stood there looking at the doors of the cubes as if working up her courage. "Would you like to try?" I asked.

She nodded and then smiled, looking relieved, as if now that she had decided to try to learn how to dream her nervousness had gone away. I had her fill out the necessary paper work and decided to put her in cube seven which was toward the back. Experienced dreamers could use cube one up front because generally they could dream even with the sound of traffic outside. Some actually preferred it because they said the background noise stimulated unusual image flows. New dreamers, however, usually did better in the back.

Her blue eyes surveyed the interior of the cubicle and lit nervously on the bed with its white paper cover.

"You can take your shoes off," I said, pointing to the chair.

"Does it help?" she asked.

I shrugged. "Some people seem to think so, and later on, if you get into lucid dreaming, you may want to use the toe stimulator." I nodded toward the wire with the small copper cuff on the foot of the bed.

As far as I know, the toe stimulators were Bruce's own invention. It became clear to him after the first two weeks of business that people had grown so unused to dreaming on their own that they needed a little help.

"We use the stimulators in connection with the EEG," I explained, pointing to the two wires at the head of the bed. "We monitor your REM sleep out at the desk. Most of the time we just let people dream and then show them how long their REM period was when they leave, just to prove they had a dream, so they don't ask for their money back. But in lucid dreaming, you can enter your own dream consciously, only at first you need help, so when we see REM sleep in a dreamer we push the toe stimulator from the desk. That sends a mild electrical impulse into the big toe, not enough to wake the person up, but to serve as a sort of subconscious notice that the dreamer is dreaming and needs to pay attention to the dream."

I could tell this talk of wires and interactive dreaming was making her nervous, so I eased up and told her she needn't wear the wires this time if she didn't want. She said, no, she wanted to do it right, which I thought was pretty brave.

She took off her shoes and put their toes against the wall, then looked embarrassed as she sat on the edge of the bed while I attached the EEG electrodes to her temples with putty. As I hooked up the toe stimulator, I thought she might bolt, but she didn't. She lay down stiffly, arms at her sides, staring wide-eyed at the ceiling.

"It helps if you close your eyes," I said with a smile as I shut the door and the red light went on.

That first day she hardly dreamed at all. She slept for about two hours, but there was only one little blip of REM on the tape.

"Is that all?" she asked. She stared at the little squiggle and looked a bit let down. She sighed, then said, "I better pick up the kids." I thought I would never see her again.

We had many walk-ins who never came back. Maybe they'd heard about us from a friend or somebody at work and they came in once to try it, found it didn't work or didn't change their lives right away and never came back. Every few months we purged the computer of names of people who never returned. The following Thursday, however, Maris appeared again. The weather was wet and cooler and she was wearing a Burberry raincoat which looked a little out of place next to the Navy surplus pea jackets of the New Agers.

"I'd like to try again," she said, with a spunky smile. "Never say die, eh?"

That day, she had a long and beautiful REM and she emerged from cube seven with a rather astonished look on her face.

"Did I do it?" she asked, looking at me rather tentatively, as if I were a teacher or a parent.

"As far as I can tell," I said, showing her the EEG printout.

"This means I dreamed?" she asked. I nodded. "But what did I dream about?"

I was utterly charmed. She came to dreaming so fresh, with so few expectations, that she didn't even know yet that if you're not careful your consciousness will swallow your dreams whole and leave nothing behind. The following week, she returned and dreamed again.

"How was it?" I asked when she emerged from cube seven looking refreshed and relaxed.

"It was lovely," she said, "I've never felt so . . ." She hesitated a second before finding the right word, "free."

I smiled and nodded.

"I dreamt I was . . ."

I put my finger to my lips. "Sometimes it's better not to say. Bruce says the gold turns to ash when it's brought out of the night garden."

"Oh, but it was extraordinary," said Maris. "I dreamt I was in school again, before I met Ted, and . . ."

I wagged my finger. "Ah-ah."

She bit her lips and smiled, embarrassed in a perfectly fetching way. She was bursting with enthusiasm, like a new convert to a religion. But I knew from experience that for certain people telling dreams could be dangerous. She bought a five coupon dream book and went off to pick up the kids.

The following week she returned again looking a little crestfallen.

"I went home and told my husband my dream, the dream I had last week. He was in it." She didn't have to say anything more. I knew what happened. He either laughed at her or he blew up. Nothing will turn gold to ash faster, and many of the suburban housewives who've shared their dreams with their husbands have never come back.

"Would you like your money back on the coupon book?" I asked.

"No," she said in a determined way. "This is something I need to do."

From that day, Maris began to change, not externally so much, but internally. She still wore the same style of clothes, at least for the first six months or so, but it's as though she began to *grow*, which is impossible, of course, for a woman her age, but as the weeks went on, she seemed to be taller, or to take up more space than she had before. I asked Bruce about this, and he said we all have the capacity to fill up much more space than our bodies actually occupy, but most of us have been taught to tuck ourselves inside ourselves the way a huge jib sail can be stuffed into a tiny bag. There's no more or less cloth when the sail's filled with wind than when it's in the bag, Bruce said, it's just a question of expansion. Dreaming lets some people out of their bag, and from the time they begin, they start to grow big and occupy more space.

Even Maris's husband noticed it. At least I assumed the rather burly business type who came in one day without an appointment was her husband come to check up on the House of Dreams. He stood in the doorway for a second and sniffed the air like a bulldog.

"This the place people come to dream?" he called out gruffly from the doorway.

I pointed to a sign on the wall near cubicle one: *Quiet, please, dreams in progress.*

He strode over to the control booth and stared at the EEG displays. He put both hands on the counter. His fingers were surprisingly short and stubby, and the flesh swelled around his wedding band. On his right ring finger, he wore a chunky university ring with Greek letters on it. He stood there like a football lineman, legs spread, feet firmly planted, as if he was ready to make a run at me, and that's when I first thought he might be Maris's husband, for I realized that in spite of his abrupt manner and rough voice, this man felt threatened by Bruce's House of Dreams.

"What is it you people do here anyway?" he asked, eyeing a pair of Birkenstocks who just then emerged from cubicle six smelling of incense and patchouli. (Bruce had a rule about dual occupancy dreaming, but we let this couple, who signed in as Vishnu and Lakshmi, dream side by side as long as there was no sex. They assured us they were into a Tantric thing and were withholding, so Bruce okayed it.)

"We give people permission to dream," I said, sliding a brochure across the counter as an attempted peace offering. Paraphrasing the brochure's language, I said, "We seek to create a dream-friendly environment where people can experience their inner unconscious selves."

The man gave a derisive snort and shoved the brochure back at me.

"Well, I don't need to dream," he said, "Suppose everybody just sat around and did nothing but dream? What then, huh? How'd the work of the world get done, eh? That's what I'd like to know."

Since these weren't, strictly speaking, questions, I didn't give any replies but merely offered to show him the cubicles and give him the chance to dream for himself.

"Me? Dream?" he asked, incredulously, "You out of your mind or what?"

And with that he left, though it took half an hour before the angry vibrations followed him out of the building.

After that, Maris's dreams became more troubled. More than once I heard anguished moaning coming from her cubicle while she was in REM. Once she cried out "Stop!" and "Help!" She was letting her hair grow and the neatly pressed khaki trousers and crisp turtlenecks gave way to looser clothes with more flowing lines. She did her first overnight some six months after her first visit. She said she had begun to dream at home, but felt she couldn't dream properly with her husband beside her in bed. She had waves and waves of REM that night, and in the morning I could hear the sound of sobbing in her cubicle. It was a long time before she could compose herself, and when she came out she looked exhausted, but cleansed in an odd way.

She did several overnights after that, but the expansiveness that was there after her first visits drastically faded. She even seemed to shrink a bit, as if she were literally getting smaller, shrinking to a size no larger than my thumb.

"It's the same principle as a white dwarf star," Bruce explained. "All that energy collapses in on itself, getting smaller and smaller without losing any force. It's a prelude to a super nova, an incredible explosion."

Maris came in for her final visit on a Thursday at one o'clock, but she did not dream. She had simply come to thank me.

"I didn't do anything you couldn't have done yourself," I said.

"I know that now," she replied, and I never saw her again.

A few months later we got a letter from the Rocky Mountain Dream Institute. Though they called it an "institute," it was more like a monastery really, situated way up in the thin air of the mountains.

"I have been here three months with the children," she wrote, "The life here is centered on dreaming. We are far from what is called civilization so we may dream more freely. We rise at night to record our dreams in private and common books. Some of the dreams are extraordinarily beautiful here, and some of the brethren illuminate them with intense and vibrant colors. Some of our dreams are large and some are very small; some are terrifyingly violent and others prophecy coming doom. In the mornings we share our dreams and ponder their meaning as we tend the garden or work in the scriptorium. In the evenings we study Macrobius or read Chaucer's dream vision poetry. Before bed, we meditate and prime ourselves for the nightly dramas that will unfold. In the time we have been here, the children, living only with books and their imaginations, have begun to dream quite naturally, and we nurture their dreams and teach them to live by their meaning. I enter my dreams more freely now, and in the morning I emerge renewed. You must come and visit if you can.

Love, Maris."